Pursued by the Panther

Pursued by the Panther

Highland Shifters Book 6

Caroline S. Hilliard

Copyright © 2023 by Cathrine T. Sletta (aka Caroline S. Hilliard)

All rights reserved.

This publication is the sole property of the author, and may not be reproduced, as a whole or in portions, without the express written permission of the author. This publication may not be stored in a retrieval system or uploaded for distribution to others. Thank you for respecting the amount of work that has gone into creating this book.

Produced in Norway.

This book is a work of fiction and the product of the author's imagination. Names, characters, organizations, locations, and events are either the product of the author's imagination or used fictitiously. Any resemblance to actual persons, living or dead, organizations, events or locations is purely coincidental.

ISBN: 979-8-3791-6264-1

Copy edited by Lia Fairchild

Cover design by Munch + Nano
Thank you for creating such a beautiful cover for my story.

CONTENTS

About this book	i
Chapter 1	1
Chapter 2	11
Chapter 3	19
Chapter 4	32
Chapter 5	41
Chapter 6	54
Chapter 7	63
Chapter 8	72
Chapter 9	88
Chapter 10	97
Chapter 11	105
Chapter 12	116
Chapter 13	127
Chapter 14	140
Chapter 15	150
Chapter 16	162

Chapter 17	171
Chapter 18	180
Chapter 19	193
Chapter 20	202
Chapter 21	214
Chapter 22	227
Chapter 23	235
Chapter 24	247
Epilogue	259
Books by Caroline S. Hilliard	273
About the author	275

ABOUT THIS BOOK

He's her true mate. But he's also the biggest womanizer she has ever met.

Fia has put off the inevitable for two years, but now her time is up. The spell she put on the gorgeous panther leader to weaken the pull of the mating bond has been burned away, and no replacement spell will be as effective.
What will the panther do when he finds out she has denied him his mate for two years? Will he hate her or love her? Or will he continue to go through women like they only exist for his pleasure, and rip her heart out in the process?

Bryson can't get the beautiful Fia out of his mind. For two years he has had his eyes on her, unable to even glance at another woman. But no matter his efforts, Fia keeps refusing his advances.
If he didn't know better, he might have thought she was his true mate. But that's impossible. The mating bond is insistent, and they wouldn't have been able to stay away from each other for more than a few days if they were fated.
For his own sake and his clan's, he needs to forget her. But before that, he will confront her about concealing her exceptional witch power from him. And perhaps make one last attempt to gain her affection before he rips her from his heart forever.

This work is intended for mature audiences. It

contains explicit sexual situations and violence that some readers may find disturbing.

CHAPTER 1

8:00 am sharp! My office.

Fia's shoulders sagged as she read the text from Bryson for probably the twentieth time, even though there could be no doubt as to what he'd meant. He was giving her an order like she was one of his panthers, and by all rights she should tell him to fuck off. She probably would have, too, if it weren't for the small matter that she had lied to him, and he had found out about it. And it wasn't a small white lie she had served him either. No, it was a big, fat, juicy lie that had completely changed his perception of her. And it was a lie he would soon come to realize was even bigger than he currently thought.

Fia had risen early that morning after getting hardly any sleep at all. It had been difficult to rest knowing her life would never be the same. She had saved everyone from Ambrosia's attack, but the cost to herself would be high. Not that she regretted saving those people; she never would. But she had hoped to live her life the way she wanted for a while longer. But that wasn't an option anymore. Bryson would soon find out who she really was to him, and then she would be bound to him forever.

True mates. A shudder raced through her body, and she fisted her hands on the table in front of her. The concept was revered among shifters, but to her it was a horrible fate. Not being able to choose whom you were going to spend the rest of your life with was like time traveling to a not-so-distant past when women were traded for business opportunities or good connections. Suddenly, her future was grim, and there was nothing she could do about it. Except perhaps delay it for a while longer.

Fia looked at the text again. Eight o'clock. She still had an hour before she had to be there, but she might as well get it over and done with. After all, what did she have to lose? Apart from her freedom, that was. Soon it would be lost, and she would never get it back. Because even if Bryson didn't want to mate her, which was unlikely, the mating bond would keep pulling them toward each other. True mates weren't meant to live apart or exist alone. That was part of the nature of a mating bond.

I'll be there in 10.

After pressing *Send* she rose from where she had been sitting at the kitchen table and headed outside to her car without waiting for an answer. It had been more than an hour since Bryson texted her, so he would already be dressed and ready, and she had a feeling he would be only too happy to receive her early.

It was only a few minutes' drive to Bryson's house.

Before Fia had time to regret her decision to arrive early, she was pulling up in front of his house.

Bryson was standing on the porch, waiting for her with his arms crossed over his massive chest. His lips were thin from how he pressed them tightly together, and he stared at her with poorly concealed fury in his eyes. The man was used to being in charge, used to everyone following his orders without objections or complaints. But she wasn't one of his panthers, and he would never get that kind of obedience from her, no matter if she was his true mate.

Fia had never tried to assess Bryson's power level for fear of revealing her own. But she suspected she was stronger than him, and if he ever tried to control her, she would use that to her advantage. He might be the alpha of his clan, but if he ever pushed her, she wouldn't hesitate to show him just how powerful she was.

Their eyes clashed when Fia stepped out of the car and started walking slowly toward the porch. She was in no hurry to be scolded for lying to him, despite the fact she had done it deliberately. She'd had a very good reason for lying, and even though he had discovered that she was hiding her power level, she wasn't going to reveal her reason for concealing it. Until Bryson found out that she was his true mate and expected her to mate him, she was all for delaying the inevitable. Being the true mate of a manwhore wasn't a fate she wanted, and she would pretend she wasn't for as long as possible.

There was no point blaming him for the situation, though. His choice in the matter was as non-existent as hers. But he had made it clear he wanted her in his bed many times in the last couple of years. So, perhaps to him this would be a welcome development.

Although, she wasn't sure about that. It was hard to picture him giving up all his women to be with her. Perhaps realizing she was his true mate would be just as frustrating and unwanted for him as it was for her. But if that were the case, they might be able to come to an arrangement. They would stay together the minimum time they had to in order to satisfy the mating bond. The rest of the time they would each live their life as they pleased without any interference from the other.

Fia worked hard to keep her expression neutral and her body relaxed while staring into Bryson's furious gaze. It was difficult not to react to his presence—it always had been.

It was a shame she hadn't gone with her first impulse two years ago. As soon as she realized she was Bryson's true mate, she had considered moving away and never coming back. But after giving it some serious thought, she had concluded the risk was too high. The spell she had put on him and herself to inhibit the mating bond needed refreshing regularly to work. And living far away, she wouldn't be able to do that, or at least it would require frequent traveling.

Fia wasn't sure what would happen if the spell wore off while she was far away. Would the mating bond still try to pull them together? And if that were the case, how would that work exactly? Bryson wouldn't know who his true mate was, so how would the mating bond work around that?

She didn't know the answers to those questions, and she hadn't wanted to take the risk of the bond alerting Bryson to her status within a short time. Instead, she had opted to stay in the area to be able to refresh the spell whenever necessary. It had worked for two years. Until the day before when the powerful protection spell, which she'd had to perform at a moment's notice, had burned away the spell she had put on Bryson and herself.

And if Fia didn't do anything about that, it was only a question of time before he would realize whom she was. So, she would try to spell him again. She already knew it wouldn't be as effective as before, and there was a chance it wouldn't work at all, but she had to try.

As she neared the porch, she could feel Bryson's power radiating off him. It was like entering a pulsing forcefield, giving her goosebumps all over her body.

Unfortunately, that wasn't the only thing his power did to her. It flowed over her like warm silk, teasing and stroking all her sensitive places. And it felt so good it took her a few seconds to remember she had defenses she could put up against his enticing power.

Without sending out more than a small amount of her own power, she coated her body with a magical protective barrier. It didn't completely stop the effect of his alpha power, but it did reduce it significantly.

As soon as she stepped onto the porch, Bryson turned without uttering a word and headed into the house, obviously expecting her to follow him. She stuck out her tongue at his back. It was childish behavior, and she knew it, but it made her feel better. And it was better than ranting and raving about her bad luck in life. Like anyone would care. The mighty alpha walking ahead of her certainly wouldn't. She couldn't help the chuckle that escaped her at the thought of her hopeless situation.

Bryson spun so fast she didn't even realize what was happening before he suddenly loomed over her with a thunderous expression on his face. "This is funny to you?" His dark-brown eyes were glowing with rage when they bored into hers, his grip on her upper arms almost bruising. "I trusted you, but what did I get for that? Lies, that's what. Nothing but lies. If you don't want me, that's fine. But you could've been straight with me."

She had to swallow past her heart beating in her throat before she could speak. Having his hands on her was threatening to melt her resolve to stay away from him and keep him in the dark about their connection. "I could've, but I chose not to."

His jaw slackened, and his eyes widened in shock at her brazen words. A full five seconds went by before he snapped his mouth shut and swore. Then, he released his grip on her arms and turned to storm down the hallway toward his office. Again he obviously expected her to follow without question. And she did. They needed to talk. She wasn't going to tell him more than she had to, but she would have to tell him something. Give him a plausible explanation for lying to him.

Fia sauntered into his office ten seconds after him and closed the door behind her. It was one of her favorite rooms in Bryson's house. Filled with light and tastefully decorated in subdued colors with private access to a patio overlooking the back gardens. Facing west, the patio was ideal for reading and relaxing on light summer evenings. Not that she'd had the opportunity to do so, but she could imagine the feeling of peace and solitude. Most of Bryson's panthers had their own houses within walking distance of Bryson's own. No more than a handful of people were staying in the large house in addition to the alpha himself, so unless there was a clan gathering, the house was fairly quiet in the evenings.

Bryson stood by the windows with his back to her, his hands in the pockets of his black military-style cargo pants. "Fia." Her name was uttered with a sigh, and he didn't try to hide the regret in his voice. Gone was his anger from before. "Thank you for saving us all yesterday. I have no doubt some of us would be dead right now if you hadn't been there and used your power to protect us. So, please don't mistake my disappointment and anger for a lack of gratitude.

"But I would like to know why you chose to lie to me in the first place, Fia, and never in two years felt the need to reveal the truth. You didn't know me back then, so being reluctant to reveal your power level to me was understandable, perhaps even prudent. But as you got to know me, you chose to keep up the charade. And the only reasons I can think of for you to do that are reasons that would put my clan at risk. And as the alpha, that is unacceptable to me. So, please enlighten me as to your reasons, because the last thing I want to do is to be forced to destroy you for being a threat to my clan."

Fia felt her eyes widen at the clear warning. For some reason she had never considered that Bryson might see her lies as a threat. The fact he was disappointed was no surprise, but feeling threatened?

Before she could think how to respond, he turned around and stared at her with his brows furrowed.

"Are you an enemy, Fia? Have I been stupid to trust you for so long? You already know I'm attracted to you. Is that something you've been counting on and using to keep me in the dark about what you are doing here? These are the questions I've been asking myself since yesterday. And if you can't give me any convincing answers, I feel obligated to re-evaluate your status as a friend to this clan and me."

Her mind was spinning. Fia hadn't been prepared for this line of questioning, focusing on her as a possible threat instead of considering her actions as just a personal insult. She didn't have any good answers lined up to explain why she had been lying for two years. Not without revealing the real reason at least. And that wasn't something she was willing to do. Not until she had no other options left.

"I'm sorry, Bryson." She let her sincerity show in her face. "I never thought you would consider me a threat for hiding my true power level. I understand and accept that you're disappointed and angry with me for downplaying what I can do. But please don't consider me a threat. If I wanted to hurt you or your clan, I could've let Ambrosia do that for me yesterday. It would've been simple to just protect myself from her attack and pretend it was all I was capable of, but instead I chose to protect everyone. And even if nothing else convinces you, my actions should prove I'm not a threat to you or to anyone else. I let my secret out to save you all because I could never watch someone else get hurt just to protect myself."

Bryson's expression didn't change as he stared at her. Her words didn't seem enough to convince him. And perhaps that shouldn't surprise her. Two years was a long time to hold onto a lie. Even though she had tried to stay away from the alpha and his panther clan, she had still ended up spending quite a few hours at Bryson's house. Like he had said, she was a friend to the clan and to him. Except she was far more than that.

"Perhaps you're speaking the truth." Bryson crossed his arms over his chest, which drew her gaze to his mouthwatering upper body. Arms, shoulders, and chest—the T-shirt he was wearing was stretched to its limits, and it was impossible not to admire all that male perfection barely contained by the thin fabric.

Fia had a recurring dream of stripping him bare and running her hands all over him just to feel his muscles play under her palms. The rumors were saying he was an amazing lover, generous and skilled, with equipment to match his performance. Combined with his looks, it was enough to make any woman salivate. And if it wasn't for the rate at which he was fucking his way through the female population...

"Fia."

The heat in his voice when he said her name made her shiver with need, and the motion made her realize she had been staring at his body for much too long. Her eyes widened as her gaze snapped up to his. She was usually better at controlling herself, but since the spell to counteract the mating bond was no longer in place, she seemed to be struggling more than usual around him.

A wicked grin spread across his face as he studied her, no doubt able to see her attraction to him in her face and body language. Which was bad, really bad.

Bryson took a step toward her with a cocky grin splitting his face and confidence radiating off him. Another swaggering step closer, and it was obvious he thought she was finally going to give in to his advances.

He hadn't yet realized she was his true mate, but she had a bad feeling he would as soon as he took in the scent of her arousal. Which meant that she either had to make him keep his distance or put a spell on him again.

"Stop!" Fia laced the word with power, and Bryson stopped so abruptly he swayed a little before finding his balance.

Concentrating on what she wanted to happen, she stared into his eyes and let her power flow slowly and delicately toward him, entering his body without him noticing anything other than a subtle sensation of hot air caressing his skin. At least that was how she'd had it described once.

The spell was meant to reduce the effect of the mating bond, and she could feel it taking effect even as his brows pushed together in confusion. It was done in less than fifteen seconds, but there was no guarantee how long the spell would last or how effective it would be this time around.

CHAPTER 2

Bryson shook his head to clear it of the strange fog that had suddenly clouded his mind. It was probably a result of everything that had happened in the last twenty-four hours as well as lack of sleep. He had been too pissed off, shocked, and hurt by Fia's obvious deception to even think about going to bed when he finally arrived home late the night before.

He had been interrogated by the police for hours. They hadn't wanted to believe he had no knowledge of what had happened at Barbara's house. But in the end, they had given up, having no indication that he had anything to do with what had happened except for the fact that he was there when they arrived. They might want to question him again at some stage, but he wasn't worried about that. He doubted they would be able to establish the cause of the blown windows and the destruction of the living room, and without the cause, it would be difficult to pin it on him.

Bryson blinked a couple of times to focus his gaze

on Fia. Desire had darkened her beautiful hazel eyes a minute ago, but it was no longer there. If anything, she looked irritated.

"As I've told you before, Bryson. I won't be your plaything." Fia crossed her arms over her chest and narrowed her eyes at him. "But perhaps I haven't spelled it out clearly enough for you. I'm not interested in being another forgotten name on the endless list of women you've fucked. Why would I? Why would anyone? You're a good-looking man, but you use it blatantly to get into the pants of almost every woman you cross paths with, including those who are married or mated. Some women even seem to be attracted to your track record, but I'm not one of them. To me it's a big turn-off."

Bryson's heart rate increased as she spoke, but at the mention of mated women, he frowned. "I've never fucked a mated woman, Fia. Ever. But thank you for being straight with me. I appreciate your reasons for saying no to me."

He sighed, and his head tipped forward as he squeezed his eyes closed. This wasn't the first time she had said she didn't want to be his plaything, but she had never been specific as to why before. At first he had thought she was just playing hard to get, but as time went by, he had started to wonder if she was looking for an offer of commitment from him. But instead of promising her anything, he had kept trying to entice her to his bed.

Bryson had always felt that commitment wasn't in his DNA, unless of course, he found his true mate. If that happened, he would have no choice but to bow to the force of the mating bond. Although, he wasn't sure he would be happy with a life tied to one woman forever.

But perhaps it was time to date someone for a limited time as a test? He had no experience with an exclusive relationship, but he wouldn't mind trying it with Fia if that was what she wanted.

Fia huffed. "What I'd like to know is why you won't give up? I've said no to you for two years, but it's like you don't hear me. And the next time I see you, you're at it again. You never stop, even though you have women lining up outside your door. Have you ever even tried going more than a few nights without fucking someone new?"

Bryson steeled himself before lifting his gaze to hers with a neutral expression on his face. There was no point denying his behavior before he met her, and he wasn't ready to reveal that he hadn't had sex with anyone since Fia snared his attention. It felt too much like admitting defeat. "Has it ever crossed your mind that I might genuinely want to be with you? And not just for sex."

Her mouth fell open for a second before she burst out laughing.

"Fia, I'm serious." Anger blossomed inside him at her reaction to his question, even though his offer probably sounded like a joke to her, and he could understand why.

She schooled her features into a serious expression before focusing back on him. "So am I, Bryson. That doesn't sound like you at all. What is it that makes me special? Is it the fact that I've actually had the audacity to say no to you—repeatedly? Or is it because I'm a witch, and you want to have one of those to use for yourself?"

It was his turn to have his mouth fall open. "I wouldn't offer you commitment just to have access to your power. Is that really what you think of me, that I use people like that?"

Fia cocked an eyebrow as she stared at him. "But you *do* use people, though. You use women for your own pleasure all the time. But I must admit I'm surprised to hear you offer me commitment. Although, perhaps I shouldn't be since I'm not sure you know the meaning of the word. How long would it last for? One night? Two nights? For your information that's too short to be considered commitment."

His anger burned hotter at her words, and he took a step closer to her before stopping himself. "I'm an alpha with a large clan depending on me. I know what commitment is, and that's why I've never offered it to a woman before you. And contrary to what you are implying, I've never used a woman in any way she didn't wish to be used. All I've ever promised is a night or two of pleasure. Nothing more. I don't need to lie to lure women to me like some deviant."

Fia visibly swallowed before averting her eyes, and a crease formed between her eyebrows. "Then why would you offer me commitment?" She didn't look at him while she waited for his answer.

"I..." Bryson frowned. He should have known the answer to her question, but he didn't. Perhaps because it was based on feelings and wants that were new to him, and he wasn't sure how to describe them in a way that made sense to other people.

Except that wasn't correct. Bryson couldn't describe them to himself either. He had no idea what it was about Fia that had him losing interest in every other woman. It made no sense and shouldn't have been possible when she wasn't his true mate.

Bryson took a deep breath before he opened his mouth to try to answer Fia's question. "Because I want to get to know you. And not just as a friend but as something more."

She tightened her lips into a straight line, obviously preparing to bite him off again, so he quickly continued before she could say anything.

"I want to make sure you have everything you need to be happy, Fia. And I want to be the one to make your eyes shine with surprise and delight whenever I get the opportunity to do something for you." His eyes widened when his own words rang in his ears, and he realized what he had just said. That didn't sound like something he would typically say. It sounded weak and pathetic, like he was a teenage boy with a crush.

Turning away from her, he swallowed hard and waited for her to burst out laughing again. It was either that or she would just turn around and walk away. A strong woman like her wouldn't settle for someone pathetic.

"Bryson?" Her tone was soft, and he could hear the uncertainty in her voice. "Are you—"

There was a sharp knock on his office door, and he felt his whole body tense in frustration. He wanted to know what Fia had been about to say, but he also knew that whoever had knocked had done it for a reason.

Taking a deep breath to calm his irritation, he turned toward the door. "Enter."

The door opened and G, his second in command,

appeared in the doorway looking grave. "You need to check the news. There's been another...incident."

"Shit." Bryson glanced at Fia before he grabbed the remote off the table and turned on the TV in the corner.

The news reporter on location had a suitably serious expression on her face while she spoke. "...serious burns to the face and neck. The identities of the victims have yet to be established, but the police can confirm that it is a man and a woman. Their deaths are treated as suspicious."

"Aviemore. Just north of Aviemore." Fia raised her gaze to his when he turned to look at her. She had her phone in her hand. "Is there a pack or a clan in that area?"

He nodded. "A pack, yes."

She nodded slowly with concern buckling her beautiful brows. "Then I'm guessing at least one of the victims is a wolf from that pack unless another shifter was visiting the area. Ambrosia is trying to increase her power, but I don't know how well it's working. When I meet her again, I should be able to tell if there has been a significant change in her power level."

Frowning, he scratched his stubbly chin. "Assuming the couple was killed after our encounter with Ambrosia yesterday. For all we know, she killed them before that. Does it say anything about when they died?" He indicated the phone in her hand.

Looking at her phone, she swiped her finger over the screen a few times. "No, it doesn't. So, you're right. She might've killed them before we met her yesterday." Fia met his gaze again. "Perhaps one of the others who were there when she attacked us noticed a difference in her power level from earlier. I never thought to ask."

"You can ask them when they arrive. I expect Leith and his friends will be here in an hour or so." After glancing at the door to confirm that G had left and closed it behind him, Bryson crossed his arms over his chest and narrowed his gaze at her. "But before that I want an explanation for why you lied to me. I accept that you didn't do it to hurt my clan, but I still don't understand why you found it necessary to hide your power level for so long. Have I ever threatened you in any way?"

Her shoulders sagged, and her gaze dropped to the floor. "No, you haven't. I hope you can appreciate that telling someone you're a witch can be difficult, but telling someone you're more powerful than most other supernaturals is downright reckless if you don't trust that person completely."

There was a hardness in her gaze when she looked at him, and her body tensed. "Most people don't respond well when they realize someone is stronger than them, and it is particularly true for powerful people considering themselves superior to others. You're an alpha and a powerful shifter, Bryson, and I wasn't going to tell you until I was sure you wouldn't use it against me or try to kill me. But as time went by, it became harder and harder to tell you simply because I had hidden it for too long already. I chose the easiest route of least possible confrontation and kept it hidden. It might've been stupid, yes, but it was easier at the time."

Bryson studied her face for several seconds after she stopped talking. She might be telling the truth, but he had a feeling there was more to it than simply not wanting to rock the boat with her revelation. There was something she wasn't telling him, but he wouldn't push her any further on the subject this morning. It would be better to let her think her explanation was accepted and let her relax in that knowledge for a little while until he suddenly asked her again when she least expected it. Because he needed to know why, and he wouldn't give up until he did.

He let his features relax into a small smile. "Okay, I can accept that. But for future reference, please remember that you can tell me anything. I won't use it against you, and I won't disclose it to anyone else. You can trust me, Fia."

Her brows wrinkled as she stared at him. Doubt was written in her eyes as she rolled her lips together, wetting them.

His eyes automatically zoomed in on her luscious mouth. He had been dreaming of her soft, full lips for two years. Kissing them, nibbling on them, and above all having them wrapped around his cock. The appendage in question twitched, and he quickly averted his eyes. This wasn't the time to have his shaft tent his pants.

CHAPTER 3

Fia noticed the desire in Bryson's eyes before he looked away. He had been staring at her lips and unfortunately his gaze wasn't the only thing that had heated as a result. She had managed to stop the shiver that wanted to race through her body, but she couldn't prevent the simmering heat that settled in her lower abdomen. As she had feared, the spell wasn't nearly as effective as it had been for the last two years, and the fact that she was getting turned on from Bryson staring at her lips for a few seconds was the least distressing consequence.

Tucking a strand of hair behind her ear, she forced her mind back to Bryson's words. "Thank you, Bryson, for accepting my explanation. I know I shouldn't have lied to you." Although she would have kept it up if she could, he didn't need to know that. "I want to ask one thing of you, though."

She waited until his gaze returned to hers before she continued. "Can you please stop pursuing me? At least until we have found and dealt with Ambrosia." It might not be long before the mating bond broke free of her spell and Bryson realized whom she was, but until then she wanted his word he would stop his relentless chase.

His jaw tensed for a second before his features relaxed into an easy smile, and he nodded. "Okay, I guess I can give you that." He frowned. "We'll probably have enough to occupy our time, anyway, until we can destroy that evil bitch."

"Yes, I think we will." She couldn't help the sigh that slipped out. This whole thing with Ambrosia was horrible and a mess, and she was wondering how long it would take for the media to catch on to the fact that there was something else going on than simple human depravity. But then people didn't believe in the supernatural anymore. They were always convinced there was a natural explanation. Except they didn't know that a lot of what they considered supernatural was just an extended part of the real world.

Fia cocked her head. "Which reminds me. What did the police say yesterday? Did they have any theories as to what had happened in the house?"

Bryson held up a hand to stop her. "I'll tell you, but it will happen during breakfast. Have you had anything to eat yet today, Fia?"

She shook her head. "But I can get something—"

"I'm making breakfast—bacon and eggs. Will you please join me?" He gave her a pointed look, making it clear that it wasn't really a question. "You need to keep your strength up. We don't know what's going to happen next."

Her eyes widened. Bacon and eggs weren't a

gourmet meal, but she had never gotten the impression he could cook. Or that he would, in fact, choose to cook. She had thought he had someone to do that for him. It would have been less of a surprise if he had asked her to make breakfast for him. "I know but—"

"No buts, not even your sexy one." He winked at her before starting toward the door. "It's time for breakfast, and I won't accept any objections."

She ended up sitting on a stool by the high table extending from the kitchen island where Bryson was frying up bacon and eggs for the two of them. He didn't want any help, so she was left to admire his large, powerful body while he worked.

The man really was a mouthwatering piece of art, with his thick muscles and his elaborate tattoos complementing his amber skin. Not to mention his gorgeous features and bad-boy vibes. She'd never had a thing for tattoos before meeting Bryson, but with him they fit like he wouldn't be the same person without them. They were a part of him just like his short black hair and his dark-brown eyes.

Need suddenly cut through her body and made her shudder with how much she wanted to touch him, kiss him, and ride him. Before she even knew what she was doing, she was on her feet. But before she could round the table to where Bryson was standing, she came to her senses and altered the direction she was heading to aim for the door to the hallway. "I'm just going to the bathroom. I'll be right back."

She ground her teeth together as she hurried toward the bathroom at the end of the hallway. Her voice had sounded squeaky and strange in her own ears, but hopefully he hadn't noticed.

After locking the door to the bathroom behind her, she squeezed her eyes tightly closed. This wasn't going well. Her desire to jump him wouldn't have been this powerful if the spell had been working as it should. But there wasn't much she could do about that.

Her pussy chose that moment to clench, and her eyes flew open when she felt wetness starting to leak out. She quickly pulled her pants and panties down to her knees to avoid having them soaked through and put a hand between her legs to stop anything from running down her thighs.

It was a mistake. Her hand was pressing against her swollen clit, and she squirmed as heat flared in her lower abdomen. She needed to do something about her raging desire, or she wouldn't be able to sit still at the table and eat like a normal person. And if Bryson caught a whiff of her arousal, it might set off his desire as well, and perhaps alert him to whom she was to him.

Fia toed off her shoes and used one hand to pull off her pants and panties. After widening her legs, she shoved two fingers inside her pussy.

She gasped as hot pleasure shot through her body, her channel so slick and ready for action that it was like she'd already come at least once. Sliding the pad of her finger over her clit made her shudder, but she clamped her mouth shut to stay silent through the onslaught of glorious sensations.

Leaning her back against the wall, Fia pumped her fingers inside her soaked channel while rubbing her clit. Bryson's face, and the way she imagined his body looked without his clothes, took over her mind, and she welcomed the enticing picture. She had always admired his looks and occasionally his personality when he wasn't trying to get into her pants.

Her whole body felt like it was burning with need and standing still was becoming impossible, but as long as she kept quiet, nobody would know what she was doing. But she had to be quick, or she had no doubt Bryson would come looking for her, wondering if she was okay. She had stormed out of the kitchen like her ass was on fire, which was sort of accurate except for the body part in question.

Rocking her hips, she struggled to stay silent as her body practically sparked with the fire growing inside her. Getting herself off was something she did regularly, and always with an image of Bryson in her head, but it rarely felt this amazing.

Her orgasm suddenly blasted through her body, making her suck in a breath through her clenched teeth. Pulse after pulse of pleasure made her see stars as she kept working her body until the bliss faded, and she sagged against the wall behind her.

Her body felt spent, and all she wanted was to go home and find her bed, but instead she had to get back to Bryson in the kitchen and pretend she hadn't just masturbated in his bathroom. *Damn. Someone just kill me already. Talk about awkward. He'll probably smell it on me.*

After quickly cleaning up, Fia sauntered back into the kitchen with what she hoped was a neutral expression on her face. Bryson glanced at her with a small smile curving his tempting lips before proceeding to fill two plates with the food he'd made—eggs, bacon, fried cherry tomatoes, and buttered toast. It looked and smelled great, and apparently her stomach thought so as well since it growled so loudly she couldn't help the laugh that burst from her.

Bryson's smile widened as his gaze lifted to hers. "Hungry, redbird? I guess it isn't such a bad thing I offered to make you breakfast then."

Redbird. He'd used that nickname for her before, and for some reason she had allowed it. Perhaps because it felt like a tribute to her long red hair.

After putting one plate down on the table directly across from where she had taken a seat, he rounded the table with the other plate in his hand. He leaned over her and put the heaped plate of food down before her, but instead of immediately moving away, he lingered right behind her right shoulder.

She frowned. "Bryson, what are—" Her words ended in a gasp when he bent his head and sniffed her neck.

A growl sounded right next to her ear, sending a shudder racing through her from her neck to her hot core. "Why do you smell so fucking good?" His voice was raspy, like he hadn't used it for days, but she had a fair idea what was happening to him to cause his voice to change like that.

His lips brushed over the shell of her ear before his teeth tugged at her earlobe, making her squirm on her stool. "Bry, please stop." Her voice was breathy, and it might have been better not to have opened her mouth at all, but she had to stop him before she started begging him to fuck her right there in the kitchen. Having his hot body so close was playing havoc with her hormones or the mating bond, or most likely both.

"Bry? I like that." He was still so close his breath

fanned the side of her neck. "Are you sure you want me to stop? Your scent says otherwise."

Turning ninety degrees in her chair, she tried to lean away from him without looking at him, but he was too close for it to be effective. "Please take a step back, Bryson." Fia made sure to say his full name this time. She had never said his nickname out loud before, and then to say it to his face. That was a slip-up she had a feeling would come back to bite her more than once.

But to her surprise, he did what she'd told him and took a step back. Except it made the situation infinitely worse when her eyes landed on the huge bulge in his pants. She had heard the rumors that he was exceptionally well endowed but for some reason it hadn't sunk in exactly what that meant. To see the evidence was a shock to her system and pulled her gaze like shoppers to a midseason sale. Somewhere in her mind there was a little sane voice telling her to look away, but it couldn't seem to reach through the noise of the rest of her mind screaming at her to jump him already.

"Redbird?" There was no small amount of glee in his gravelly voice. "You're drooling."

"I…" Like in a daze, she dragged her gaze away from his groin and tipped her head back to meet his eyes. He was grinning at her, and she blinked a couple of times while trying to process what he had just said.

His large hand cupped her chin. "Can I kiss you?" His dark-brown orbs were practically black with desire as he bent his head slowly toward her.

His mouth was only an inch from hers when her brain finally came back online. "No." The word left her mouth just as his lips brushed against hers, light as a feather.

Bryson lifted his head just enough to comfortably meet her shocked stare, his hand still holding her chin. "No?" The inflection in his voice made it sound like he didn't believe her.

"No!" She narrowed her eyes at him. "I don't want to kiss you." She steeled herself for his response, but he surprised her when he simply shrugged and let go of her chin.

"Okay." Without a word of protest, he rounded the table before sitting down on the stool across from her and grabbing his knife and fork. Giving her an easy smile, he indicated her plate. "Then eat. You need breakfast to sustain your feisty spirit." He winked at her before digging into his food.

It took her almost a full minute to recover enough to pick up her own knife and fork. She was still hungry, but with her mind and body in complete turmoil, it was hard to think about putting something into her mouth. At least something other than his... *No! Not going there.* But she must have made a sound because Bryson suddenly barked out a laugh, making her jerk in surprise and lose her knife on the floor.

"I'll get you another one. Just leave it." He was up and moving before she could protest. The grin on his face was a clear indication that he was enjoying her struggling resistance to him. And from what she could see when her traitorous gaze lowered down his body, it had done nothing to diminish his desire.

Pulling in a deep breath, she closed her eyes and waited for him to walk up behind her to deliver a clean knife. She wanted to resist him, at least for a while longer. Just a few more days to try to come to terms with him becoming her mate. She frowned. That wasn't right. It was the other way around. *She* would become *his* mate.

***

Bryson couldn't hide his grin at the pained expression on Fia's face when he returned to the table with another knife for her. Her eyes were closed, and she was clearly trying to fight her desire. But the whiny moan she had made just seconds ago had sounded very much like a confirmation that she was soon going to join him in his bed.

Finally, his years of trying to seduce her might be paying off, and it was about fucking time, because he was about to go insane with lust for her. She was continuously on his mind, whether he was awake or asleep, and no matter how much he jerked off to a fantasy of her, it was never enough to satisfy his desire for the real thing.

He had been hungry for sex since he was old enough to feel that kind of desire, but he had never wanted a particular woman like he wanted Fia. She had taken his breath away the first time he saw her, and she had never really given it back. But that might be about to change.

"Here's your knife, redbird. Are you all right?" Sliding the knife across the table toward her, he tried to contain his wicked grin. The last thing he wanted to do was to push her away when she was finally showing signs of caving. Even her clear "no" to him when he asked to kiss her didn't bother him when her scent and body language were so clearly in his favor.

Her eyes opened, and she stared at him for a

second, before her gaze dropped to the knife on the table. "Thank you." Her voice was husky, and she cleared her throat before continuing with a frown. "I'm fine."

His grin widened. "Good. Then eat up. Leith and his friends will be here soon, and we can't have you wasting away now, can we?"

Bryson went back to eating his own food. He was ravenous, although it wasn't food he wanted. But it would have to do until further notice.

He couldn't wait to show Fia the surprise he'd had done for her. It was something he had already been thinking about for a while when he met her, and seeing her had made up his mind to go through with it. He was looking forward to seeing her reaction. Hopefully, she would be pleased and not horrified. But he couldn't be sure until he'd actually revealed it to her. He didn't know her well enough to foresee how she would take it.

They ate in silence until the sound of cars outside reached his ears. He recognized the purr of Leith's V12 engine, and the other cars most likely belonged to Leith's friends.

Glancing over at Fia's plate, Bryson was surprised to see it was almost empty. She must have been really hungry considering he had given her a full plate. And she must have enjoyed his food. That had a smile curving his lips. He wouldn't mind feeding her every day if he was only given the chance to do so. But for that to happen, she would have to stay the night.

She lifted her gaze to his when he stood. Smiling, he indicated her plate. "You can stay here until you're done. There's no rush. I'll go greet our guests, and you can join us in the living room later, okay?"

Fia shook her head and stood. "No, I can't eat another bite. Thank you, Bryson. I didn't think you could cook, but apparently you can." A small smile tugged at the corner of her lips.

He chuckled. "I can do a lot of things, but you'll have to stick around to find out." He didn't let his gaze linger to see her reaction. Instead, he quickly cleared off the table and put the plates and cutlery in the dishwasher before heading out of the kitchen.

Leith and Sabrina both smiled when they approached the porch. Accompanying them was everyone who had tried to stop Ambrosia the day before. Trevor, a powerful wolf alpha, with his human mate, Jennie, following him. Duncan, another wolf alpha, and Julianne, his human mate. Michael, a wereserval from America, with his mate, Steph, a powerful witch. And lastly Callum and Vamika, both wolves and by the way she was following behind him as they approached the porch, it was clear they had finally had time to mate.

A sting of pain ran through Bryson's chest, and he rubbed his skin through his T-shirt like that would do anything to alleviate the discomfort. The pain had been coming regularly since their encounter with Ambrosia the day before, and he was starting to wonder whether her magic had affected him more than he had thought.

"Leith." Bryson gripped the man's forearm, and Leith returned the gesture in the traditional greeting between alphas, before Bryson turned to bow to the man's mate. "Sabrina." The famous Loch Ness monster and his mermaid mate, both rare and powerful creatures. Bryson was privileged to be one of just a dozen or so people who knew their real natures. They were secretive about what they were and for good reason.

Bryson proceeded to greet the rest of the alpha couples in the same fashion before bowing to the others in their party.

Another car pulled up just as Bryson was about to turn around and head into the house. Henry, the wolf alpha from the pack located northwest of Inverness, smiled at them through the windshield before stepping out of the vehicle.

After greeting Henry, Bryson led them all into the living room like he had the day before. Fia was already seated in the chair at the opposite end of the long table from his own. He would have liked to have her closer, but this wasn't the time to tell her that.

Bryson headed over to his chair and sat down. "Please have a seat." He studied the various mated couples while they made their way over to the couches lining the long table. They were all holding hands or touching each other like it was as vital to them as breathing. And perhaps it was, considering they were all true mates.

In fact it was a rare sight indeed to see so many true mated couples gathered in one room. Most shifters never found their true mate. And it was considered such an unusual occurrence that most shifters never even bothered to look for the one designed for them. Instead, they chose someone to mate, like a human would choose someone to marry. Except, of course, for the small matter that mating was permanent whereas marriage wasn't.

As soon as everyone was seated, Leith leaned forward in his seat and locked eyes with Bryson. "There has been a breakthrough since last night. Hugh, the alpha of the panther clan northwest of Glasgow, called this morning. He recognized the photo we sent him of Ambrosia. She is the mate of one of his panthers."

CHAPTER 4

Bryson's lips curled into a smile. "So, the bitch has a name now?"

Leith gave a short nod. "She does. Amber Johnson. Hugh had never heard of the name Ambrosia before, so it does not appear she has been using it as an alias until recently. At least not that he was aware of."

Bryson nodded slowly. "Okay. But I take it she's not with the clan at the moment."

"That is correct." Leith's brows creased. "And her mate is not there at present either. The couple left to stay at their cabin on the west coast months ago, and the alpha has not seen them since. But apparently, that is not uncommon for them.

"Since Hugh received Ambrosia's, or Amber's, picture he has been trying to call her mate, but the man's phone is switched off, so Hugh has not been able to reach him. The alpha was planning to head over to the cabin to check on them this morning, but I told him he would be better off with some of us going with him. We do not yet know where Amber and Mary went yesterday after they left Barbara's house. But for all we know Amber has taken Mary back to her father."

"Not her father." Henry shook his head as he looked at Leith. "Mary is human. Amber's mate can't be Mary's father."

Leith frowned. "You are right. I did not consider that. Perhaps Hugh knows who Mary's father is. I did not think to ask, nor did I ask how long Amber has been mated."

Bryson nodded and swung his gaze around to all the couples and the three of his panthers seated around the table. "So, I guess the question is who's going to visit the clan down south. If no one objects, I'd like to be one of the people going, particularly considering they're panthers. I've met Hugh a few times before, and he's a good alpha. I'm sure he'll help us in any way he can, particularly considering it's in his own best interest to stop Amber from killing more shifters."

"I think it's a good idea for you to go." Sabrina smiled at him before turning her head to look at Fia at the opposite end of the table from him. "And I think Fia should go with you. She might be able to detect whether Amber is there before you actually knock on the door. Am I correct?"

Fia's face was a blank mask when she nodded, her eyes on Sabrina. "Yes, I should be able to do that. But are you sure you don't want to go yourself?"

Bryson's shoulders tensed, and he was about to tell Fia that he'd like her to go with him when Sabrina beat him to it.

"No. Amber still thinks I'm dead, and I'd like to keep it that way."

Leith visibly flinched, and Sabrina threw him a soft smile before turning back to Fia. "If I approach her clan, word might get back to her that I'm still alive. But it won't come as a surprise to her if you're the one looking for her, not after what happened at Barbara's house. And she might think twice about attacking you again, considering how you blocked her last time."

Fia bit her bottom lip as she nodded slowly. She glanced at Bryson for a second before her gaze traveled around the table. "I think it might be a good idea if someone else comes with us, just in case she's actually there."

Bryson hid a smile as he studied her face. Perhaps it wasn't visible to everyone else, but he could see the desperation in her eyes. She wanted someone else to travel with them, and he was betting it was because she wasn't trusting herself to be alone with him. Not even in a car, which would be where they would spend most of their time.

His mind wanted to elaborate on what might happen while they were alone, but he quickly pushed the thoughts away to avoid ending up with a throbbing erection while having visitors. Instead, he tried to come up with a good excuse why no one else should join them, but once again Sabrina spoke in his favor.

"It's better if the rest of us stay here or go back to Leith's house." Sabrina's gaze was firmly on Fia as she spoke. "As Leith said, we don't know where Amber and Mary are. They didn't take Amber's rental car, so we don't even know how they left the area. Or, have you had a chance to look into that, Callum?"

The man in question shook his head with a small smile, and he pulled his mate closer to his side before he answered. "No, not yet. I've been too busy spending time with my beautiful mate. But I'll look into it as soon as we're done here." He frowned. "I can't imagine it would be easy to travel with Mary. Barbara had to give her a sedative to be able to handle her alone inside the house. Unless Amber can calm her somehow, she'll have a hard time controlling her daughter. Mary's agitated and unpredictable."

Vamika looked at her mate before turning her head to look at Bryson. "I can call the local hospitals and mental institutions and check if they've had anyone admitted in the last twenty-four hours. Amber won't be able to carry out her sinister plans while simultaneously looking after her daughter."

"Do you have a picture of Mary?" Bryson looked at Callum. The young wolf had already shown he was good at finding relevant information and tracking people.

"No, but I'll look into it first thing. Shouldn't be too difficult now that I have her mother's name, and I know what Mary looks like."

"I'll help you." Vamika smiled up at her mate. "I know more about computers than I let on. I had to be able to hide my tracks while living with my old pack. And whatever I don't know, I'm sure you can teach me."

Callum lifted an eyebrow at her with an amused smile on his lips. "And you waited this long to tell me, baby girl?" He bent and whispered something in Vamika's ear, which made her snort and tighten her grip on Callum's thigh.

Bryson smiled at the newly mated couple. It was a shame to interrupt their flirting, but they had work to do. "Good. I can have some of my panthers show Amber's and Mary's pictures to a few people in the area around Barbara's house." He met G's gaze, and the man nodded his acceptance of the task. "Perhaps someone noticed in which direction the two women went and if they got a lift with someone or acquired some kind of transportation. Amber might've used her powers on some people, but I think it's unlikely she was able to erase everyone's memory of her and her daughter. And with her daughter's erratic behavior, they should've been noticeable, unless of course, Amber used magic to calm her. But even so, they were in a hurry and might've attracted attention."

Bryson sighed. "But we have to make sure to avoid the police. They let me go last night, but I'm not convinced they're done with me. And if they become aware that friends of mine are asking questions, they'll be back to try to pin the whole incident on me. They'll have no evidence to support their claim, but I'd rather avoid having to test my lawyer's strength against theirs."

***

Fia nodded along with most of the other people in the room, but she was struggling to follow the conversation. Her hands were fisted tightly in her lap as her mind was spinning with the fact that she would be stuck in a car alone with Bryson for hours. And as if that weren't bad enough, they would have to spend the night down south before driving back the next day.

She had been trying to think of an excuse to leave Bryson's house and go back to her own to be alone and get some more sleep. But it didn't seem like that was going to happen anytime soon. Not when she was going to have to spend time with the one person she wanted to stay away from. In all honesty *wanted* probably wasn't the correct word, which had been proven this morning when she'd had to fight her own body to prevent herself from ripping Bryson's pants off and riding him on the kitchen floor.

How long would she be able to be alone with him before she caved to the demands of the mating bond? And how long would it take for him to realize she was his? She feared the answer to those questions would be hours and not days if she couldn't find another way to quell the call of the mating bond.

Fia shuddered when a mixture of panic and desire raced through her body. If only Bryson had been a complete asshole to her, perhaps it would have been easier to dismiss the mating bond as an unfortunate duty she would just have to put up with occasionally while living her own life the rest of the time. But even though he might have been arrogant in how he pursued her, Bryson had never treated her badly or lied to her.

Fia already knew what was going to happen, though. She would fall hard for Bryson, and when he strayed, which he inevitably would, he would break her heart. But the horrible part was that the mating bond wouldn't disappear even if her heart was broken. It would keep demanding they fuck and spend time together, and it would gradually tear out her insides and leave her an empty husk.

"Fia." Bryson's voice penetrated her thoughts, and based on his tone, she realized it wasn't the first time he had tried to get her attention.

"Yes." She nodded as she lifted her gaze to his, but her expression was too wooden to give him a smile.

He studied her face with a frown before his expression relaxed into a smile. "I was saying I think it might be time for us to leave. It will take us several hours to get there."

She nodded again, unable to come up with another response. Hours with only a few inches between them. She was so fucked in every meaning of the word.

Bryson rose from the table, and she followed suit. After exchanging a few words with his panthers and some of the other people around the table, he headed toward the door.

Fia walked as if in a daze when she followed him to his office. Assuming he was going to pick up a few things he needed for their trip, she continued toward the couch to wait for him to finish packing.

"Fia, are you all right?" He was suddenly right in front of her, staring down at her with concern in his eyes. "You look pale, and you're shivering. What's wrong? Is there anything I can do?"

Shaking her head, she tried to give him a reassuring smile. But from the way he frowned in response, her effort wasn't very successful. "I'm fine. You just go ahead and pack or whatever you need to do, and I'll sit here for a minute."

She started for the couch, but before she made it one step, his hand wrapped around her upper arm to stop her.

"Not so fast there, redbird. You're clearly upset, and I want to know why." Bryson turned her to face him, but she stared straight ahead at the tattoos covering his throat and didn't meet his eyes.

She didn't resist when he placed a finger beneath her chin and tipped her head back until their gazes locked. "Fia, talk to me. Please." There was concern written in his eyes. "Have I done something to hurt you? Whatever it is, please tell me. I can't fix what I don't know. And whatever you may think of me, I don't want to hurt you."

Bryson seemed so genuinely concerned that her throat clogged with how much she wanted him to actually care about her. Her stomach knotted, and her eyes pricked with the threat of tears, as an overwhelming desire to throw her arms around his neck and hold him tightly swamped her. It was by sheer will alone that she tore out of his grip and turned away from him. "Please leave me alone for a minute, okay? Go do whatever you need to get done so we can leave."

Her whole body was tense while she waited for him to approach her again—to press her for an answer to his questions. She sighed in relief when he walked past her and disappeared out the door of the office before closing it behind him.

This trip was going to be a nightmare, but it would be okay if she could only get a handle on her emotions. At the moment they were all over the place, greatly helped along by the insistent mating bond.

"Okay, Fia, just breathe. You can do this. You *have to* do this." Her mumbled words sounded weak in her own ears, but she repeated them in her head like a mantra while she stiffened her spine and focused on her breathing.

By the time Bryson returned, she felt more relaxed

and centered. This was just another challenge she would have to conquer. And she had a plan for how to do that. She would pretend to sleep in the car while going through every spell and adjusted spell she could think of that might help her in this situation. There had to be something she could use, and she would find it.

CHAPTER 5

Fia was trying to relax in the passenger seat of Bryson's sleek sports car, but it was proving more difficult than she had thought. He was so close she could feel his hot alpha power caress her skin, and it was keeping her on edge, unable to concentrate on anything other than his presence.

They had swung by her place for her to pack a few things for their overnight stay, and as usual her mother had been more than a little enthusiastic about talking to Bryson again. It was grating on Fia's nerves the way her mother always spoke about him like he was some kind of hero or gentleman or something.

Fia had tried to remind her mother several times about the stories firmly establishing Bryson as a womanizer, but it was like the woman didn't care. At least she didn't see the problem with his behavior like Fia did. According to her mother, his respectful manner toward her was a compliment to his character, and that was all that mattered in her book. Apparently, the man could do nothing wrong as long as he showed respect for his elders.

At almost thirty Fia was way too old to live with her mother, but it had been a comfort to them both since they didn't know a lot of other witches, and there was quite a lot about their lives they couldn't disclose to other people. Fia had tried for several years to live a life among normal humans while hiding her true self, but after a disastrous engagement she realized it wasn't the kind of life she wanted. Her being a witch wasn't the reason she had ended up leaving her fiancé, but the break-up had led to her decision to leave the life she used to have. Instead, she and her mother had made a life and a business together, and while the two women certainly had their differences, they weren't significant enough to prevent mother and daughter from being great friends.

Contrary to many parents, her mother had never interfered in Fia's romantic life, leaving her daughter to make her own choices when it came to men. Except for some reason, when it came to Bryson. Fia couldn't count the number of times her mother had hinted or outright told her to go on a date with the man. And in this she was as persistent as the man himself. It had been the source of several arguments between Fia and her mother in the past couple of years, causing Fia to avoid the topic of Bryson around her mother if she could help it.

If only Fia could have avoided the man as well, but she had to reinforce the spell at least every month to make sure it remained stable and effective. Due to his persistent pursuit of her, though, she never had to make up an excuse to see him. It was rarely more than two weeks between each time he sought her out with a new scheme to get into her pants.

His efforts hadn't paid off for him but seeing him regularly had been wearing on her defenses. Every time her eyes landed on him, she was reminded of how amazingly good-looking he was and how her body wanted him desperately. Thank God she had a good battery-operated lover, or she might have given in to him months ago. But based on her observations that morning she would have to invest in a larger vibrator. The old one just couldn't compare to Bryson's cock, and she knew it would feel deficient after seeing his real size.

Need suddenly tore through her and made her channel clench, and a moan escaped her before she could stop it. Holding her breath, she waited for Bryson to comment on her sound or scent while she silently cursed herself for letting her thoughts wander. To think about the man's cock while seated beside him in the confined space of his car was a rookie mistake she should have made sure to avoid.

"Are you awake or are you dreaming?" Bryson's deep voice made her shiver as its timbre seemed to vibrate against her skin. "And what's with your scent today? I can't remember you ever smelling this delicious before."

And your voice has never sounded so fucking sexy before. She couldn't tell him that, though. But it was the truth, and she had no doubt it was the mating bond speaking. At least partially the mating bond. Some of it was probably just her. Even without the mating bond, she would have been attracted to Bryson, but perhaps it would have been easier to resist her temptation to fuck him.

Opening her eyes, Fia turned her head to look at him. If he had been less of a fuckboy and not her true mate, she might have enjoyed letting him work to capture her attention for a while before finally giving in to him. She had no doubt they would have had fun together. But his track record wasn't something she approved of or wanted to be a part of, and she had no intention of ending up mated any earlier than strictly necessary.

Bryson glanced at her with a mischievous look in his eyes. "Were you dreaming just now, or were you fantasizing about me?"

Her eyes widened in shock, even though she should have anticipated his question. He was nothing if not straightforward, but that didn't mean she didn't feel called out.

After he glanced at her again, his smile widened. "You *were* fantasizing about me. Good to know. Then I suppose you're not as immune to me as you've been pretending to be."

She sighed in defeat. There was no point trying to deny her attraction to him. It would only make him more relentless in his gloating. "I'm not always able to control my physical reactions, but that doesn't mean I welcome them. They're an unfortunate nuisance. I'm not sure you understand what I'm talking about, since you never seem to quell any of your impulses—healthy or not."

His sudden burst of laughter startled her. "What is it I do that you consider unhealthy? Having sex? For your information that's considered part of a normal healthy lifestyle even for humans but particularly for shifters. Denying that part of myself would be unhealthy."

The blatant reminder of his lifestyle made her flinch, and she turned her head to look out of the passenger-side window. He would never understand where she was coming from, and that was one of the main reasons why this mating bond was a curse, and she had been struggling against it for so long. "I don't want to be a part of your healthy lifestyle as you call it. I'll fight it for as long as I can."

"Fight it? What exactly do you mean by that?" She could practically hear the frown in his voice and bit her lip in irritation when she realized her choice of words. "Is that your way of saying that you're attracted to me, but you don't want to be with me? You don't have to promise me a lifelong commitment to have sex with me, Fia. I don't understand why you would turn me away if you wanted me. You're not a virgin, are you? And even if you were, I'd make sure you had an amazing first time."

"I'm not a virgin." She turned to stare at him. He really was clueless as to how she saw him, even though she had tried to tell him more than once. "For your information I've had several great lovers, but none of them have been fuckboys." It was stretching the truth a bit, considering only one of her previous lovers had been any good between the sheets, but Bryson didn't need to know that.

Bryson flinched before his eyes narrowed and his jaw muscles tensed. Perhaps he had finally gotten the message about what she thought of his womanizing. It was about time. Not that she expected it to make any difference to his future behavior. It was part of his lifestyle as he had just told her. But at least she had made her point, and perhaps it would cause his behavior toward her to change.

"Is that why you haven't said yes to me? Because I've had sex with other women before you?" His expression was guarded, and his voice was controlled, but the tension in his jaw gave away his irritation. "You just told me you've had several lovers. Were they all virgins before you? And what happened to them after you were done fucking? Did any of them mean anything to you beyond sex, Fia?" His hands tightened on the steering wheel until his knuckles turned white, and the steering wheel creaked in protest.

Fia studied him for a few seconds while considering how to answer his questions. He was clearly pissed off, but she didn't really understand why he was so angry. She had turned him down for two years, so it wasn't like anything had changed. "I went out with one of them on and off for a year, but we were never serious about each other. But then there was Paul."

She bit her lip and dropped her gaze to her lap, not quite sure what to tell him. Perhaps she should have avoided mentioning Paul at all, but Bryson might as well know. "We had been engaged for two months when I found him fucking another woman. He told me it was only sex and that it didn't mean anything, but it meant something to me. That was three years ago. It took me moving away before he understood I didn't want him after what he did."

"What an asshole." There was barely controlled rage in Bryson's voice.

Bursting out laughing, she turned to look at him. "That's rich coming from you. Do you really think women haven't been hurt by your so-called healthy lifestyle? Then you're truly naive."

Fia jerked in her seat when his hand slammed down on the steering wheel with a crack, and his power enveloped her whole body like hot water in a tub. His voice was low and menacing when he spoke. "I never make promises I don't intend to keep. In fact, I make sure people know exactly what they can and can't expect from me. A commitment is binding and shall be treated as such. It can be broken if necessary, but honesty and compassion is required. Which is one of the reasons I don't make any commitments I haven't carefully considered the implications of."

She stared at him as his power stoked her need and made her squirm in her seat. Did that mean he actually knew what he had offered her that morning, and it wasn't just a spur-of-the-moment kind of thing?

But even if that were the case and he had meant it when he spoke of commitment, she wasn't ready to believe him and accept his offer. He hadn't shown any signs of stopping his lifestyle of fucking everything in a skirt after he started chasing her, and to her that would have been a natural thing to do if he really wanted to be with her. Unless his wanting to commit to her was a recent development, perhaps as recent as the last twenty-four hours and a direct result of her spell being burned away.

***

Bryson wanted to punch the fucking asshole who had hurt Fia, and he would if he ever found out who this Paul was. The man had clearly destroyed her trust in men, and Bryson had no trouble seeing how. What he didn't understand was how Paul had wanted to fuck someone else when he had a woman like Fia committed to him. It was inconceivable.

Fia wasn't just beautiful; she was strong and resourceful. She didn't need a man to support her or take care of her to thrive, and that was something Bryson found utterly irresistible. He wanted to be the man she desired and wanted to spend time with, not because she needed his strength or money but because she wanted him for the person he was.

For a while Bryson had thought Fia's continued resistance to his seduction was purely based on the large number of women he'd fucked, which he felt was hypocritical when she had freely admitted to having had several lovers herself. But that wasn't the reason, at least not the main one. Fia feared being hurt again. She was scared of being stomped on by someone who claimed to care about her. And perhaps she thought Bryson's history with women meant he would do the same to her that her asshole ex-fiancé had done.

He glanced over at her. She was staring down at her fisted hands in her lap with a tight expression on her face. He wished he had known about this earlier. It would have made a difference to how he approached her, but it was too late to do anything about that now.

"I'll never do anything like that to you, Fia. I've already told you I want to spend time with you, and that means exclusively you. As long as we have a mutual agreement to date or whatever you want to call that kind of relationship, I won't so much as look at another woman. And why would I want to, anyway, when the only one I want to be with is you?"

She huffed. "You'll have to forgive me for not believing you, Bryson. During the last couple of years while you've been trying to get into my pants, you must've fucked at least a hundred other women. I take your behavior as evidence that you don't really have any interest in me at all apart from fucking me once or twice."

Bryson stiffened. Fia had a point. She didn't know what he'd been going through for the last couple of years. There had been no other women, but that was a fact he had hidden well to avoid appearing weak and escape questions from his panthers. He hadn't outright lied about it, but he had made an effort to let everyone think he was still acting the way he used to with women. And now his deception had come back to bite him in the ass, and he wasn't sure what to do about it.

Would Fia believe him if he told her the truth? Or would she think it was a convenient lie to persuade her to give in to him. She might even decide to talk to one of his panthers to check if he was being honest with her, but none of them would be able to confirm his claim since none of them knew the truth.

Perhaps he should postpone telling Fia until he had told his clan, but that would mean waiting until he got back late the next day. And he didn't really want to wait that long to tell the beautiful woman next to him the truth and perhaps increase his credibility in her eyes.

Staring straight ahead, he gripped the steering wheel tightly and swallowed hard. "This might be difficult for you to believe but—"

Fia's phone started ringing, and she dug into her purse to find it. A crease developed between her brows when she stared at the screen, but whatever she saw wasn't enough to prevent her from answering. "This is

Fia."

"Fia, it's so nice to hear your voice again. I'm in Inverness, so I'll be around shortly. It's about time we catch up, don't you think?" The smug male voice was loud enough that Bryson could hear every word, and it had him grinding his teeth. From the way Fia paled he had a fair idea who was calling her.

It took her a few seconds of stunned silence before she responded, but when she did, her voice was thick with rage. "No, there will never be a time for that."

"Oh, baby, don't be like that. A man has to be able to make one mistake without being shunned forever. It's time we made up and moved on. I still love you, you know, and I want your fine ass back in my bed where it's supposed to be."

Bryson just about broke the steering wheel while listening to the asshole's arrogant words. If he could have physically hurt someone through the phone, he would have.

Fia chuckled, but there was no amusement in the sound. "You had your chance, and you blew it. I don't love you anymore, and there is no point coming to my house because I'm not there." She looked relatively calm if you didn't count the white-knuckled fist resting on her thigh.

The man laughed. "Still playing hard to get, huh? Just tell me where you are, and I'll meet you there."

Bryson snatched the phone out of Fia's hand. "Fuck off, asshole! She's with me now, and if you so much as think about approaching her, I'll hurt you." His voice was little more than a growl, and he squeezed the phone so hard in his hand that the casing cracked.

"Who the fuck are you?" Fury darkened the other man's voice.

"I'm Bryson, and you can consider this your last warning. Call her or approach her and you'll wish you were dead."

The line went dead, and Bryson slowly handed the phone back to Fia. "I assume that was Paul. How often has he been calling you?" His voice vibrated with his anger, and he pulled in a deep breath to try to calm down. He wanted to strangle the guy, and he probably would if he ever saw him. Hopefully, Paul had gotten the message and wouldn't be contacting Fia again.

A deep frown marred Fia's face. "I haven't heard from him for a few months now. Before that he called me every few weeks, but I always managed to talk him out of coming to see me."

Bryson loosened his grip on the steering wheel. It was already cracked, but breaking it completely would mean a delay. "Why do you even answer when he calls if you don't want anything to do with him?"

She shrugged. "Because I don't want him to turn up on my doorstep unannounced. And he might if I don't answer his calls."

It made sense. What didn't make sense was Paul waiting this long to insist on visiting Fia if he really cared about her. But there were more important aspects to consider. "Has he ever physically harmed you in any way?"

Shaking her head, Fia turned to look at him. "No. And before you ask, he used to be a nice man. Warm, attentive and positive. But he changed after we got engaged. Gradually, he became colder, and he started to take me for granted, treating me more like property than someone he cared about. It hurt when I found him with another woman, but by then I had already decided to break the engagement. The cheating was just the tip of the iceberg that made it easier to leave immediately without having to come up with another explanation."

Bryson breathed out a silent sigh of relief. At least the asshole hadn't laid a hand on her, because that would have earned the man a slower and more painful death than he already deserved for treating her the way he had. "If he ever calls you again or tries to contact you in any other way, you will tell me, okay?" He phrased it like a question, but it really wasn't.

A small smile tugged at her lips while she stared straight ahead. "Bryson, I appreciate your help but—"

"It wasn't a request, Fia." Anger made his voice rougher, and he released some of the power he had been trying to keep in check. "You *will* tell me."

Fia tensed and visibly swallowed before she nodded, but she didn't turn her head to meet his gaze.

It wasn't good enough, and Bryson let more of his power fill the space around them. "Tell me yes."

She gasped and squirmed in the seat beside him. "Yes." The word was breathy and filled with so much desire that the need he had successfully controlled for a while broke free and his cock swelled rapidly.

Before he could think better of it, he reached out and put his hand on her thigh. She jerked in response but didn't pull away or tell him to remove his hand. "Redbird, I can practically taste your desire. Do you want me to…stop?" He had meant to stop the car, but belatedly he realized she might think he was asking whether she wanted him to stop touching her.

Her eyes were big and round when her head snapped around, and she finally met his gaze. "I... That's..." Her hand landed on top of his, but instead of pushing it away like he had expected, her fingers curled around his and tightened like she desperately needed something to hold onto.

Bryson's mouth went dry, and he couldn't come up with a single thing to say. She had never touched him like this before, and even though she wasn't doing anything other than holding his hand, it was enough to play havoc with his control. All he wanted to do was stop the car and pull her onto his lap, but he didn't want to risk doing something that would provoke her into pulling away from him again. He needed to let her stay in control. If she wanted more from him, she would let him know.

"Bryson, can we stop?" Her voice was husky, and she squirmed and squeezed her thighs together.

"Of course," he rasped. *Fuck yes!* His cock hardened even more as he slowed the car.

She turned back to look at the road ahead. "I mean in the next town. I need to go to the bathroom." Pushing his hand off her thigh, she released her grip.

It was like having a bucket of ice water poured over his head, and it took him a few seconds before he could answer in a relatively calm voice. "Okay, sure." He forced a smile as he stared straight ahead. He had let his desperate need for her convince him she was ready to give in to him. *Fuck, I'm an idiot. A desperate idiot.*

CHAPTER 6

Fia stared straight ahead and didn't say a word while Bryson kept driving for another ten minutes before they entered a small town. Or town was probably pushing it, seeing as it was just a few houses and a gas station.

He pulled into the service station and parked. Without looking at her, he nodded toward the entrance. "Go on. I'll just wait here."

Nodding, she got out of the car and hurried into the small building. The toilet was in the back, and she breathed out a sigh of relief when she locked the door behind her.

Fia didn't really need to go, but she desperately needed to be alone if only for a few minutes. Bryson's power had been near suffocating in the car, and it had turned her on to the point where she started wondering if she was going to come right there in the seat.

Her clit was throbbing against the seam of her

jeans, and if she hadn't had the foresight to put on a panty liner, her wetness would surely have soaked through and made a wet patch between her legs. She wasn't going to do anything about her need in a gas station restroom, though.

After using the toilet, she splashed some water on her face to freshen up and try to force herself to think about something other than Bryson waiting for her in the car. But the man was firmly stuck in her mind, and his protective behavior when Paul called added to her attraction to him. She'd had no idea how hot it was to have someone step up and take charge like that, and the fact that she knew Bryson would make good on his promise to hurt Paul if he ever showed up only made it hotter.

Fia pulled in a deep breath and held it for a few seconds before letting it out slowly. *Relax, Fia, and focus. No more drooling over the gorgeous panther. He's a fuckboy, remember?* She gave herself an encouraging smile in the mirror before she left the bathroom.

Bryson studied her face with a pensive expression on his face when she climbed back into the car. It was a bit unnerving, but instead of letting it get to her, she gave him a bright smile.

His eyes narrowed, but he didn't say anything, and as soon as she put her seat belt on, he pushed the accelerator, and they were off down the road.

Fia focused on the scenery that flew by as they sped along the A9. The panther clan they were going to visit was located not far from Glasgow, which was a bit ironic, considering Paul lived in that city. But he was currently in Inverness, and he didn't know where she was, anyway. Hopefully, Paul had left Inverness by the time they got back the next day, because as much as she would love to call Bryson on her ex's ass, she wouldn't. It would mean owing Bryson for protecting her, and that kind of debt wasn't a good idea.

"Fia, I..." Bryson stopped and sighed, and she turned her head to look at his profile as he stubbornly stared straight ahead. "I meant what I said earlier, that I'd like to be with you, spend time with you. We can take it slow and have dinner, talk, you know, just get to know each other better. And I won't try to seduce you or mention one word about sex. I promise. It will be up to you when or if you feel ready for that next step with me."

Her jaw slackened in shock as he spoke. This man was completely different from the Bryson she had known for the last two years. Was it her past experiences and Paul's behavior that had prompted him to change his strategy? Or was being with her so important he was willing to try anything to gain her favor? It was hard to know what to believe, but she definitely preferred this strategy to the last one of constantly trying to persuade her to come to his bed with a poorly hidden confidence that she wouldn't be able to resist for much longer.

"Does that sound like something you would be willing to try?" He turned to meet her gaze for a few seconds before turning back to keep an eye on the road.

Fia didn't know what to say. Her body was screaming *yes*, but her mind was more reluctant, particularly considering spending time with him was irreconcilable with keeping him at arm's length. She was still trying to come up with a way to subdue the mating bond, and an agreement to spend time with him would be counterproductive in that respect.

"I don't know, Bryson." She stared at his profile, taking in the tenseness in his jaw and shoulders. She felt bad turning him down when he had asked so sweetly, but she didn't really feel like she had a choice if she wanted to avoid ending up mated to him within a few days. They would be mated eventually; any other outcome was unlikely, but if she could come up with a clever way to postpone it for a few more years, she would do it.

"I think you might be better off focusing on someone else than me. I'm clearly not your type." The words almost choked her on their way out, but she knew she would be better off if Bryson mated someone else instead of her. No matter what the bond kept telling her, she would be off the hook if Bryson mated another woman. Mating was forever, and there was no changing that fact.

Frowning, Bryson glanced at her with something reminiscent of pain in his eyes. "What if you are exactly my type, and I'm yours? We don't know unless we try."

Biting her lip, she looked away. This had to be the mating bond speaking. He'd never acted like this before, like she was important to him. All she had ever been was a piece of ass, and knowing that had made it relatively simple to keep turning him down. But this new Bryson was much harder to say *no* to.

"You really don't want me, do you?" There was definite pain and resignation in his voice, and she almost turned back to look at him.

But she resisted the urge. Agreeing to spend time

with him would only make this more difficult, while staying firm in her decision would hurt less in the long run.

He didn't say anything more, and she kept staring out the passenger-side window. Her body was tense, and her stomach kept churning like she had eaten something that didn't quite agree with her. But it would pass in time. Hopefully.

They had been driving for quite a while when he broke the awkward silence between them. "Okay, I need ice cream."

The statement was so out of the blue Fia couldn't help the snort that escaped her. Smiling, she turned to him and met his gaze.

Bryson was smiling back at her with his eyes shining with warmth and happiness, and she felt an almost overwhelming desire to melt into his strong arms. She was tall for a woman, but she would still just about drown against his large frame, and it would feel so good to just lean on him for a while and let all her fears and worries go, knowing he would take care of her no matter what happened.

"Fia, what's wrong?" Dark-brown eyes were staring at her from a face suddenly lined with concern.

She blinked a couple of times and realized tears had filled her eyes, and one had escaped down her cheek. Looking away, she swiped at the stray tear. "I'm fine. I don't know why I…" No reasonable explanation came to mind, except that this true mate thing had been grating on her for a long time, wearing her down slowly, and she was so tired of it. All she wanted was a break from worrying about what was going to happen.

"There's no doubt you need ice cream." The smile

in Bryson's voice made her turn back to look at him, and she couldn't help smiling when she saw the glint in his eyes. "The turn-off to Perth is coming up in just a couple of minutes. I know of the perfect place."

"Thank you." She chuckled through her tears. "I think you might be right. Ice cream sounds good." The tension in her body seeped away as her gaze lingered on his profile, until she caught herself staring at his lips. She quickly turned to stare at the road instead.

Why did he have to show her all these new sides of himself? The warm, humorous, hurt and don't forget protective sides of his character. The seductive side had been possible to ignore, at least for the most part, but all these other traits weren't as easily dismissed. They greatly improved his personality in her eyes.

Bryson obviously knew where he was going, driving confidently through the streets of Perth until he pulled to the side and parked. Before she knew it, he was outside, opening the door for her, and she returned his smile when he reached out a hand to help her out of the car.

They walked down the street side by side until he indicated a small cafe tucked between two shops. "Just in here. They have the best ice cream I've ever tasted."

It had never occurred to her that he might have a sweet tooth. He was a panther, a carnivore, and apart from that morning they hadn't shared many meals together, but she had assumed desserts weren't something he particularly enjoyed. But then she had always been more focused on staying away from him than getting to know him.

"What would you like?" His large hand pressed gently against the small of her back. "I think I've tasted all the various flavors, and every single one is fantastic. You can't go wrong no matter what you choose."

Fia stared at all the colorful flavors spread out before her, but she struggled to focus when the warmth of his hand seeped through her shirt and heated her skin. She wanted to lean back against it, but instead of giving into the urge, she stayed still and tried to concentrate on the task at hand. "I think I'll go with banana and dark chocolate." Her voice was a bit husky, but she pressed on, pretending she didn't sound like she had just woken up. "In one of those waffle cones, please."

"I'll have the same, and please make them extra-large," Bryson's dark voice rumbled beside her.

The woman behind the counter smiled. "Coming right up."

"Excellent choice." Bryson's murmured words next to her ear made a shiver race through her body, and she folded her lips between her teeth to stop the moan that threatened to escape her.

This wasn't going well. Her resistance was going to crumble if she stayed this close to him for much longer. They needed to move on as soon as possible. Because once they arrived at their destination, they would be among other people, and it would be easier to focus on something other than Bryson's hotness and charming attentiveness.

"Here you go. Enjoy." The woman gave them a bright smile and handed over two massive ice creams.

Fia's eyes widened, and she chuckled as she felt the weight of the thing in her hand. "Thank you. I didn't expect it to be quite this…enormous."

The woman just smiled, probably having heard the

same thing many times before.

Bryson laughed as he steered Fia toward the high table by the front window. "Don't worry, I'll finish it if you can't."

She turned to gape at him. His ice cream was just as large, and she wasn't sure she could finish even half of her own. "That's impossible. You'll throw up."

His eyes sparkled with amusement. "I have a particular weakness for ice cream. One of these is nothing. Two is better. But I've been known to put away more than that."

Shaking her head slowly, she stared at him. "Ice cream is one of my weaknesses, too, but I certainly don't have your capacity."

"Not many do." He stuck out his tongue and lapped at the ice cream slowly and methodically while keeping his eyes locked on hers.

Fia couldn't look away from him, and she couldn't eat. The sight of his tongue caressing the ice cream like he was pretending it was something else made her want to find a hotel immediately. And she had no doubt he was doing it on purpose and was fully aware of its effect on her.

It took all her willpower to tear her gaze away and focus on her own ice cream.

A deep chuckle sounded from beside her, but she resisted the urge to look at him again. Nothing good would come of letting herself get trapped in his snare.

As predicted, she couldn't finish more than half of her ice cream, but true to his word Bryson devoured it without trouble. The man could certainly put it away for someone who didn't look like he had an ounce of fat on him, but then he was a shifter. Their metabolisms were known to be significantly higher than a human's.

Bryson had barely stopped chewing when he rose from his stool and nodded toward the entrance with a smile. "Ready to get back on the road?"

Nodding, she stood before following him toward the door.

Opening the door, he indicated for her to walk out ahead of him, but as soon as she had passed him, he reached out and braided his fingers with hers before following her out the door.

Caught off guard, she let it happen, but as soon as they were outside on the sidewalk, she turned her head to look at him.

Bryson stared straight ahead with a small smile creasing his lips as they moved toward the car, like walking hand in hand with her was perfectly normal and something they had done countless times before.

CHAPTER 7

Bryson reveled in the feeling of her small hand securely laced with his, and for every step he took that she didn't tear her hand out of his grip, he silently cheered. He kept his gaze trained straight ahead and didn't talk, to avoid doing or saying anything to provoke her into pulling away from him.

He had wanted Fia for two years, but the longing had never been as intense as it was in the last few hours. He wanted to be in her presence constantly. Except it was more than that. He *needed* to have her close, and letting her out of his sight for even a minute had his heart speeding up in agitation.

Perhaps he had been wrong for the last two years in concluding she wasn't his true mate. Because this had to be mating behavior. But it still didn't make sense that it hadn't taken effect sooner. He should have known within days of meeting her. But instead his need for her had been ebbing and flowing like the tide, though never dying completely.

"Bryson." The sugary sweet voice snapped him out of his thoughts, and his gaze quickly found the tall blonde who had called his name. She was walking straight toward him with a wide and arrogant smile on her face.

"Tanya." His tone reflected his annoyance, but she didn't seem to notice as she continued toward him until he had to stop to avoid crashing straight into her.

Fia yanked her hand out of his, and he wanted to growl at Tanya for destroying the progress he had finally made with his redbird, but he controlled his reaction in favor of handling this situation correctly and expediently.

Tanya reached out toward him while she gave him a self-satisfied smile, but he quickly took a couple of steps back to stay out of her reach. He might be forced into exchanging a few words with her, but there was no way he was going to endure her touch.

Again she didn't seem fazed by his reaction. Lowering her hand, she kept smiling like he had just told her he was happy to see her. "It's so nice to see you again. I had planned to call you, but I've been so busy with modeling jobs all over Europe, you know?" She pursed her lips and fluttered her eyelashes, and he almost rolled his eyes. "Are you staying in Perth for a few days? You should come and stay at my place. I—"

"No, thank you." His lips twisted in a disgusted sneer, and he barely contained a shudder at the mere notion of touching her again. They had met in Edinburgh while he was there on business not long before he met Fia, and they had ended up spending a couple of nights together, even though she was annoying as hell.

Tanya had been someone to satisfy his hunger for sex and that was all. Just like the rest of the women he'd been with. Harsh but true. But they had all been eager to be fucked, so it wasn't like he ever had to beg for it. For most women one look was usually enough to have them crawl into his lap. And that was something he had been proud of. Until he met Fia and other women's attention became a nuisance and an exercise in evasion without being obvious.

Tanya's eyes narrowed, and she shot a glance at Fia, who was standing a couple of yards away. "I'm sure she'll find her own way home. You and me, though." She grinned up at him, but her smile looked a bit strained this time. "We're dynamite, remember?"

"No." He didn't elaborate before taking a step to the side to pass her. She had been nothing special, or more accurately, less than average, but telling her would only be cruel. He would never say anything like that to a woman. If a woman gave him her body, the least he could do was pretend she was fantastic, no matter if she was or not.

But Tanya apparently wasn't done yet. She took a step to the side to block him from moving past her while her face twisted in anger. "What's so special about her? You said I was amazing in bed."

Bryson crossed his arms over his chest and broadened his stance. Staring down at her, he tried not to show his distaste for her and her behavior. "I told you I didn't want anything more than sex, and you were happy with that. I want Fia to be my woman if she'll have me." He lifted his gaze to meet Fia's, but that was the wrong thing to do.

Tanya hissed, and before he realized what she

intended, she stormed over to Fia and pushed her.

Fia clearly didn't anticipate the woman's actions either and wasn't prepared for the impact. Stumbling back a few steps, Fia managed to gain her footing, but by the time she came to a stop, she was in the road with a car heading straight for her at a speed too high for the busy city street. The driver wasn't going to be able to stop in time.

Bryson didn't think he had ever moved that fast. He snatched Fia out of the road with only a fraction of a second to spare before she would have been seriously injured or perhaps even killed when the car hit her.

Holding her tightly to his chest, he laid his cheek against the top of her head. His heart was racing a million miles an hour as images of Fia's broken body in the middle of the road flashed through his head. "Are you all right, redbird?"

His eyes landed on Tanya, and he let his fury show when their gazes met. He wanted to kill Tanya, but it would have to wait until he'd made sure Fia was okay.

"Yes, I'm fine." But Fia's voice sounded shrill and wobbly like the shock of what had just happened was just starting to take effect.

"I'm so sorry, Fia." He tensed against the pain that flared in his chest. "I should've seen it coming and prevented her from touching you." It was his fault Fia had almost died. Anticipating things like this was usually something he was good at, but he had just failed miserably.

Fia struggled in his arms, and lifting his head, he loosened his hold on her. Beautiful almond-shaped hazel eyes met his when she tipped her head back.

"Don't take the blame for a crazy woman's actions, Bryson."

Tilting his head to the side, he studied her face. She looked like she meant what she had just said, and it surprised him. He had expected her to pin this on him due to his track record with women.

Bryson didn't know how to respond, so he just nodded. He was at least partially to blame, even if Fia didn't want to tell him to his face. She seemed to be doing okay, though, which meant it was time for him to deal with Tanya.

The blond woman was still standing a few yards away, glaring at him and Fia like she hadn't almost killed someone. He didn't usually take the time to get to know the women he fucked, but this one had to be crazier than most of the women he had been with. Being jealous after two years of not even trying to contact him had to be a sign of insanity.

His lips curled in distaste as he narrowed his eyes at Tanya. He had always had qualms about killing women. But for her he might have made an exception if they had been somewhere else than the middle of a busy city street.

After letting go of Fia, he closed the distance to Tanya in a few long strides. Towering over her, he did something he had hardly ever done before and was completely against the rules of shifters.

It was easy to see when she noticed the change. Her jaw slackened, and her eyes widened in fear, but instead of backing away from him like he had expected, she just stood there staring at him.

His head was bent to prevent other people from seeing his animal eyes and his extended fangs. But

Tanya saw them clearly and judging by her reaction, she didn't think his change was a party trick.

Bryson leaned in and spoke softly in her ear. "The next time I see you, I'll kill you." Then, he let his features change back to human before he walked back to Fia and swung her up into his arms.

Fia made a small noise of protest, but he ignored it and hurried to his car. He wanted her to be as far away as possible before Tanya recovered from her shock and decided retaliation was in order. He didn't consider it likely due to Tanya's obvious fear, but he wasn't going to take any more chances with Fia's life.

After having placed Fia resolutely in the passenger seat, he rounded the front of the car while scanning the surrounding area. Tanya was nowhere to be seen, but that didn't mean she was no longer a threat.

He got in and started the car before taking off down the street at an elevated speed. Keeping his eyes on the road ahead, he ground his teeth together while pondering what had just happened.

It was the first time one of his previous fucks had assaulted a woman he was with, but it might not be the last. And with the number of women he had fucked, it was only a matter of time before they ran into the next one. He had never regretted his lifestyle before, but then he had never expected it to have consequences like this. *Fuck, I'm a stupid asshole.*

Taking a deep breath, he glanced at Fia sitting next to him. She was silently staring straight ahead with a neutral expression on her face. It was impossible to tell what she was thinking, but he desperately wanted to know. And he wanted to know why the thought of her death made him feel like he would have wanted to die as well. "How are you feeling, Fia?"

She shrugged without sparing him a glance. "Fine." Her voice was toneless and dead and gave him no clue as to how she was actually feeling.

Trepidation settled like a vibration in his gut. She had allowed him to hold her hand, which he had considered immense progress. But that was before Tanya had shown up and destroyed everything. Were they back to how it had been for the last two years with Fia rejecting every move he made? Or was this just a small setback? He didn't know, and he didn't think this was the right time to try to find out. She probably needed some time to process what had just happened without him pestering her with questions.

***

Fia's mind was spinning. If not for Bryson's quick reflexes, she would have been injured—seriously injured. But all she could think about was how a permanent injury would have affected her relationship with Bryson. Would he still have wanted her if she became paralyzed? And how would such an incident have affected the fact that they were true mates? She didn't have the answers to those questions, and she couldn't ask Bryson. And why should she care, anyway, when she resented the fact that she was his true mate?

Fia had read about true mates in one of her mother's old books about known supernatural species, a rare book that had once belonged to her grandmother. It had contained enough information that Fia had realized who Bryson was to her, but she suspected there was a lot she didn't know yet about the mating bond and its consequences.

She had wanted to ask Sabrina a few questions about it, but with everything that had happened and the risk of revealing her status to Bryson, she had decided against it. And with their sudden trip, there had been no time for it anyway.

But Fia was quickly coming to realize that she needed to find out more to be able to avoid making a mistake, and she would make a point of contacting Sabrina when they got back the next day. If the blonde somehow understood Fia's connection to Bryson, Fia would just have to find a way to swear her to secrecy for the time being.

But there was no reason to expect that Sabrina would discover what was the basis for Fia's questions. With everything going on with Amber, questions about mating should be expected from someone like herself who didn't have firsthand experience with it. But even if there was a good reason for her questions, she still couldn't ask Bryson directly. The consequences would be too high if he realized the real reason she wanted to know.

Bryson's white-knuckled grip on the steering wheel made it clear he was still agitated about what had happened. And the way he had resolutely grabbed her and carried her to the car had shown her the urgency with which he wanted to get her out of there. There was no doubt he was shaken by what had happened, but then most people would have been. It didn't have to mean she was special to him beyond the fact that they had known each other for two years.

He had been adamant he wanted to be with her, but she didn't trust his intentions, and she still didn't think they were on the same page about the meaning of commitment. He might think he knew what it meant, but she had a feeling his version of commitment had an expiration date that wasn't nearly as far into the future as it was for her.

Fia let out a silent sigh. It was a bit of a catch-22 situation. She wanted him to prove himself to her before she said yes to be with him, but he wouldn't be able to prove himself unless she agreed to be with him. And hence the reason why her mind was spinning.

Turning her head to face the passenger-side window, she squeezed her eyes shut. With everything that was happening, this wasn't the right time to make a decision about Bryson and herself. It would need to wait until the issue with Amber was resolved, and Fia had a clear head to think about this logically and determine whether she was ready to take the risk. Until then she would have to suppress the call of the mating bond as best she could.

CHAPTER 8

Bryson scanned the area carefully as they drove up the long driveway toward the farm, which was the base for Hugh's panther clan. It was a big farm with fields spread out in between lines of trees. And sheep were dotting the green pastures, grazing peacefully and giving the place a languid country charm.

The panther alpha in question came out onto the porch just as Bryson parked the car in front of the big farmhouse. Hugh was a large man, almost as wide as Bryson himself. But in contrast, Hugh's fair skin wasn't covered in tattoos, and his long red hair was gathered in a braid down his back.

Hugh's mate, Kynlee, exited the house right behind her mate before coming to a stop beside him on the porch. The curvy blonde wore a warm smile that broke into a laugh when her mate snaked his arm around her waist and yanked her close to his side.

Bryson didn't look at Fia or say anything before he exited the car. He probably should have, but the silence between them had felt awkward after what had happened in Perth, and he simply didn't know what to say apart from stating the obvious that they had arrived at their destination.

As soon as he stepped out of the vehicle, Bryson met Hugh's gaze and nodded. Hugh didn't follow the old customs, so the greeting ritual wasn't something he expected or wanted. In fact the man felt the official greeting was too formal and made people feel like they were less valuable if they weren't an alpha.

Bryson respected Hugh's opinion, but he didn't agree. The old customs weren't meant to be used as a form of segregation. The rules were there to help each clan member understand their position and responsibilities and how those fit into the total structure of the clan.

Everyone was important and valuable in a clan, and yet everyone was different. Each person's position was determined based on the individual's strengths and weaknesses. The responsibilities should suit the individual and thereby empower them, but that meant taking great care when assigning responsibilities.

The result was a clan that worked like a well-oiled machine and could handle any type of crisis without needing a lot of time to prepare and plan, simply because they were always prepared, and they had a working plan where everyone already knew their role.

Bryson had been told several times by other alphas, including Hugh, that he ran his clan like a military captain would a company of soldiers. And they were mostly right, but he didn't see anything wrong with that.

"Welcome, Bryson." Hugh smiled before moving

his gaze to Fia. "About time you mated. Congratulations."

Bryson's spine stiffened as his head snapped around to look at Fia. And just like he had expected, she paled as she stared at Hugh with wide eyes.

"Oh, I thought…" Hugh's voice faltered as his mate tsked at him. "Damn, I'm sorry."

Bryson sighed before he swung his gaze back to Hugh. The damage was already done, and there wasn't much he could do about it. Not in the presence of Hugh and Kynlee anyway. "It's fine. An honest mistake. But, no, Fia is not my mate. Only my…travel companion." Bryson would have been happy to present her as more than that, although mating wasn't what he had in mind at this stage.

"Welcome, Fia, and please accept my apology." Hugh sighed. "I hope I'll make a better impression from now on."

"It's okay." There was a smile in Fia's voice, and Bryson's gaze was drawn back to her. "Like Bryson said, an honest mistake. Don't worry about it."

"Thank you. You're most gracious." A wide grin split Hugh's face in half as he bowed. "But then I wouldn't expect anything less from a fellow redhead."

Hugh's mate laughed and swatted at him. "No flirting, you big oaf. I'll have your hide, and you know what that means."

"Oh, I can't wait." The big red-haired man waggled his eyebrows at his mate. "Is that a promise?"

Kynlee laughed and swatted at him again. "You're incorrigible. Are you going to invite our guests into the house, or am I?"

Hugh swept out his arm in a welcoming gesture.

"Please come join us in the living room."

"Thank you." Bryson nodded his acceptance and started toward the porch. Fia soon filed in beside him, and they mounted the steps side by side.

Hugh and Kynlee led the way into the living room. It was a large room toward the back of the house, decorated in various shades of brown and beige, and with large windows overlooking a vast field of grazing cattle of the long-haired Highland variety.

Bryson took a seat at one end of a long leather couch, and to his surprise Fia sat down next to him with only a couple of inches preventing their thighs from touching. He glanced at her, but she was staring straight ahead and didn't meet his gaze.

The alpha couple sat down across the low table from them, and Hugh had barely sat down before he locked eyes with Bryson. "I haven't been able to get ahold of Erwin yet. His phone is switched off, and according to the phone company he hasn't made or received any calls in months." The big man sighed and shook his head.

Bryson leaned forward in his seat, resting his forearms on his knees. "Am I correct in assuming that Erwin is Amber's mate? And does he usually go off the grid like this?"

"Yes, Erwin is Amber's mate." Hugh shot a glance at his mate. "I don't contact him often when they're staying at their cabin. Ever since he mated Amber seven years ago, he's been a different man. Temperamental and difficult, and to be honest every time they take off for the cabin, the rest of the clan breathes a sigh of relief."

"But does he usually turn off his phone while

staying there?" Fia frowned.

"Not that I have experienced before." Hugh sighed again. "I usually have to call him a couple of times before I can get him talking, but he always either picks up the second time or returns my call within a day or so. I've never experienced total radio silence before, and I'm starting to think something has happened to him. Either Amber has hurt him, or she is keeping him prisoner. Because killing him wouldn't be an option, considering they're mated."

Bryson nodded. "What's your impression of Amber?"

Kynlee's mouth twisted in distaste. "Unpleasant if I have to put it politely. I could definitely come up with worse words to describe that woman. Thankfully, she didn't want to stay in this house, so they adopted the small cottage in the western field. And we had no objections to that. In fact, I think I would've moved out if she insisted on staying in this house."

Hugh put an arm around Kynlee's shoulders and kissed her temple. "Oh, I wouldn't have let her, love. I might be a jovial man, but there are limits to what I can tolerate." The alpha turned his head to look at Bryson. "To give you an example, when they were fighting inside the cottage, it could easily be heard all the way up here almost two-hundred yards away. I would've killed her before I let her stay in this house."

The corners of Bryson's lips tugged up into a grin. "I can understand that. So how far away is their cabin? Leith mentioned it was located somewhere on the west coast, but that doesn't narrow it down much."

"A little south of Oban." Hugh smiled. "It's not accessible by car, so we'll have to walk for about half an hour from the nearest road to get there. It's a beautiful place, but it always surprised me that Amber wanted to stay there with Erwin for any length of time. I got the impression she was a city girl, and the cabin is primitive without electricity and running water. I wouldn't have thought a small cabin like that would suit her, but then I didn't think she would accept living in the small cottage down in the western field either. She did, though, if you disregard the frequent fighting."

Bryson glanced down at Fia's sandals before looking at Kynlee. "Do you think Fia can borrow some appropriate footwear? We didn't exactly plan for a hike, and I don't want her breaking a leg or something worse out there."

"Of course. How about you?" Kynlee lifted an eyebrow at him.

"I'll be fine. I usually come prepared." Lifting one of his feet to show them his combat boot, he grinned. "But thank you for asking."

Kynlee chuckled before she rose and swung her gaze to Fia. "Come on, Fia. Let's find you something to wear. I'm sure I've got something that'll fit you."

"Thank you." After getting to her feet, Fia followed Kynlee, and Bryson couldn't help how his gaze immediately zoomed in on Fia's ass and stayed there until she disappeared out into the hallway.

No sooner had the women left the room than Hugh leaned forward and narrowed his eyes on him. "Are you playing hard to get, or is she? Because there's definitely something going on between the two of you. The way she looks at you…" Hugh shook his head slowly with his lips pressed into a hard line. "You shouldn't be stringing her along. She's too good for that."

Bryson's eyes widened at the accusation. "I'm not the one—" He cut himself off when he realized what he was admitting to. But judging by Hugh's grin, he had already said too much.

"Ah, I see." The big red-haired man chuckled. "It's as I thought then. Struggling with your past, is she? You do have a reputation a lot of decent women find offensive. I believe you have a lot of work ahead of you if you intend to win her over."

Bryson sighed and let his head tip forward. "I'm finally starting to realize that. I didn't think my past would matter that much, but for Fia it does, and I don't know how to convince her I would never look at another woman while committed to her." He didn't know why he blurted this out to Hugh. He didn't know the man that well, but it felt good to tell someone he could trust who didn't belong to his own clan.

G was a great friend and second in command, and they discussed practically everything except Fia. Bryson hadn't told G anything about his almost obsessive attraction to the beautiful redhead, and he had no intention of doing so either.

To tell his second in command he hadn't had sex in two years might be okay if a bit embarrassing. But telling G that it was due to Bryson pining for a woman who didn't want him was entirely different. It felt too much like failure.

"Well, a lot of wooing and groveling might be in order. Although, I can't quite picture you doing that." Hugh chuckled again, and Bryson lifted his head to glare at him, which made the man burst out laughing.

"You have to forgive me, Bryson, but you've never come across as the groveling type." Hugh struggled to contain his laughter. "But it might be time for you to learn. I have a feeling she'll be worth it."

"What makes you say that?" Bryson stared at the other man. They hadn't even been there half an hour, and Fia hadn't spoken more than a few words since they arrived.

Hugh shrugged. "Exactly what I said. Just a feeling I have."

Bryson turned his head to look out the window. Hugh was right. Fia would be worth it, but that didn't mean she would accept him. He had obviously been wasting his efforts for the last two years by focusing on seducing her instead of befriending her. But that didn't mean she would be any more accepting of his past with his altered strategy.

∞∞∞

Fia glanced at Bryson for what must have been the hundredth time. He had been quiet since they left the farm and headed toward Oban, and she hadn't been able to think of anything to say to break the silence between them. His expression was neutral if a little pensive, but there was nothing in his demeanor to suggest what he was thinking. And thereby lay the problem.

She wanted to talk to him about what had happened in Perth, but his focus might be on their impending visit to Amber's cabin. They had been on the road for almost two hours since leaving the farm, so based on what Hugh had said, they should arrive any minute. Not at the cabin, though, but at the place they would have to park their car before their half-hour hike toward the craggy coast where the cabin was located. But thankfully, they wouldn't have to try to find the place by themselves. Hugh, the red-haired panther alpha, and his lovely mate were in the car ahead of them, and the couple would show them the way to the cabin.

It was impossible to predict what they would find when they arrived. But there was no reason to believe Amber would be there at the moment. Fia couldn't imagine the nasty witch had time to be stuck at a primitive cabin. The woman was too busy trying to increase her power by killing shifters. Unless Amber's mate was still at the cabin, and the mating bond demanded she visit him regularly.

"Did you bring sunscreen?"

Her head snapped around to stare at Bryson. The question was so out of the blue it didn't immediately register what he had asked. "Um…yes, I always bring sunscreen."

"Good." A small smile formed on his lips, and he looked relieved.

Chuckling, Fia cocked her head as she let her gaze rest on his profile. "I hope you haven't been worrying about that this whole time. You've been awfully quiet."

His smile died, and he didn't meet her gaze. "I wasn't sure you wanted to talk to me after the incident in Perth. I'm really sorry about what happened. If I had suspected for a second that she would—"

"Bryson, it wasn't your fault, and I'm fine because you saved me."

He jerked and swerved halfway into the other lane before regaining control of the car. Then, his gaze dropped to his lap with a shocked expression on his face, and she realized why. Her hand was on his thigh, and she hadn't even realized she had put it there.

Fia yanked her hand away and turned to stare straight ahead. Her hand was practically burning with the feel of his tensing muscles against her palm, and her heart was trying to pound its way out of her chest. What on earth had made her touch him like that? She had never done anything like that before. But then he had never seemed vulnerable before and had been trying to take the blame for something that wasn't his fault. Sure, he had obviously fucked the woman, but it had sounded like it was a while ago, and the woman hadn't tried to contact him since.

"Fia." His voice was soft. "Thank you for saying that. I realize my past is more off-putting to you than I thought it would be. And to have it literally intrude like that…" He paused just long enough for her to turn to look at him. "There's something I want you to know, and it will probably sound unbelievable to you. But I swear it's the truth."

Turning his head, he met her gaze for a moment. "I haven't been with another woman since I met you. Tanya was one of the last, and that was a few weeks before I laid eyes on you for the first time."

Frowning, she shook her head slowly. That couldn't be right. She had never actually seen him with another woman, but his nighttime endeavors had been talked about among his panthers frequently, and it had to be because they had witnessed women coming or going. Why else would they talk about it like it was a fact?

"I know you probably don't believe me, and it's my own fucking fault for pretending I was still acting the way I used to." Bryson sighed. "Even my panthers think I'm still up to my old shit, so I have no one who can vouch for what I'm telling you is the truth. But it is. I haven't fucked a woman for two years because I haven't wanted anyone but you. Perhaps that makes me weak or obsessed, but so be it. The only one who gets my blood pumping is you."

Fia stared at him, but he didn't turn to look at her again. Was it possible he was telling the truth? Two years was a long time; she would know. But it must have felt longer for him, since he was used to having a new woman in his bed every few nights. It was hard to believe he had been able to pull off that kind of deception with people living in the same house as him. Someone must have noticed that he behaved differently, or he was a better actor than she had given him credit for.

Or he was lying to her. She let herself really study him. His whole body was tense like a spring ready to snap, making his impressive muscles bulge. His power was subdued but pulsing, like he was struggling to keep it under control. It didn't take a genius to realize that he was anxiously awaiting her response to his revelation, but she wasn't quite sure what to say. Did she believe him? Perhaps, she wasn't sure. But no matter what she believed, she felt an almost irresistible urge to touch him and soothe the worried lines from his gorgeous features. A compulsion that was no doubt a result of the mating bond.

Dragging her gaze away from him, she took a deep breath to try to contain her need to touch him. Only to suck in a breath when a thought suddenly struck her. Had he been affected by the mating bond this whole time? Was that why he didn't want anyone else? She had never considered that the bond might have that effect. But did it? *Damn it, I need some answers.*

"Fia, please say something. Anything." There was pain in his dark-brown eyes when he finally turned to look at her. "If you don't believe what I've just told you I understand but please tell me."

She swallowed hard and tried to come up with something to say, but the truth was she was still stunned by his words. "Bryson, I don't know what to say. And truth be told I don't know what to believe. I don't know how many times I've heard one of your panthers talk about your numerous conquests. How have you been able to hide what you have been doing, or rather not doing, from them for so long? It sounds like an impossible feat."

His sigh was deep, and his whole body seemed to deflate. "Yes, I guess it was a long shot to hope you would believe me. I should've told someone. Even just one person speaking in my favor would be better than no one. But I've been...embarrassed that I couldn't..." His lips tightened into a hard line when his words faltered, and he wouldn't meet her gaze.

Her eyes widened when she realized what he wasn't able to say. But her expression quickly tightened into a frown. Was that the reason he hadn't been with another woman in two years, that he couldn't get it up? Whether it was the result of the mating bond or not didn't really matter if that was the only reason he had stopped fucking his way through the female population of Scotland. It actually made it worse, if the only reason he wanted her was because Fia was the only woman who gave him an erection.

"We've arrived."

Bryson's short declaration pulled her out of her head and back to reality just as he parked next to Hugh and Kynlee's car. *Shit.* Fia wasn't ready for this, not with all the conflicting feelings Bryson's admission had created. But at least they were half an hour's walk away from the cabin, and she still had some time to get a grip on her emotions and prepare for the worst-case scenario—meeting Amber again.

Exiting the car, she pasted a smile on her face. Perhaps if she could manage to get Kynlee alone for a while, Fia could get some answers about the mating bond. But she had her doubts it would be possible with two possessive males around.

But then it was best to push her questions to the back of her mind for the time being and concentrate on the task at hand. It was impossible to predict what would meet them at the cabin, so she had to be prepared for a range of scenarios.

After pulling the bottle of sunscreen from her bag, she quickly applied the thick lotion to her face, neck, and arms. The rest of her body was covered by clothes and wasn't at risk of being burned by the summer sun. She checked to see that she had her water bottle before hooking her bag over her shoulder.

"Are you ready?" Hugh gave them a big smile. "The trail is rocky and steep some places, but you'll be fine as long as you watch where you're going."

Fia nodded. She wasn't worried about the hike even if it was steep. "Please let me know a few minutes before we get there. I want to be in front when we approach the cabin just in case."

Bryson took a step toward her with a deep crease between his brows. "Fia, let me—"

"No." Their gazes locked, and she shook her head firmly. "I can't have any of you standing in my way if Amber attacks. She might not be there, but we won't know that until we check."

Bryson's jaw tensed, and he looked like he was going to protest, but after she shook her head again, he sighed and turned to look at Hugh. "Lead the way."

"Sure thing." The red-haired alpha started down the trail with his mate following right behind.

Fia hurried after the couple, leaving Bryson to bring up the rear. Something she soon regretted when she felt his gaze burning into her back, or more correctly her ass. Her heart soon sped up, and it had nothing to do with their moderate pace.

Her mind soon reverted to what Bryson had told her in the car, and she found herself pondering the effects of the mating bond. She had known true mates, and regular mated couples for that matter, had to spend time together, and sex was a necessary part of the relationship, but beyond that she was pretty clueless as to how it worked. Did the mating bond prevent the mates from being attracted to someone else? It had been true for her since she met Bryson, but that didn't prove it as a universal fact.

And what about love? Did feelings factor in at all, or was the bond only linked to carnal desire and procreation? All the mated couples she had met had been affectionate toward each other, but again it didn't prove that the opposite didn't happen.

Fia prided herself on her multitasking skills, but

apparently she had been too busy thinking to really see where she was going. Before she even realized what was happening, her foot slipped on a rock, and her face suddenly raced toward the ground at an alarming speed.

Her nosedive was abruptly stopped when an arm came around her waist and yanked her up. Her back slammed against a hard chest, causing the air in her lungs to leave her body in a woosh.

"I've got you." Bryson speaking right next to her ear had his breath fan the shell of her ear, and a delicious shiver raced down her spine. "You have to be more careful, or you'll end up hurting yourself. I'd offer to carry you, but I've got a feeling you would object to that."

Images of him carrying her like he had in Perth assailed her already-tortured mind, and she closed her eyes against the conflicting emotions and need that hit her with the force of a truck. Heat from his body penetrated her skin and shot to her core, making her squirm in his arms.

"Fia?" He spun her around in his arms until she faced him. "What's wrong?"

Tipping her head back, she opened her eyes. She had been in his arms after the incident in Perth, but with the shock of what had happened, the effect of having him so close hadn't been the same as it was this time. And the impact it had on her was probably showing in her eyes.

Bryson's gaze met hers, and the concern in his eyes quickly changed into stark hot desire. Then, his gaze dropped to her parted lips, and she couldn't help the moan that escaped her.

She craved his mouth on hers, and more than the light brush of a kiss he had ended up giving her when she had told him no at breakfast.

CHAPTER 9

The need Bryson had been trying to control since the day before flared to life with a vengeance when he saw the heat in Fia's eyes. He knew she had been turned on before, but having her in his arms while she looked at him like she wanted to jump him was threatening to shred his control completely.

Every muscle in his body tensed, and his focus narrowed to Fia's mouth, her soft lips, which he had wanted to kiss for far too long. But he shouldn't, not when they were only minutes from the cabin of a powerful witch.

Fia moaned, and the sound made him suck in a breath as it resonated through his body, turning his already hardening cock rock solid in an instant.

He had to taste her, if only for a few seconds. Nothing else was as important as feeling her lips against his and tasting her mouth.

Tightening his arms around her, Bryson bent his head and slanted his lips over hers, groaning when the scent of her arousal hit him square in the nose, and the taste of her exploded on his tongue. *Mine.* The word popped into his mind and made him pause for half a second before dismissing it.

Her arms wrapped around his neck and locked him in place as she eagerly responded to his kiss. Her breasts were mashed against his chest, and he shuddered as his hands itched to fondle the soft mounds.

He could have drowned in the sensation of her lips sliding against his, their tongues playing a wicked dance, and the sounds of her throaty moans. He probably would have if Hugh's voice hadn't shattered the moment.

"As much as I respect you, Bryson, this isn't the time or the place to get it on with your wet dream. Pardon my French, Fia."

Fia yanked her head back, her mouth open and her eyes wide, and a beautiful crimson color rising fast into her cheeks. "I… I…"

"You're beautiful." Bryson gave her a small lopsided smile. "And thank you for finally letting me kiss you. I have wanted to taste your lips for a very long time."

She wrinkled her eyebrows as she kept staring up at him, looking like she didn't know how to respond.

Chuckling, he let his arms fall to his side before taking a step back. "You'll have to forgive me if I walk funny for a while, though. That's just what you do to me."

Her eyes dropped to his groin when he adjusted himself. His cock was testing the strength of the fabric of his pants. What wasn't noticeable was the way his balls had drawn up so tightly to his body he almost expected them to crawl inside.

Fia abruptly turned around and started walking, and Bryson let out a sigh, not sure whether it was a sigh of relief or regret, but perhaps a little of both. He didn't know what she felt about what had just happened between them, but at least she had let him kiss her, and that was a significant improvement from how she had kept him at arm's length since they'd met.

As soon as he remembered how she had ended up in his arms in the first place, he quickly closed the distance between them. She clearly hadn't been paying attention to where she was going, and with what had just happened between them, her focus probably hadn't improved. Hence the importance of staying right behind her in case she tripped again. And it had nothing to do with his need to be close to her.

They hadn't walked for more than a few minutes when Hugh stopped and turned around. "We're almost there. Are you sure you want to take the lead?" He frowned at Fia before moving his gaze to Bryson. "Erwin isn't much of a threat, but based on what I've been told about Amber's powers and her affinity for killing, I would feel more comfortable—"

"Please don't take this the wrong way, but I'm the only one here who can stop her." Fia's voice was soft yet firm.

Hugh's eyes widened, and he opened his mouth like he was going to object, but Bryson shook his head.

"She's right, Hugh." Bryson stared at the other man. "I don't know if Leith told you, but Fia is the only reason we weren't seriously injured or killed yesterday. But we should be prepared to go up against

Amber as back-up, since we have no idea what we'll meet at the cabin. There have been no indications she has an accomplice, but we are on her turf here, and if we have learned anything so far it is that we shouldn't underestimate her. Neither her power nor her willingness to kill without hesitation."

Hugh frowned, and his jaw muscles tensed before he turned to look at Kynlee. "You stay behind me." His voice was firm and filled with power, unlike his jovial behavior from earlier.

Kynlee nodded and put her hand on her mate's forearm. "I will, baby, but you have to promise me to be careful and not take any chances."

"Of course." Hugh's eyes softened as he looked at his mate. "Always."

***

Fia took the lead down the path, and she could feel Bryson right behind her. He was so close she could feel his power beating against her back, but she didn't let it distract her. Not when she had no idea what would happen next, and she was the only one strong enough to handle Amber.

She didn't know the full extent of Amber's power, but she knew the bitch had the ability to control someone's mind, at least to a certain degree. Preventing the witch from focusing on any of the others in their group was important. Fia needed Amber's attention to stay firmly on her to ensure everyone's safety.

But they were at a disadvantage as Bryson had pointed out earlier. They were on the witch's turf. Amber knew the cabin and the surrounding area well, and they didn't. And for all they knew, the bitch had installed cameras or other kinds of sensors that would warn her of someone approaching. Amber could have set up a magical barrier as well, but Fia would have noticed if she had. There had been no sign of any magic used in the area as far as Fia had been able to detect. But that was no reason for them to relax their vigilance.

After rounding a craggy outcrop, Fia came to an abrupt stop. A small, cozy cabin was nestled against the natural rock wall behind it. The stone walls and slate roof blended perfectly with the surrounding area, and Fia imagined it would be near impossible to spot the cabin from the sea below even though there was nothing to obstruct the view.

The place looked deserted like no one had been there for weeks. But looks could be deceiving, and Fia wasn't about to take any chances.

She approached slowly while keeping an eye on the door and windows. There was no detectable movement or sounds, but then she wouldn't have expected there to be if the person or people inside already knew they were approaching.

Fia moved closer until she was about fifteen feet away from the corner of the building. Using her power, she scanned the cabin and the surrounding area for power signatures, and it didn't take long for her to detect two distinct people inside the cabin. Neither of them was familiar, which meant Amber wasn't one of them. Either the witch wasn't present at all, or she had the ability to disguise her power completely. It wasn't an ability Fia had heard of before, but that didn't mean it was impossible.

Keeping her eyes trained on the cabin, Fia spoke

barely above a whisper. "There are at least two people inside the cabin, none of which is Amber. But I can't guarantee the witch isn't hiding in there as well."

"Are any of them human?" Bryson spoke close to her ear, and she had to fist her hands at her sides to maintain her focus with him so close.

She swallowed hard before answering. "No, but there may be humans in there as well. They don't have a power signature that I can pick up, so I can't tell."

"Okay." He pulled back before conveying her words to Hugh and Kynlee.

Fia studied the cabin while considering what to do next. She needed to enter the small building, but she would have to be prepared for an attack as soon as she opened the door.

"Bryson," Fia said in a low voice and soon felt his presence right behind her.

"Yes, I'm here."

She spoke without turning to look at him. "I want you to join me as I approach the cabin slowly. When we're close enough, you rip the door open and get out of the way."

His hands closed around her upper arms, and she sucked in a breath at the contact. "I don't like it. You'll be too exposed."

Fia shook her head firmly. "It's the only way. We need this to end, and hopefully we can do that here and now without exposing any more people to danger."

"Fuck!" Bryson swore under his breath, and his hands tightened around her arms for a second before he let her go. "Okay, but you have to be prepared for anything. If Amber is in there, she'll come at you with everything she's got this time. She already knows how powerful you are, and she won't hold back."

Fia nodded. "I know, but I don't think she held back the last time either. The difference now is that she knows who she's up against. But I don't know whether that means she'll try to take me down or run. She has a history of running if she can, and that's one of the reasons you need to stay out of the way. If she gets past me, she won't hesitate to hurt you or even kill you to get away."

"If she gets *past* you." Bryson's voice was filled with concern. "Amber knows she's cornered in there, and that makes her more desperate. And consequently, more dangerous. Perhaps it would be better if you stay here while I open the door. The longer distance between you might help her remain calm and consider more options. I'm scared of what she'll do if she is left with no viable options other than to kill you."

Fia pulled in a deep breath while considering Bryson's words. He was right. Giving Amber no choice other than to try to kill them wasn't a wise move. There had to be at least a perception of an out, and Fia staying farther away from the door when Bryson opened it might be enough to give that perception. The only flaw in that plan was that Bryson would be directly in the line of fire if Amber decided to open the door before he reached it.

Tightening her fists, she nodded slowly. "Okay, but it will put you at risk. You have to promise me to keep an eye on the door while you approach, and if someone opens it, you get out of the way immediately. Run or dive to the side. I won't be able to focus on attacking if I'm worried I'll hurt you."

"I promise." His low rumbling voice next to her ear made her shudder as her whole body heated. "Are you ready?"

"Yes." Keeping her eyes trained on the door, she nodded. "Please tell Hugh and Kynlee to stay back."

"I will." Bryson pulled back, and she heard him convey the message to the couple behind them.

There had been no movement inside the cabin since they arrived, judging by the location of the power signatures. They were both stationary, but there could be a multitude of reasons for that. They could be sleeping peacefully, or they could be cocked and ready to attack. But no matter the occupants' reasons for staying still, it didn't change Fia's strategy.

Bryson passed her on his way to the cabin door, and she barely resisted her urge to grab his arm and yank him back. Fear latched on to her spine with its icy claws and sent her heart rate straight up. Watching him walk into a possibly lethal situation had her whole body tense in preparation to attack whoever tried to hurt him. He wasn't supposed to be there. She was. She was the one who was supposed to be in front protecting him and the others.

Fia stared at the door while letting her magic swirl in preparation inside her. Attacking someone in front of Bryson without hurting him was possible but difficult. Particularly if the person she attacked retaliated, and Fia had to shield Bryson and the others at the same time as she kept up her attack. But she would do it if there was no other way.

Bryson ascended the two stone steps to the cabin door before quickly yanking the door open and moving to the side.

Nothing happened. There was no one standing inside the door, and Fia sensed no movement inside the cabin. It was like the people inside didn't even realize the door had been yanked open. But there was, of course, another explanation that was more likely. The people inside were waiting to attack until Fia or one of the others stepped inside. The door wasn't wide enough for more than one person to enter at a time, which meant the people in there didn't have to deal with all of them barging in at once.

Fia took a deep breath to center herself. At least Bryson had moved away from the cabin and was safe. Whatever happened next, she would be the one at the front. If someone attacked, they would have to get through her before they could reach the others.

She started toward the door while trying to make out the room inside, but it was difficult to see with the sun shining and the darkness inside the small stone structure.

Fia was no more than four feet from the door when a clanking sound startled her, and she froze. It had come from inside the cabin on the right and sounded like chains being dragged along the floor.

It was impossible not to get a bad feeling. Were the people inside the cabin tied up? Or was the sound just a trick to make her believe someone needed her help? It was impossible to tell from where she stood, so she held her position and listened.

CHAPTER 10

Bryson's fists were so tight his nails were cutting into his palms. It was taking everything he had to stay still and let Fia approach the cabin alone. He had felt her power, and the rational side of his brain knew she could probably handle whatever came at her, but even with that knowledge, he couldn't seem to calm down.

His muscles were straining, and his stare was locked on the cabin door. He was prepared to run to Fia's aid immediately if necessary. And he almost did when a sound from inside the cabin broke the silence. Someone seemed to be chained up inside, but he didn't know whether that meant they were up against another threat or if it was just another of Amber's victims.

It might be Erwin, but it could just as well be someone else. But why would Amber feel the need to restrain someone who wasn't her mate? She hadn't been reluctant to kill people before.

What he did know was that he didn't want Fia to

enter the cabin and face whoever was in there alone. But he had no other choice. Getting between Fia and the people inside might cause Fia to focus on protecting him instead of herself. It was a frustrating situation with no good options, and he hated it.

Fia took another step toward the open door, and his whole body jerked as his instinct to remove her from danger tried to take over. He managed to rein it in—barely—but he wasn't sure how much longer he would be able to do that. His panther's fur was rubbing beneath his skin and threatening to break through and push him into his change, and not for the first time the thought that Fia might be his mate crossed his mind.

The beautiful redhead ascended the stone steps, and upon reaching the open door, she leaned a little forward to look inside. Her gasp at whatever she saw had barely left her mouth before he was right behind her. His hands closed around her upper arms, and he yanked her back against his chest, before he even realized what he was doing.

Bryson froze, expecting hell to break loose. But nothing happened. Silence reigned, and Fia remained where he had her pressed against his front. She didn't make any move to get out of his hold on her.

"What did you see?" He spoke low close to her ear.

She pulled in a shaky breath before answering him. "Two people, one male and one female, both emaciated and in chains."

"No chance of anyone else hiding in there?" His muscles were still bunched and ready for a possible attack.

"No." Fia shook her head. "There's only one room

and nowhere to hide."

"Okay." Though, he wasn't ready to relax just yet, not before he had surveyed the inside of the cabin himself. Until then he reserved the right to be cautious and protective. "Please stay here while I go inside and check."

Fia shook her head, and he clamped his jaws together in frustration. The fact she was powerful didn't negate his need to protect her.

Her hand came up and brushed over his, which was still wrapped around her upper arm. "You have to let me go, Bryson. I don't think these people are any threat to us, but you can follow me inside if you'd like. Just stay behind me until I've double-checked that it's safe."

"Fine," he grumbled before relaxing his grip on her arms. Bryson wasn't used to letting someone else take the lead into a possibly dangerous situation, and he certainly didn't like the feeling of relinquishing control. But he knew it was the right thing to do in this situation, and he realized that if he wanted Fia, he would have to get used to being with a strong, capable woman. He was a powerful alpha, even though there were a few who were more powerful than him. But the truth was that Fia was more powerful than he was and not by a small amount either.

Fia entered the cabin, and he followed directly behind her, quickly scanning the room inside to ascertain for himself there were no immediate threats.

Bryson swallowed hard at what he saw. Fia had given him a short account of what she had seen, and from her behavior and tone he knew it was bad, but it was still worse than he had expected.

The male was lying on a bed in the far left-hand corner, on top of dirty covers. He was hardly more than skin and bones, and if Fia hadn't told him she had sensed two power signatures, Bryson would have believed the man to be dead.

The female lying on her side on the floor next to the wall on the right didn't look in much better shape, but the dull glow in her brown eyes as she tracked their movements spoke of her consciousness.

Fia had been right that there was no one else in the cabin, and he finally let himself relax. After heading back to the entrance, he stuck his head out and indicated to Hugh and Kynlee that they could come inside. "Amber isn't here and probably hasn't been for a while, but I think you'd better come and have a look at the two who are."

They both nodded and hurried toward him, concern written in their faces.

Chains suddenly clanked behind him, and he spun just as Fia screamed in pain. The skeletal female was no longer lying barely conscious by the wall. She was halfway on top of Fia, pinning her body to the floor. The woman's teeth were buried in Fia's wrist, her throat moving as she swallowed.

Bryson was there in a fraction of a second, grabbing the female by her throat. She let go of Fia when she could no longer swallow. He didn't hold back when he threw her against the wall, but the damage was already done. Fia's wrist was torn open, and blood was spurting from her open vein. She would bleed out quickly if he couldn't stop the bleeding.

Unfortunately, the healing abilities of a shifter couldn't be transferred to another person. A human mated to a shifter would heal faster than a regular human, but not nearly as fast as a shifter and not nearly fast enough to survive something like this without immediate treatment. Thankfully, there was another solution.

Quickly moving over to where the female vampire lay crumpled on the floor, he clamped one hand around her throat while he used the other to lift her wrist to his mouth. In an ironic quid pro quo, he tore into her wrist until her blood flowed into his mouth. Then he let her go and hurried back to Fia where she was lying, whimpering on the floor, cradling her damaged wrist.

Her eyes widened when he grabbed her wrist and covered the wound with his mouth. He couldn't explain to her what he was doing while he let the vampire blood he had gathered in his mouth do its magic. Fia's blood mixed with the vampire's in his mouth for a few seconds, until the healing properties in the vampire blood started taking effect, and the wound started to close.

Bryson held Fia's gaze while he let the wound heal, trying to convey with his eyes that she would be okay, and there was no need to worry. It didn't take more than thirty seconds for the wound to seal completely, and he pulled back slowly, letting some of the vampire blood stay on her skin to make sure there would be no remaining scar.

Fia kept staring at him, clearly still in shock after what had happened. She had already known about shifters when he met her, but he had no idea whether she knew about vampires.

I'm such a fucking idiot. No matter what she knew he

should have made sure to check the people in the cabin before turning his back on Fia. The only blessing was that she was going to be okay. There would be no lasting injury except for the shock the incident had given her. And he could have spared her that if he had practiced what he preached and not just assumed everything was okay.

"Thank you." Fia's whispered words made him wince and shake his head.

"Don't thank me. I should've checked. This is my fault, and I'm sorry." His heart sank as he looked away. He had probably blown his chances with Fia, and he couldn't blame her. It was entirely his own fault.

Fia moaned as she sat up, and his eyes snapped to her face. She looked pale and tired, which wasn't a surprise. Her wrist might be healed, but she would be feeling the effects of the blood loss for a while.

"Let's go outside." Bryson didn't wait for her response before gathering her in his arms. He met Hugh's gaze on the way out of the cabin, and the man nodded. There was a bench seat made from a long flat stone just to the right outside the door. Bryson took a seat with Fia still cradled in his arms. Settling her across his lap, he wrapped his arms around her and held her close, tucking her head against his shoulder.

He should probably have put her down beside him to let her keep her distance, but it felt so good touching her after what had just happened. It reminded him how abruptly a human's life could be torn away. Even a powerful witch like Fia was much more vulnerable than most supernaturals.

Anger surged inside him, and the reality of what could have been the outcome settled in his bones. He wanted to scream, rage, and tear something apart with his bare hands just to alleviate the almost crippling fear that threatened to choke him. He had been so close to losing her, and he knew with absolute certainty that the grief would have killed him.

Fia was his mate, his true mate. Why he hadn't realized it before he had no idea, but it was suddenly so clear. And with the knowledge, all his uncertainty and doubt fell away. He had a purpose in life that surpassed any other, and it was to claim Fia as his mate. She was above and beyond everything else in his life, and he wouldn't rest until she agreed to be his.

Bryson didn't realize how thoroughly he was inside his own head before Fia's hand on his cheek brought him back. She was staring up at him with a considering expression on her face that made his whole body tense with apprehension. Whatever she was thinking, it couldn't be anything good. At least not for him.

Fia suddenly leaned in and kissed his stubbly cheek, and his eyes widened at the unexpected gesture. "Please don't blame yourself for what happened, Bryson. I should've been more careful."

He gave her a small smile as his heart swelled in his chest. She seemed to be taking this better than he was. "Have you met a vampire before?"

Her brows wrinkled, and her hazel eyes swung to the open door before she shook her head. "No. I read somewhere that they exist, but as far as I know I've never met one. I didn't realize they looked so…human."

Bryson nodded as he studied her beautiful face. *Mate.* No wonder he had been drawn to her for two years and not able to move past that no matter how many times she'd rejected his advances. "Most supernaturals do. It's how we have been able to stay hidden throughout the ages."

"Of course, I realize that." Fia met his gaze again. "I guess I've just watched too many movies. What are we going to do with her? She's obviously dangerous. Is every vampire like that?"

Frowning, he pulled her tighter against his body. The shock of almost losing her wasn't out of his system yet, and the realization of whom she was had added to it. "She's been starved for who knows how long. I would like to blame her for what she did to you, but the truth is she's in survival mode and was only acting on pure instinct. When she's been fed, she'll return to her normal self. Whether she's a decent person or not remains to be seen, but her attacking you isn't an indication of who she really is. But until she has been fed, she has to be restrained, or she'll attack anyone who gets close enough."

Fia cocked her head, and a small smile curved her lips as she stared at him.

"What?" He narrowed his eyes at her, unable to tell what she was thinking.

Her smile widened. "You keep surprising me. I thought I had you all figured out, but apparently I was wrong. I was prepared to talk you out of killing her, but instead you're being rational about this."

CHAPTER 11

Bryson's heart fluttered in his chest, and he smiled. It sounded like Fia's perception of him had improved. And he couldn't help thinking it supported his case. "Does that mean you'll say yes if I ask you out for dinner?" He winked at her.

Fia chuckled before closing her eyes and resting her head against his shoulder. "I think I have to leave that decision until I feel better. Right now I could do with a nap."

He nodded, even though she couldn't see it, before kissing her forehead. "Right after you've had something to drink, redbird."

She nodded against his shoulder. "My water bottle. It's in my bag."

Smiling, he leaned his cheek against her forehead for a second just to bask in the feel of her. "Do you mind if I lay you down to rest here while I get your bag?"

"No, that's fine."

Bryson rose with her in his arms, before laying her down on the stone bench. "Don't fall asleep just yet, okay?"

Fia gave him a small smile and mouthed *okay*.

After storming into the cabin, he grabbed her bag, which was still lying on the floor where she had lost it. Fia's eyes were closed when he returned outside, but they blinked open when he put a hand behind her neck and lifted her head. "Now drink." He placed the top of the bottle to her mouth and let her drink until she indicated she was done.

"Will you be okay here while I help Hugh and Kynlee inside?" He studied her face, but she seemed okay apart from being a bit pale.

"Yes." Her voice was soft, like she was seconds away from falling asleep.

"Okay, I'll check on you every few minutes."

Her nod was barely noticeable, but it was there. And Bryson forced himself to turn away and walk back into the cabin.

Hugh and Kynlee were both standing beside the male on the bed, and they raised their heads to look at Bryson when he entered.

"How is she?" Kynlee's face was filled with concern. "I saw what you did. Quick thinking."

He nodded. "She's tired, but she'll be okay." Then, he swung his gaze to the unconscious man on the bed. "How about him? Is it Erwin?"

"It's Erwin." Hugh sighed. "And he looks a damn sight worse than he did the last time I saw him. I've tried waking him, but there is no response. We'll have to take him with us, but I'm not sure exactly what to do about him. If he doesn't heal, well…"

Bryson frowned. "I know someone who might be able to help him. It will depend on what is wrong with him, of course, but if Steph can't heal him, perhaps she can tell us what's wrong. It might be just a lack of food and water for an extended length of time, but it's just as likely that Amber did something to him to render him unconscious. If Fia was in better shape, she might've been able to tell us whether he has been subjected to some kind of magic. But that will have to wait until she's recovered."

Hugh nodded before turning to look at the female vampire still lying by the wall where Bryson had left her. "What do we do about her? She'll attack whoever tries to carry her, but we can't leave her here either."

Scratching the stubble on his chin, Bryson considered their options. There might be an easy solution to their vampire issue. "If you stay close and ready to intervene, I'll let her feed from me. It might not be enough to bring her out of crazy mode, but it's worth a try. If she's still just as desperate afterward, we'll have to tie her up properly using that chain as a bit to prevent her from ripping someone's throat out. It won't be pleasant for her, but if she's usually a decent person, she'll be happy to know she didn't inadvertently kill or maim someone while not in control."

"Are you sure you want to risk her feeding from you?" Hugh studied his face. "It might have repercussions."

Bryson nodded. "I know, but I don't think I'm at risk."

Hugh lifted an eyebrow at him, but Bryson shook his head to stop the man from voicing his question.

Fia was most likely asleep and wouldn't hear him, but he was reluctant to mention the word mate in the same sentence as her name. She hadn't even agreed to go out with him yet, so he would prefer to keep the fact that she was his true mate to himself until she was ready. Mentioning it too soon would only scare her away.

Although, there was an issue with that. The mating bond wouldn't let him wait for long to claim her. If he was lucky, they might have a week, but that would probably be pushing it.

"All right." Hugh nodded. "Whenever you're ready. I'll be right beside you."

"Good. I'll just check on Fia first to make sure she's still okay." Bryson exited the cabin and approached the stone bench. Fia was fast asleep, her breathing calm and even. All he wanted was to grab her and take her home, but they wouldn't be able to leave for a few hours yet.

Walking back into the cabin, he headed straight for the vampire. She looked unconscious, but he wasn't stupid enough to believe it. The minute he was close enough that the scent of his blood roused her instincts, she would lunge for him. It was in her nature to do anything to survive, but he was prepared for it this time.

Bryson went down on his knees before approaching her slowly. He didn't take his eyes off her for even a second. Vampires were extremely fast, and he needed to catch her to be able to control where she bit him.

Hugh was right behind him and no doubt ready to help if necessary, and Bryson would probably need it when he had to remove her. There was only so much blood he could give the female without weakening himself, but she wouldn't want to let go. She would need more blood than he could give her for her to fully recover, but that would have to wait until they got back to Hugh's farm.

He was two feet away from her when she moved. Her speed with which she launched herself at him would have impressed him if he wasn't busy controlling her attack.

Driving the side of his forearm into her open mouth, he slammed her down on her back on the floor before straddling her waist. She bucked against him to throw him off her, but as soon as her teeth sank into his flesh, and his blood started flowing into her mouth, she calmed down and grabbed ahold of his forearm with both hands.

If she had been human, she would have taken some serious damage being handled like that, but as a vampire it wasn't even enough to give her a bruise. This way he had full control over her movements, and it would be difficult for her to gain the upper hand.

Bryson let her feed until he felt it starting to affect his strength. "It's time." He glanced at Hugh before closing his hand around her throat and squeezing. Hugh put his hands on her shoulders and used his weight and power to keep her in place.

The female acted just like Bryson had expected when she was made to let go of her food source. Thrashing her head from side to side, she snapped at Hugh's arms in frustration, and bucked against their combined efforts to hold her down.

Bryson studied her glowing red eyes to check for

any sign she might be regaining her sanity while putting pressure on the bleeding wound on his forearm.

"I think we'll have to tie her up." Hugh looked at him. The man's muscles were straining from keeping the agitated female pinned to the floor. "She doesn't show any signs of calming down."

Nodding slowly, Bryson sighed. He had hoped the female would regain enough sense and composure to be able to communicate and perhaps even walk to the car using her own two feet. But it didn't look like that was going to happen. She had been starved for too long and needed more blood to recover.

"Let's give it a couple more minutes until the bleeding has stopped." The woman was slamming her knees repeatedly into Bryson's back trying to dislodge him, but it would take more than that to persuade him to move off her.

Hugh lifted an eyebrow at him, his face red. "Easy for you to say. I'm doing all the work here. You're just sitting there nursing that scratch on your arm."

Bryson laughed. "Why don't you stuff your arm in her mouth then? She'll calm down, and you can relax for a while."

"Not happening." Kynlee glared at Bryson from where she was standing by Erwin's bed and crossed her arms over her chest. "My mate will not feed the vampire."

"You're mated, aren't you? Shouldn't be a problem then." Bryson couldn't help teasing Hugh's mate, even though he would never have allowed Fia to feed the bloodsucker if he had been given a choice in the matter. He wasn't worried for himself, though, since he knew exactly whom he belonged to, and no vampire would be able to change that no matter how hard they tried.

Kynlee visibly bristled, but her mate spoke before she could say anything.

"Don't tease her. That privilege is all mine." Hugh grinned and winked at his mate.

Bryson expected Kynlee's temper to flare even hotter, but to his surprise she laughed. "Oh, baby, sounds like someone's going to be in the doghouse tonight." Then, she winked back at her mate before marching out of the cabin.

"Fuck." Hugh's grin disappeared and was replaced by a scowl as he turned to Bryson. "This is your fault, you know, and I'll come up with a way to get you back. Just you wait and see."

Shaking his head slowly, Bryson chuckled. "We'll see about that." He wasn't worried about what Hugh would do. Kynlee wouldn't stay mad at her man for long, if she even was mad at him. She might just be giving him a hard time. And as soon as Kynlee was back in Hugh's arms, this would all be forgotten.

Bryson looked down at the female still struggling beneath him. Her long brown hair was matted and resembled a bird's nest, and her face was gaunt with skin the color of ash. Her appearance would improve significantly when she was back on a stable diet of fresh blood, and hopefully, she would turn out to be a decent person. But until that happened, they would have to restrain her using chains or a solid cage. There was no other way.

"Okay, let's do this." Bryson looked at Hugh, who nodded back at him. "I'll hold her down until you can get that chain into her mouth. Then I'll lift her so you can wrap the chain around her entire body. We can't have her arms and legs flailing if we're going to be able to carry her back to the car."

Using all the thick chain they could find in the cabin, including the length used to restrain Erwin, they worked methodically until they had secured the chain around the female's skeletal body. She wasn't happy and gnawed on the chain in her mouth until Bryson cringed from the sound, but it wouldn't hurt her, and she probably wouldn't remember any of it once she regained her awareness.

Leaving Hugh to keep an eye on the female and Erwin in the cabin, Bryson went outside to check on Fia. But he needn't have worried.

Kynlee was standing by her side, and as soon as he exited the cabin, she turned to look at him. "She's still sleeping, and she seems to be warm enough."

"Good." Bryson sighed as he went to stand next to Kynlee. "I fucked up, and she could've died because of it. It was damn lucky the vampire went for her wrist and not her throat, because if—"

"Stop." Kynlee gave him a stern look. "There's always a what if, but all you can do is learn from it. It's no use beating yourself up for what could have happened. It didn't. End of story."

Bryson chuckled in surprise. "That's something a guy would say. Women are typically—"

"Don't even go there." Kynlee's eyes narrowed into slits. "Presumptuous shit like that is what will drive women away. Is that why no woman has stayed with you for more than a few minutes?"

Shock made him gape at her, and it took him a few

seconds to come up with a response. "I've never wanted a woman to stay with me until..." His gaze lowered to Fia's beautiful face. Was that what people thought, that women left him because he didn't treat them right or gave them what they needed? It wasn't what he had heard, but then he had never asked people what they thought of him or his behavior. Most men seemed to admire him, but women? He had assumed they did as well.

"It was a joke, Bryson." Kynlee's voice made him look back at her. Her head was tilted to the side as she studied his face. "I didn't expect you to take it seriously. You had no problems teasing me just a few minutes ago."

He nodded slowly before lowering his gaze to Fia's motionless form. Fisting his hands against the fear that settled like a brick in his gut, he didn't try to find any words to explain himself to Kynlee. Her teasing words had reminded him his future was lying on the stone bench in front of him, but he might not be able to persuade his true mate to accept him because of his history with women.

Hugh's mate disappeared into the cabin, and Bryson was left alone with his thoughts and fears. He didn't like the feeling of helplessness that made his shoulders slump. All he wanted was to wake Fia and beg her to be his. But this wasn't the time for that. Pushing her wouldn't make her accept him any faster. On the contrary, it might make her pull away. He needed to be patient, but patience wasn't his strong suit.

Time crawled at a ridiculously slow pace while the sun crept toward the horizon. They took turns watching over Erwin and the vampire in the cabin and keeping an eye out for anyone approaching while waiting for the sun to set. They couldn't leave the cabin with the vampire while the sun was up unless they wanted her to fry.

Bryson sent a message to Leith, telling him what they had found at the cabin and that Amber's location was still unknown. Leith texted back immediately. Apparently the monster and his friends weren't any closer to discovering her location either. Amber's daughter, Mary, hadn't been admitted to any of the local hospitals or mental institutions, and Callum hadn't been able to find any signs as to where they had gone. It was frustrating and unnerving for everyone.

As soon as the sun disappeared, Bryson rose from where he had been sitting on the stone bench by Fia's feet. It was time to finally leave the cabin, and he wanted to get out of there as soon as possible.

Kneeling next to the bench, he caressed Fia's cheek before tucking a stray lock of hair behind her ear. He wanted to wake her with a kiss, but taking liberties wasn't the way to win her affection and trust.

"Fia?" She was sound asleep, and he felt bad having to rouse her. But they needed to get moving, and he wanted to convey their plan to prepare her for what was going to happen.

Bryson curved his hand behind her neck before massaging gently. "Fia, little redbird, please wake up. It's time to leave."

She blinked her eyes a few times before focusing in on his face.

"There you are." He smiled at her, taking in her adorable, sleepy expression. "How are you feeling?"

Yawning, she stretched one arm above her head before returning his smile. "Better, I think. But it's hard to tell when I've just woken up. Ask me again in a few minutes, and I might be able to tell you."

Bryson laughed. "Well, we're ready to leave, and you'll be hitching a ride on Kynlee's back unless you feel up to walking. I'll be carrying the vampire, so I won't be able to carry you as well. That would be a bit much even for me." Getting to his feet, he winked at her before turning away and walking into the cabin.

CHAPTER 12

Fia let her gaze follow Bryson's big muscular form until he disappeared through the door. This day's events had shown her sides of him she hadn't seen before, softer sides, and it was changing her perception of him.

Perhaps she should have taken some time to get to know him earlier. It wouldn't have changed the fact that he was a fuckboy, but it would have opened her eyes to his other qualities and given her a more complete picture of whom she was saying no to. And if it were true the only woman he wanted was her and had been since they met, it might be a good enough reason for her to consider accepting a couple of dinner invitations.

Pushing herself up into a sitting position, she squeezed her eyes closed as her head started spinning. It wasn't unexpected, considering her blood loss, but apart from the dizziness, she wasn't feeling half bad. And there was only one person she had to thank for that—Bryson. His quick thinking and reactions had saved her, because she had been too shocked to even contemplate using her magic against the vampire. So much for being a powerful witch.

"Are you feeling better?" Kynlee's voice made Fia open her eyes and lift her gaze to the woman's face. She hadn't even heard her coming out of the cabin, but then shifters had a profound ability to move silently just like their animals.

Fia would have loved to see Bryson as a panther. She had seen a couple of his clan members in their panther forms but never him, and she couldn't help but think he would be magnificent.

"Fia?" Kynlee's voice snapped her out of her thoughts and made her realize she hadn't answered the woman.

"Thank you. I feel much better." Trying to stretch out the kinks in her back from lying on the hard stone bench, she smiled up at the woman. "Still a little tired and a bit dizzy, but apart from that, I feel fine." And the tiredness was probably due to her hardly sleeping the night before.

"Good." Kynlee smiled. "I'll be carrying you back, so there's no need to worry about your dizziness." The woman turned to face the other way before going down on one knee. "I'll have my hands underneath your thighs, so you won't need to use a lot of strength to hold on. Just wrap your legs around my waist and your arms around my shoulders, and we'll be off."

A sound from the cabin made Fia turn her head just as Bryson exited with the female vampire hanging over his shoulder. The vampire was wrapped in chains, but what got Fia's attention was Bryson's muscles in his arms, shoulders, and chest moving and bunching.

He had changed into a tank top before they left for the cabin, and it showed off his upper body in a way that made it impossible to look away from all that ripped brown and tattooed flesh. The need to touch him was almost overwhelming. She wanted to feel his hard flesh under her hands and sliding against her bare breasts as he thrust…

"Redbird." His grin was wide and knowing when her eyes snapped to his. "You'd better close your mouth before you swallow a bug."

Mortification made her face flame, and she quickly turned away from him. He already knew how she was feeling, so there really wasn't any point in hiding her reaction. But she couldn't bear to see the self-confident look on his face. She hadn't yet agreed to go out with him, but to him her reaction might be a confirmation she would. And he would most likely be right. But she wasn't going to tell him that just yet.

Instead of climbing onto Kynlee's back, Fia rose and took a few tentative steps. She felt a little wobbly, but it wasn't bad, and she really wanted to use her own two feet instead of being carried like a child.

Fia turned to the woman, who had risen and was studying her with wrinkled brows. "I think I'd like to walk and see how it goes. I'm not sure I can make it the whole way on my own feet, but I'd like to try."

Kynlee nodded and smiled. "I understand, and I'll be right behind you just in case you need help."

"Thank you. That sounds perfect." Fia returned the woman's smile just as Hugh came out of the cabin carrying Erwin over his shoulder.

"Are you sure?" Bryson's brows pushed together as

he stared at Fia, his eyes looking darker than usual. "I won't be there to help you this time if you stumble."

Fia cocked her head at him. "You heard Kynlee. She'll be right behind me and will help me If I need it. There's no need for you to worry your pretty little head about me." After winking at him, she turned and started walking toward the path.

"Wait!" Bryson's sharp command made her stop and turn to look at him. "I'll be in front, and you'll walk right behind me. We'll take this nice and slow, and if there's anything, and I mean anything at all, you tell me, okay?" While he spoke, he came to stand right in front of her, staring down at her with a stern expression on his face.

It was obvious he wouldn't accept any arguments, so she just nodded.

Giving her a short nod, he walked past her and continued toward the path at a leisurely pace. Fia fell in behind him with Kynlee directly behind her. And judging from the sound of their footsteps, Hugh was following directly behind Kynlee.

Fia made sure to concentrate on where she put her feet. It was getting dark, but there was still enough light to see the path in front of her. It had only taken them half an hour to get to the cabin, but at the pace they were going, it would take longer to get back. By that time it might be completely dark.

She wasn't worried, though. If necessary, Kynlee would help Fia when it got too dark for her human eyes to see where she was going. Shifters had better senses than humans even in their human forms, and cats were known for their excellent night vision.

It took a shorter time than she had expected to get

to the narrow dirt road where the cars were parked. While keeping her focus on the path in front of her, she had only glanced at Bryson's ass a handful of times, which wasn't bad, considering how it was directly in front of her the entire time and absolutely worth staring at. The man was a walking commercial for men's health and fitness, and the power emanating from him just made him more irresistible.

Bryson and Hugh unloaded their cargo in the backseat of Hugh and Kynlee's truck since Bryson's sports car didn't have a backseat.

"You just go ahead." Bryson looked at Hugh. "We'll be along shortly. I have a couple of things I want to discuss with Fia before we leave."

Fia felt her apprehension rise, and she wanted to tell Hugh and Kynlee to wait. But Bryson turning to pin her with his stare stopped her, and the couple got into their car and left before she could tear her eyes away.

Whatever Bryson wanted to say to her, it must be something other than wanting to secure her agreement for a dinner date. Because that could have been discussed in front of the others surely.

Suddenly, being left alone with him felt like a threat. Not because she was scared of him. He would never touch her if she told him not to. And therein lay the problem. She wasn't confident she would be able to say no to him if he came on to her again. Her resistance to him was rapidly disintegrating, and one of the reasons was the way he had saved her life twice in a matter of hours. It was hard to turn your back on a man who jumped to your aid without hesitation.

"Fia." His voice was rougher than normal when he

took a step toward her.

Swallowing hard, she took a step back as her heart rate increased.

"Fia stop." He took another step toward her with his gaze locked on hers, and unable to pull her gaze away she took another step back.

Narrowing his eyes on her, he kept coming, but he quickened his steps, and she could no longer move backward fast enough to maintain the distance between them.

Within seconds he was right in front of her, and his hands gripped her hips and stopped her progress. "I want to make a few things clear before we leave here, redbird, and you're going to listen to me." His expression brooked no argument, and he used his height and bulk to reinforce the effect of his commanding tone.

Fia couldn't come up with a suitable response, so she didn't give him any except continuing to stare into his dark eyes.

"I know you haven't agreed to be with me yet, and I know you haven't dated anyone else in the time I've known you." Bryson's power wrapped around her as he spoke, causing her body to heat up fast. "But let me be perfectly clear to avoid any misunderstandings. I'm determined to win you, and I'll allow no other man to vie for your affection. If anyone tries, I'll make sure they understand who you belong to. You might not want me yet, but I'll keep trying until the day you understand we're perfect for each other. And that day will come, mark my words."

Bryson had tried to seduce her countless times since they met, and she had found his methods annoying more often than not. But for some reason his declaration of ownership had her wanting to climb him like a tree and tell him she was ready to be fucked—hard. Whether it was the mating bond speaking or just him she had no idea, but if he didn't move away from her soon, she didn't think she was going to be able to resist him for much longer.

"Are we clear?" He bent his head slowly toward hers while holding her gaze, and she wet her lips in anticipation. But instead of kissing her, he grazed her jaw with his nose and sniffed.

Her eyes widened, and her whole body tensed when he groaned, the sound vibrating down her spine until it reached her core, her channel clenching in response. "Yes." Her voice was high-pitched and unrecognizable.

Chuckling, Bryson lifted his head to stare down at her. "That's a word I haven't heard from you very often. I like it."

She cleared her throat and tried to come up with a sassy response, but it was like her brain had turned to mush, and all she could think of was how much she wanted him to push his large cock inside her. Her sheath was aching with her need to be filled, and her clit was swollen and ready for his touch. But she wouldn't ask for it, no matter how much she wanted him. She would rather burn with unsatisfied desire than ask him for his touch.

This time when he bent his head toward her, though, she didn't let him deviate from the path to her mouth. Gripping his shoulders, she pushed up on her toes and pressed her mouth to his. The feel of his hot lips against hers sent a shiver through her body, and she parted her lips and pushed her tongue into his mouth to play with his.

He responded but more languidly than she craved. Caressing her tongue with his own, he slid his hands to the middle of her back before pulling her closer.

There was no mistaking the hard ridge in his pants. Bryson wanted her just as much as she wanted him, but then she hadn't expected anything less. Though, his kiss was too slow and controlled, like he had all the time in the world. Perhaps he was so sure he had won her over that there was suddenly no rush to get into her pants.

Impatient need made her shudder, and she broke the kiss to stare up at him. Her eyes widened when she saw the heat in his eyes. He was definitely as turned on as she was, so why didn't he initiate something more?

"If you want more from me, you'll have to spell it out, redbird. I'm not going to do anything unless you tell me what you want." Bryson's intense gaze never left hers while he stood completely still.

"I..." She swallowed down the moan that wanted to escape. After saying no to him for so long, it felt odd to voice her desire, even though he already knew how turned on she was. He could smell it on her. But the fact that it was up to her to tell him what she wanted was enough to render her mind temporarily blank.

Tipping her head forward, she closed her eyes and rested her forehead against his shoulder. Staring into his eyes had been unsettling, and she needed a little break from his intensity to be able to decide what to do next. Saying yes wasn't just a big step, it was a step that would change her life forever. And even though

Bryson might be a better man than she had realized, she was still reluctant to give up her own freedom. Or was she? It was hard to think with him so close.

His skin was so warm. The darkness had brought a chill to the air, but it didn't seem to affect him, and she wanted to soak in his warmth and closeness. And his musky peppery scent. Without even thinking about what she was doing, she stretched out her tongue and licked his smooth skin.

Bryson shuddered, and his hands pressed her more firmly against him. "Did you just taste me?" His voice was a dark rumble that seemed to vibrate through his chest.

Fia sucked in a breath, and her eyes popped open. "Um, yes…" *And you taste good.* But she didn't tell him that. She had just licked his chest. What was wrong with her?

His hands suddenly closed around her head, and she didn't resist when he tipped it back. She had noticed the heat in his eyes before, but it was nothing compared to the molten glow in them now. "Can I make you come, Fia? Please say yes. I want to taste you." His stare was mesmerizing, and all she could do was nod.

She wanted him inside her more than anything she could think of, and he had finally given her a chance to tell him that without using words. Somehow it felt like less of a commitment, which was so hypocritical she inwardly cringed. The truth was she was reluctant to commit to him, so why did she expect him to commit to her?

But the second his lips crushed against hers, she forgot everything else. His tongue thrust into her mouth and dominated her own, leaving her shivering with need and gasping for breath when he finally pulled back.

Bryson didn't give her a chance to come to her senses before he lifted her and moved her to the roof of his car. "Lie down." The growl in his voice made her channel clench again, and she did as she was told without any objection.

After quickly undoing her jeans, he started pulling them down her thighs along with her panties.

The whole experience was out of this world hot until a scraping sound made her freeze and put her hands on his to stop him. "Bry, stop! I'm ruining your car." The paint was being scratched to hell by the small metal studs adorning her back pockets, and there was no way she was going to be able to pay for the repairs.

Bryson stopped, but instead of answering, he leaned forward and pressed a kiss to her bare belly button, making her suck in a breath as her pussy clenched. "Those scratches will stay there to remind me of the day my girl finally let me pleasure her. They will help me remember how lucky I am. Now let go of my hands, redbird, so I can taste your sweet pussy and make you feel good."

Meeting his gaze, she pulled her hands slowly away from his large warm ones. His words were probably the most romantic thing anyone had ever said to her, and they had come from the big alpha panther she hadn't believed had a romantic bone in his body.

He tugged her jeans and panties down her legs, until they were wrapped around her ankles, before lifting her legs to hook her knees over his shoulders. His gaze zoomed in on her bare pussy, and she swallowed hard against her sudden self-consciousness.

What if he didn't like what he saw? Or how she tasted? He had been with so many women, most of them far more experienced in bed than she was. She would never be able to measure up to his expectations.

"Relax, my sweet redbird." His gaze lifted to hers as his hands caressed up the outside of her thighs until they reached her hips. "And you'll have to forgive me if I'm a bit rusty. I haven't touched a pussy in two years." His smile was a bit feral, but it still took her breath away. And his words helped push her anxiety to the back of her mind. Whether that was his intention or not she didn't know, but it was sweet all the same.

CHAPTER 13

Bryson was determined not to let his apprehension show. But he hoped his words gave him an excuse to try again if his performance wasn't up to par.

The rational side of him knew he would be fine, but the importance of showing his mate he could give her what she needed, in bed and in life, was paramount. Fear of having her turn away from him in disappointment or disgust was threatening to choke him, and he didn't know what to do about it since he had little experience with this kind of anxiety. The only times he had known something vaguely similar was when Fia had rejected him, but even that had been nothing compared to this.

Get a grip, asshole. You know what you're doing. Just focus on her pleasure, and you'll be fine. Leaning in, he kissed her inner thigh before trailing kisses slowly up her soft skin toward her soaking wet cunt. Her delicious scent was flooding his senses, and his cock twitched when she let out a long moan.

He wanted inside her so badly it hurt, but he wasn't going to. Not yet. This first time was all about Fia's pleasure and learning her body, and he wouldn't let his own need distract him.

Kissing along the crease between her thigh and her pussy, Bryson couldn't help the low growl settling in his throat. He was going to bury his face in her cunt soon, but he wanted to hear her beg for it first.

As if on cue, she uttered one word barely loud enough to qualify as a whisper. "Please." The muscles in her thighs and ass tightened, and she shifted her hips to the side, putting her pussy right in front of his mouth.

He grinned but didn't oblige her. "Repeat that a little louder and call me Bry." Their gazes met, and he almost chuckled at the pained expression on her face. Combined with the heat in her eyes it was a most compelling look.

"Please...Bry," she murmured. Then she bit her lower lip.

His fingertips dug into her hips at the sight. He wanted to be the one to bite that lip. Just the thought of feeling that plump flesh between his teeth made his gums ache.

Forcing his gaze back up to hers, he leaned in and slid the tip of his nose over her clit once, making her gasp. "Louder."

She hesitated for just a second. "Please, Bry." Her voice was shaky but louder this time.

Chuckling, he dipped his tongue between her folds and licked slowly up the seam of her cunt, before he flicked the tip of his tongue over her clit a few times.

Fia shuddered and moaned, and she lifted her pelvis

off the car roof to chase his mouth when he raised his head.

"Now scream it."

This time she didn't even hesitate before she yelled at the top of her lungs. "Please, Bry. Fuck me!"

He almost choked on his own tongue as need surged through him, making him press his hard cock against the side of the car in desperation.

Burying two fingers deep inside Fia's tight sheath, he moved them around until her hips jerked and she mewled. Having found her sweet spot, he lowered his head and sucked her swollen clit into his mouth.

She gasped and whimpered, and he basked in her glorious sounds while pumping his fingers inside her, making sure to hit that spot inside her every time. Alternating between sucking and flicking the tip of his tongue against her clit soon had her grinding her pussy against his face and letting out short yells.

Bryson needed to bury his cock inside her silky, wet cunt more than he needed his next breath, and the tight confinement of his pants wasn't helping any. Reaching down with the hand that wasn't busy pleasuring his mate, he quickly undid his pants and wrapped his hand around his straining shaft.

While stroking his length, he pumped his fingers into Fia's velvety sheath. She had asked him to fuck her, and just the thought of thrusting into her was enough to push him toward his climax.

He intensified the suction on her sensitive nub, and it didn't take long before her pussy clamped down on his fingers, and she screamed his new nickname as she started coming.

His cock jerked with his release, and he growled his

pleasure against Fia's clit, making her scream a second time as her thighs shook with the intensity of her pleasure.

Bryson kept up his attack on her sensitive parts until her muscles relaxed and her ass hit the roof of the car. Lifting his head, he met her hooded gaze before pulling his fingers out of her cunt and putting them into his mouth.

Her eyes widened as he made a show of licking his fingers clean. But he didn't need to exaggerate the effect her taste had on him. He had just painted the side of his car with his cum, but his cock was already hard and ready for more. It might be due to the mating bond and the need to claim his true mate, or just the fact that he had wanted her for so long.

Fia might have begged prettily for him to pleasure her, but she hadn't agreed to a date yet. Telling her she was his true mate would have to wait, and until then he couldn't risk fucking her. If he accidentally claimed her during sex, he was about two hundred percent sure she would hate him for it.

"That was... Thank you, Bryson." She bit her lower lip again before looking away.

"Anytime, Fia." He kept his eyes on her face, but she turned her head back to look at him. "But you're to call me Bry from now on."

That brought her gaze back to his. "Not when others are present. It's too…intimate."

He laughed. "Why? Because you'll remember how you just begged me to make you come?"

She sucked in a breath. "Yes." The word was no more than a whisper. "Bryson, I—"

Whatever she was going to say was swallowed by a

gasp when he abruptly yanked her off the roof of the car and flipped her around until she was on her feet and bent over his arm, her bare ass gloriously displayed.

His hand connected with one of her ass cheeks with a crack before he shoved two fingers inside her drenched pussy, making her squeal. "What's my name?" His voice was a dark rasp.

Pumping his digits inside her, he made sure to graze his knuckles against the extra sensitive area inside her. It should have been his hard shaft inside her, but he couldn't risk it.

"Bry." She moaned his name. "Please, I want your cock."

He groaned, and if he hadn't been so desperate to mate her, he would have happily obliged. "Not today, redbird, but soon I promise." After pulling his fingers from her pussy, he spanked her again, making her scream his name. Using three fingers this time, he pushed them inside her only to have her internal muscles immediately clamp down and seize his digits as she shuddered and whined with her orgasm.

Fia was breathing heavily and hanging limply over his arm by the time she came down.

His jaw was clamped shut, and all his muscles were straining with how desperately he wanted to come again. It was like the orgasm he'd had minutes ago hadn't even happened. His cock was a throbbing steel bar poking into his stomach, and his balls were pulled up so tightly they were threatening to crawl inside his body.

Bryson lifted Fia into his arms and cradled her against his chest. Her legs obviously weren't holding her, and he needed to have her close. Letting her go wasn't an option, and after moving over to the front of his car, he sat down on the hood and rested her ass on his lap.

With how unresponsive she was, he wasn't prepared when she suddenly moved, and her hand wrapped around the head of his dick. But she let go of him just as quickly, and her eyes widened in shock.

Before she could do anything more, he quickly lifted her off his lap and put her on the hood of his car before standing and giving her his back. He closed his pants over his erection while wincing at the discomfort.

"Bry, what the hell was that?" Fia scooted off the hood and gripped his arm to turn him toward her without even bothering to pull her pants up. "Do you have a piercing?"

Bryson turned to face her and met her gaze. "Let's leave that question for later, okay?" Her reaction had his spine stiffening with apprehension. He had wanted to surprise her, but perhaps he had misjudged her reaction to something like that. What if she hated it?

She shook her head firmly while staring up at him. "No, Bry, tell me. I have no experience with piercings. I've only seen pictures."

"Pictures?" Jealousy suddenly tore through him, making him narrow his eyes at her. "You have been studying pictures of other men's cocks?" He barely resisted the urge to rip his pants open and push his dick inside her just to show her whom she belonged to.

She burst out laughing, and he couldn't help the snarl that forced its way out of his throat. "Calm down. It was before I even met you." But the huge grin on her face did nothing to appease his anger.

"The hell I will." He gripped her upper arms and pulled her closer until their noses were less than two inches apart. "The only cock you will see from now on is mine. Are we clear?"

She chuckled. "Show me then."

Bryson froze when he realized his mistake. He didn't want to show her yet because he didn't know how she would react. But then she had already guessed he'd had some work done, and she didn't seem frightened by the prospect.

The sound of a car approaching made him turn his head and scan the road. Lights could be seen through the trees. It was still several hundred yards away, but he quickly bent and pulled Fia's panties and jeans up her legs. "Someone's coming."

He didn't know whether to be relieved or disappointed at the disruption, but it was probably for the best, considering pulling out his still rock-solid shaft would only tempt him to fuck her. And if she begged for it, he might not be able to say no to her this time.

"Get in the car, Fia. We're leaving." Without looking at her, he rounded the car and opened the driver's side door.

"What's this?"

He glanced over at her where she stood staring at the passenger-side door. "What do you think?"

She chuckled before lifting her gaze to his. "You came all over your car." Then she frowned. "Why didn't you come inside me? I asked you to fuck me, and I'm on the pill so…" She shrugged.

His body tensed again as he narrowed his eyes at her. "Why exactly are you on the pill? You've been telling me no for two years, and I know you haven't been with anyone else in that time. Were you planning on fucking someone else, or have you just kept taking them since before we met?" He wasn't sure he wanted to hear her answer, but he needed to know.

Her whole body tensed, and she quickly looked away. "I... I just wanted to be prepared, that's all."

His eyes were fixed on what he could see of her face. "Prepared for me or someone else?" His heart sped up while he waited for her answer. If she said someone else, he wasn't sure what he would do.

"Just...prepared." She shrugged again.

Light swept over them from the car approaching, and Bryson bit back the question on the tip of his tongue. "Get in the car, Fia." His voice was hard, but he couldn't help it. He got in and waited for her to open the door and take a seat beside him.

After lingering a few seconds that felt like an eternity, Fia finally opened the door and got in.

Bryson wanted answers, but he didn't want to discuss this until the car approaching had passed them. He would never hurt her, but if she had been planning to fuck someone else, he would make a scene and come across as threatening. And he didn't want the people in the car to get the wrong idea and try to take her away from him, because that would end badly for everyone.

The car crawled past at a snail's pace, and he was just about ready to explode with impatient fury by the time it finally disappeared around a bend down the road.

Squeezing his eyes shut, he took a deep breath to try to calm down enough to speak rationally. It did nothing to alleviate his tension, but he hoped he would be able to talk without too much of a growl in his voice.

***

Bry's power was filling the car with an intensity that made Fia squirm in her seat. He was obviously furious about the possibility that she had been thinking of someone else. But if she admitted that she had only been thinking about him, he would automatically take that as confirmation that she wanted to be with him. And she hadn't quite landed on that conclusion yet. Or at least she wasn't ready to admit it.

A lot had happened in the last couple of days, and she needed a little time by herself to decide what to do about it. And when. She didn't feel ready to sign her life away, but then would she ever be? It was a crucial decision, but she was definitely closer to saying yes now than she had ever been.

"Fia, please explain." Bry's voice was almost shaking with barely controlled fury. "Is there someone else?"

She couldn't lie to him. He didn't deserve that. Shaking her head, she turned to meet his gaze before answering him truthfully. "No, there's no one else."

"Thank fuck." He squeezed his eyes closed before leaning forward and resting his forehead on the steering wheel. His shoulders sagged as he breathed out in a deep sigh.

Fia frowned and bit her lip as she took in his obvious relief. She wanted to reach out and touch him. Run her hand over his thick shoulder, up his neck and into his short hair to massage his scalp. She wanted to show him she cared about him and only him, but she didn't. It felt like it would be too intimate even after what they had just shared.

A full minute went by before he sat back and started the car. He didn't say anything and didn't look at her as he turned the car around, and they started up the dirt road.

The silence was awkward, but she couldn't think of anything to say, so instead she stared straight ahead while trying to go through everything that had happened that day and analyze it all.

The biggest question she had was whether her fight against the mating bond had been the right choice. If Bry had been speaking the truth when he said he hadn't been with another woman since he met her, did that mean it was how the mating bond worked? That none of them would be attracted to anyone else ever again?

But then why had he asked whether she wanted someone else? He would have known she didn't. Except he didn't yet know they were true mates, did he? Which made it a reasonable question for him to ask. But shouldn't his possessiveness have tipped him off that they were mates? He was a shifter and knew more about mating than she did, and with her spell barely working, he should have worked things out by now. It was all so confusing.

All these questions were proving her earlier conclusion that she needed to talk to someone about true mates and how the mating bond worked. Fia hadn't previously had anyone to talk to about this that wasn't a part of Bry's clan, but she did after meeting

Sabrina and the other true mated couples. And she needed to take the time to talk to one of them as soon as possible. It was becoming more urgent by the hour because she didn't think she would be able to resist Bry for much longer. But before taking the final step, she needed to know all the consequences of mating him.

It was dark, and there weren't a lot of houses along the main road, but there was the occasional one with lights in the windows. Turning to look out of the passenger-side window, Fia came face to face, so to speak, with the dried evidence of Bry's pleasure. She hadn't even noticed he came since she had been too busy enjoying what he was doing to her, but she was happy he did. Just the thought of him pleasuring himself, made a spark of desire rekindle inside her.

What confused her was what happened afterward. He hadn't wanted to show her his piercing, and she couldn't help but wonder why. He had just had his face buried between her legs, but for some reason he didn't want her to see his cock. It was strange and at odds with his typical confidence.

Her lips stretched into a naughty grin as she turned to look at his profile while he stared straight ahead. He had been pestering her with indecent invitations for two years, so perhaps it was time to return the favor. "So about that piercing, why won't you allow me to see it? What are you hiding? Are you embarrassed because it's pink and floral?"

His jaw tensed, and he didn't turn to look at her. A few seconds went by without him responding to her questions, and from the look on his face, he was pondering what to tell her. And perhaps what not to tell her. "I'll show you later, Fia. It just wasn't the time and the place."

She burst out laughing, and he winced, probably realizing how lame his excuse sounded. If it could even be called an excuse. "Really? That's all you're going to give me after you practically devoured my pussy? You'll have to do better than that, Bry."

His head snapped around to look at her, his eyes wide. Then, he seemed to realize he was the one driving and yanked his gaze back to the road. "I... As I said, I will show you later." He visibly swallowed before continuing. "It was meant to be a surprise, okay? And I don't just want to show it to you, I want you to experience it. It's supposed to feel good for you."

"Supposed to?" Fia frowned as she studied his face. He looked apprehensive, but that couldn't be right. "I can't imagine I'm that different from every other woman. If your previous hook-ups liked it, why would I be any different?"

"I had it done for you, Fia." There was a crease between his brows when he glanced at her. "No one else has even seen it, let alone tried it, so *supposed to* is the correct term until I know for sure. But if you don't like that kind of thing, I'll remove it before we...if we..."

His voice died, and she was taken aback by the concern lining his face and the tension in his shoulders. If she didn't know better, she would have said he looked scared, but she had never thought Bry was even capable of that feeling. At least not when it came to his own body and performance in bed. His arrogance had been one of the things that had helped her keep her distance.

CHAPTER 14

Fia shook her head to try to clear her thoughts. She wasn't sure how to feel about him having something like that done for her. He didn't really know her and had no idea what she liked. So, why would he even contemplate having a piercing done for her?

"I'll remove it, Fia, don't worry. You don't even have to see it."

His words made her frown. "No, I don't want you to remove it, and I already told you I want to see it."

"Then why did you shake your head?" He glanced at her with one eyebrow raised.

"Because I don't understand why you would get your cock pierced for me when I kept turning you down. Are you sure you weren't going to do it anyway, and it was just the timing that made it so no one else got to test it?" She kept her eyes on his face to judge his reaction. Perhaps her question was harsh, but she did want to know the answer.

Bry sighed, and his shoulders sagged. "I guess that's

a reasonable question. To tell you the truth, I had considered it before I met you, but I didn't really have the motivation to go through with it, considering the possible complications. But when I met you, that changed. Your pleasure is important to me, Fia, and anything I can do to increase it, I'll do. And..." He visibly swallowed. "I wanted to give you something I've never given anyone else before."

All she could do was stare at him, his gorgeous profile, his amazing body, his pierced cock. Not that she could see that last part of his anatomy, but there was a definite bulge in his pants that indicated he was at least sporting a semi.

Just the thought of how it might feel inside her made her squeeze her thighs together. The way Bry had made her explode using his mouth and fingers, it was hard to imagine it could get any better, but she couldn't wait to let him try. A cock piercing hadn't been high on her agenda of things to try before, but for some reason it was suddenly at the top of her list and climbing.

"Fia, if you keep staring at my crotch like that, I might have to stop and jerk off before I can concentrate on driving." There was a note of challenge in his tone, like he was intending to shock her.

But shock wasn't what reverberated through her. Her gaze rose to his face, and she moaned at the image he had just put in her head. She would love to watch him pleasure himself, his hand stroking his large cock, the tension in his body at the mounting pleasure, the expression on his face when he came—all of it. And she already knew she wouldn't be able to watch him without touching herself.

His eyes widened when he saw the expression on her face. "Fuck. I didn't expect that to turn you on. I thought... Damn, I want you in my bed, redbird. I'll make you come so hard you see stars. And I won't let you rest until you beg for mercy."

Fia shuddered at his words and the way they made her channel clench with need. But she wasn't done questioning him. "Why me, though? What's so different about me that you wanted to give me something special?" She already knew they were true mates, but except for the last two days, the mating bond shouldn't have affected him much. At least that was what she had thought. But she was coming to realize that she might have been wrong in her assumption.

Bry smiled but didn't meet her gaze. "I've already told you I want to be with you, and I've never wanted to commit to anyone before. It took me a little while to understand what I wanted, but it was there from the first time I met you."

She nodded slowly. It was what she had expected based on what he had told her earlier that day. But his response didn't answer all her questions about the mating bond and how it worked. And before she knew more, it was best not to tempt fate by teasing him and letting herself get too aroused to resist him.

Something he had said suddenly registered, and she frowned. "What did you mean by complications? You're a shifter, so why—"

"Exactly." Bry gave her a wry smile. "I change form, and what happens to the piercing during a shift is unpredictable. Which is one of the reasons why piercings aren't that common among shifters."

Her eyes widened as she stared at him. "What do you mean by unpredictable?"

He chuckled. "How painful it is during the change and whether it stays the way it's supposed to. They use a special silver platinum alloy that's not automatically rejected by our bodies, but it's impossible to know what happens until you shift."

She swallowed hard at the mention of pain. "The piercing is still there, so I assume it hasn't been an issue for you."

"Not apart from the burn when I change, but it's worth it."

Fia's eyes were glued to his face. "It's painful and you still want it?" Just the thought of having something burning down there... *No. Just no.*

Grinning, he glanced at her. "It's only painful when I change, and even then it doesn't last long. I'd suffer more than that to ensure you had a good time."

All she could do was shake her head slowly in shock. Because what was she going to say to that? Thank you? It was time to find something else to talk about. "Um, okay. What's going to happen to the vampire?"

Bry chuckled but didn't object to her change of topic. "Hugh will gather some of his single panthers to feed her. Hopefully, she'll be sane enough to talk by tomorrow morning. She wasn't there of her own free will, and I for one want to know how Amber managed to capture her. And of course whatever the female can tell us about that evil bitch will be helpful."

Fia nodded before she frowned. "Why only single panthers? What would happen if a mated panther fed her?"

"Most likely nothing." Bry shrugged. "But vampires can bond with the person they feed from. It's something they can control, but with a starving vampire who's not in control of their powers, it's a bit of a risk."

Fia's mouth fell open as she stared at him.

Chuckling, he glanced at her. "Don't worry. If she had bonded with you, I would've smelled it on you. And I seem to remember we were quite close not that long ago." He winked at her.

"Okay, so I guess I don't have to worry about being a vampire's plaything. That's good to know."

"It is." Bry's voice was deeper than before. "Because if you are going to be anyone's plaything, you're going to be mine."

She sucked in a breath as a spark of need shot through her. *Damn him for stoking my desire like this.* But two could play that game. "Unless of course we switch it up and you become my plaything."

Bry let out a growl before turning to look at her with heat shining in his eyes. "If you really mean that, just say the word. I'll be more than happy to oblige you."

She bit her lip as a shudder raced through her. "You would accept that? Being someone's plaything?"

His lips stretched into a grin while he shook his head slowly. "Not someone's, Fia. Yours. I've never even considered being someone's plaything before, but I'd be happy to be yours."

***

Bryson glanced at Fia. She looked stunned, like she hadn't expected his answer. And if he were being honest, he was a bit surprised himself to find out he wouldn't mind that kind of arrangement with her. He had always preferred to be the one in charge in the bedroom as well as out of it, but that was before meeting his true mate and feeling firsthand what it meant to really want to be with someone in every way.

She became silent after his declaration, but it didn't feel like a bad kind of silence. Her focus seemed to turn inward and with everything that had happened that day and the day before, he wasn't surprised. She probably needed time to process everything, so he chose to stay quiet and let her have the time she required.

The landscape flew by as he drove a bit too fast while considering how to tell Fia that she was his mate. She had come a long way toward accepting him just in the last few hours, but breaking monumental news like that had the potential to scare her away. There was no doubt she was attracted to him, but it wasn't the same as committing herself to him for life.

They would spend the night at Hugh's house, and he hoped Fia would choose to share a bed with him. He wasn't going to be able to say no to having sex with her in that case, even though he would have to be careful and control his instinct to mate her. The mating bond was already urging him to claim her, and having sex would only increase the compulsion.

Except *already* wasn't correct, considering how long it had been since they'd met. It was the one thing he really couldn't understand. The mating bond should have taken effect immediately and not waited two years before suddenly waking up. He had never heard of such a delay ever happening before, and he couldn't help thinking that something unusual must have happened to prevent it from manifesting at once.

By the time they parked in front of the farmhouse, Bryson had explored every conceivable explanation for the delay in the onset of the mating bond, but he had yet to come up with a plausible one. It was a mystery, and he doubted he would ever get to know the reason. But at least the bond had finally taken effect, and he knew why he had been obsessed with Fia for so long.

Smiling, he turned to look at the beautiful woman next to him. She had a wrinkle between her brows as she stared at the house. "Are you all right? We'll get you some food. It's been way too long since you ate anything, and you need to replenish your strength if you're going to keep your promise."

She turned to him with her brows raised in confusion. "Promise? Which promise?"

Bryson chuckled. "To make me your plaything. Or are you going to go back on your word?"

Laughing, she rolled her eyes. "Are you sure that's what you want? You don't strike me as the submissive type."

"I'm not, but that doesn't mean I won't do it for the right woman. Who knows, I might even enjoy it?" He winked at her, hoping she would agree. If she was the one with the reins, it might be easier to suppress his instinct to claim her.

Fia chewed on her bottom lip while studying his face. "I'll tell you after we've had something to eat. I'm not going to make any decisions on an empty stomach."

Bryson laughed at her delaying tactics, but he couldn't fault her for her logic. "Wise woman. I guess I'll ask you again after we've eaten then."

She just smiled at him before she opened her door and got out.

Kynlee came out of the house just as they stepped onto the porch. "There you are. I was starting to get worried that something might've happened to you." The woman studied both their faces, seeming to look for evidence that something was amiss. When she didn't find it, she smiled and shrugged. "Okay, you're here now. Come on in. I'm sure you're hungry."

"Thank you." Fia smiled, and Bryson nodded his thanks as well. "Food would be perfect, actually. I'm starving."

Kynlee nodded before turning and heading back into the house. "Good."

Bryson indicated for Fia to enter ahead of him, and she gave him a small smile before following Kynlee into the house.

The large kitchen with dining section was decorated in the same brown and beige colors as the living room, except a few items in other colors seemingly strategically placed to break up the monotony.

The scent that met them was heavenly and made Bryson's stomach growl. Apparently, Fia wasn't the only one who was starving.

Hugh was already at the table, serving up a hearty stew into large bowls. The man smiled when they entered the room. "Finally. I was starting to regret our decision to wait for you to join us for dinner."

"Everyone else has already eaten." Kynlee walked up to the chair next to Hugh and pulled it out to sit down. "Take a seat and help yourselves. And please don't be shy. If you want anything to go with the stew, please ask. We usually eat it like this, but we're open for variations."

"Thank you. It looks and smells fantastic." Bryson pulled out a chair for Fia across from Hugh before taking a seat next to her. There was a large bottle of water and a selection of soft drinks on the table. "What would you like to drink, Fia?"

She gave him another small smile. "Just some water please."

After filling her glass and his own, Bryson offered the bottle to Hugh, who took it with a nod. "So how's the vampire doing? Has she calmed down yet?"

Hugh nodded. "Surprisingly, yes. The female fed from two of my panthers before she pulled away and didn't want to feed from anyone else. She thanked them politely and asked to be left to rest for a while."

"Is she still tied up?" There was a look of concern on Fia's face, but Bryson was unable to tell whether it was because she was afraid of the vampire or if she was concerned about the female's wellbeing.

"No. I don't think she means us any harm." Hugh scratched his chin. "But I have a couple of my panthers looking after her for the time being. They'll bring more people to feed her if necessary. There are several who have volunteered. I have a question for you, though, Fia." Hugh cocked his head while looking at her, and Bryson narrowed his eyes at him while wondering what Hugh wanted from his redbird.

Fia didn't seem concerned at all. "Of course, ask away."

Hugh smiled. "Would you mind checking on Erwin after we've eaten? He's still unresponsive, and it might be because he's dehydrated and starved, but I would like to know if Amber has put some kind of spell on him. Would you be able to detect something like that?"

"Yes." Fia nodded. "I should be able to feel any magic still affecting him, and of course, I'll be happy to check."

Bryson smiled. He should have known Hugh's question would be innocent. *Fuck. Only a few hours since I found out I have a true mate, and already I'm turning into a jealous idiot.*

Hugh's smile widened. "Thank you. Erwin might've been an asshole the last few years, but he's still a part of my clan." His smile disappeared and was replaced by a frown. "I can't save him from his mate, though, and I've got a feeling she's going to be his demise."

Fia visibly swallowed. "That's one thing I can't help with, I'm afraid. If I could, I would."

Bryson felt his whole body tense at Fia's words. Or perhaps not her words as much as her dejected tone when she said them. It almost sounded like she had tried that before and failed. But that couldn't be right. Who would want her to change or remove their mating bond?

CHAPTER 15

They ate, and their conversation centered around everyday things, but Bryson found himself struggling to participate. Something was nagging at him, but he couldn't quite put a finger on what it was. It was just a feeling he was missing something.

As soon as they were done eating, they cleared off the table before Bryson and Fia followed the alpha couple up the stairs to the bedroom where they had put Erwin.

The man on the bed looked more dead than alive, but it was going to take more than a lack of food and water to kill him. Although, he might need to get liquid and nutrients intravenously to recover enough to wake up, unless Fia could help him somehow.

Fia moved over to the bed, and Bryson stayed right beside her. There was no way he was going to let her get attacked again. The chance of that seemed extremely remote, but things could change quickly, and he wasn't going to make the same mistake twice.

Staring at the man on the bed, Fia shook her head slowly with concern wrinkling her brows. "How long do you think he's been like this? I don't know how long it takes for a shifter to get to this state of emaciation, but I would assume weeks have gone by since he last had a proper meal."

"Weeks is probably right." Bryson took in Erwin's skeletal features.

Fia turned her head and looked up at him. "You should remove your hand from my back. I need to use my power to detect any magic used on him, and I don't want it to affect you."

Bryson removed the hand he had put on her lower back without even realizing it. He had felt her magic the day before when she protected them all from Amber, and it had blasted through him like he had just opened the door to a raging furnace. It hadn't felt uncomfortable, though, quite the opposite in fact. It had left him with a throbbing erection.

The realization made him grit his teeth. Was that how it had affected everyone else as well? Because that would be a serious problem.

He spun to look at Hugh and Kynlee, who were still standing right inside the door. "I think it might be better if you wait outside while Fia works." His tone was harder than he had intended, and Hugh raised an eyebrow at him in question.

"That's not necessary." Fia's voice brought his attention back to her. "They'll be fine staying in the room. This won't require a lot of power."

Bryson narrowed his eyes at her. "But won't they be...affected anyway?"

She tilted her head to the side as she stared up at

him. "If you're asking whether they will feel anything, the answer is no."

He stared at her for several seconds before he gave her a short nod and turned back to Hugh. "Okay, then I guess you can stay."

"Well, thank you." Hugh's lips curved into a grin, and there was amusement in his eyes, like he was taking great pleasure in Bryson's behavior. But thankfully, he didn't say anything.

Fia put her hand on Erwin's chest and stood still while her gaze lingered on the man.

A few seconds went by before her eyes widened, and she pulled her hand away. But instead of explaining what she had found, she just stood there, staring at Erwin like he had given her a shock.

"What did you discover?" Bryson studied Fia's expression.

"He…" Her voice sounded choked, and she cleared her throat before starting again. "He's affected by Amber's magic. She's put a spell on him to suppress the mating bond."

Bryson frowned. "I thought that was impossible. You said—"

"I said I couldn't help with that, not that it was impossible." Fia's body was tense, and her tone was clipped. "And it doesn't mean the bond is gone, only that the effect of it is much reduced."

Bryson froze as he stared at her profile. She had yet to look at him after what she had discovered, and he desperately wanted to see her eyes. A dread like he had never felt before settled like a molten rock in his stomach, and he needed to see her eyes to make sure his suspicions were groundless. She couldn't have, could she? It was impossible.

"Is that what's keeping him unconscious?" Hugh's voice came from right behind Bryson. "And if so, can you remove it?"

Fia bit her lip before she answered. "I don't know what's keeping him unconscious, but I don't think it's the spell. He might have some injuries we can't see, or it's simply dehydration. I'm not a healer, though, so I can't tell if he's got any internal injuries. Steph would be able to. We can ask her if she'd like to help. I'm almost certain she would."

"I would really appreciate her assistance." There was warmth in Hugh's voice. "Can you remove the magic affecting him?"

Fia nodded slowly before she turned to look at Hugh without giving Bryson as much as a passing glance. "Yes, but I'm not sure it's a wise thing to do unless we're prepared. With the bond in full effect, Amber will be pulled to him. I'm not sure how long she would be able to stay away, but I'm sure you do."

Hugh looked back at Kynlee before returning his gaze to Fia. "Good point. Probably a maximum of two days before she'd turn up, but for all we know, she would come as soon as she felt the change. And I don't want her back on my doorstep before I'm ready to receive her."

"Then I think it's time to contact the others." Fia turned toward Bryson, but instead of looking into his eyes, she fixed her gaze at a point on his chest. "Can you call and ask them to come here as soon as possible? Unless of course it's better to transport Erwin somewhere else where we have the advantage when she arrives and can avoid collateral damage."

"I think I know a place."

Fia looked at Hugh when he spoke. Apparently she didn't have any qualms about meeting *his* gaze. "Okay, then perhaps we should get everyone to meet us there."

"No." Bryson couldn't prevent the harshness in his tone. "We'll invite them here first so we can make a sound plan for how to kill her."

Fia's eyes widened, and she took a step away from him. "That...sounds like a good idea."

"Then I'll call them." He turned to look at Hugh, who was frowning at him. "Right after I've spoken to Fia alone. Is there somewhere we can talk privately?"

"Of course." Hugh studied Bryson's face with concern tightening his expression, but thankfully, the man didn't ask any questions. "Please follow me."

The red-haired alpha turned around and headed toward the door, and Bryson put his hand on the small of Fia's back before starting after him. She didn't resist or protest, which was a consolation if a small one.

Hugh took them to a small bedroom at the corner of the house, which the man assured them was sufficiently far away from everyone else staying on the second floor so nobody would accidentally overhear them.

As soon as Hugh closed the door behind him on his way out, Bryson rounded on Fia. She was chewing on her bottom lip and wouldn't meet his gaze. "Tell me that's not what you've been doing to me for the last two years."

"I... I assume you're talking about the spell Amber used on Erwin." She swallowed hard before raising her gaze to his. "I can't tell you that, but it was—"

"So, you have known we are true mates since we met?" Bryson didn't even know how he managed to get the words out. His chest seemed to have caught fire, a raging inferno burning his heart and lungs to a crisp.

"Yes, but—" Tears gathered in her eyes, and she choked on her words.

Just minutes ago he would have been moved by her tears. But not now. Not when he was struggling to even breathe through the pain in his chest. She had resisted his advances since day one, but she hadn't distanced herself from him completely, and he had taken that as a positive sign. A possibility that she would come around someday. But all this time she had known and willfully chosen to use her power to prevent the mating bond from working its magic. And to do something like that could only mean she didn't like him, perhaps even hated him.

"Bry, I'm sorry." With tears flowing down her cheeks, she took a step toward him and reached out a hand as if to touch his face.

But he quickly stepped back out of her reach. "Sorry doesn't cut it, Fia. Not for something like this. I chose to trust you, but all you've done to me is deceive me. About your power, about who we are to each other, and God only knows what else. But I'm sorry. I'm sorry I'm so unworthy in your eyes that you chose to destroy the most amazing thing a couple can ever experience."

Bryson didn't wait around to see if she had any response to his words. After flinging the door open, he stormed out of the room, down the stairs, and out onto the porch before ripping his clothes off and changing into his panther.

**

Fia stared at the door that had slammed shut after Bry had flung it open. She wanted to run after him but what was she supposed to say when she caught up to him? All the reasons she had for keeping him in the dark about being his mate were lame and petty, not to mention selfish.

She had never considered Bry's feelings before using her magic on him. But in her defense, she hadn't really known the meaning of a mating bond, and she suspected there was more to it than she had assumed. At least from what she had experienced in the last few days, there were a lot more emotions involved than she had thought.

She shuddered as she recalled the utter devastation in Bry's eyes when he discovered her betrayal. If she had been in doubt of his feelings for her before, she wasn't anymore. And based on his words, it was obvious he already knew they were true mates before they'd entered Erwin's room. Although, she had no idea how long he had known and why he hadn't told her about it.

Fia shuddered again but for an entirely different reason. Pain ripped through her chest, sending her gasping to her knees. It felt like someone had just stabbed her in her heart and twisted the knife for maximum damage.

She must have blacked out for a little while, because the next thing she knew, she was lying on her back on the hard floor with Kynlee shaking her and yelling her name. Her eyes felt heavy, but she managed to crack them open to stare up at the concerned blond woman.

"Are you all right? What happened?" Kynlee's brows were pushed together, and her eyes were dark with worry. "Did Bryson hurt you? I saw him run out of the house and change, but I didn't think him capable of hurting you. Quite the opposite in fact. I thought he wanted you to be his mate."

Tears formed in Fia's eyes before rolling down her temples and into her hair. "I did something horrible." Her voice was little more than a whisper. "He didn't hurt me. I hurt him."

"Oh." Kynlee looked a bit taken aback before giving her a doubtful expression. "What did you do?"

Squeezing her eyes shut, Fia took a deep breath before answering. "I put a spell on him."

"Okay. I assume he didn't know, and he was hurt by that. It would explain him needing some time by himself. I'm sure he'll be back soon, though, and you can talk this through and put it behind you."

Fia opened her eyes and shook her head slowly. "I'm not sure he'll be ready to forgive me anytime soon. If ever."

Kynlee gave her a small smile. "It can't be that bad. It probably hurt his pride more than anything else."

Fia shook her head more firmly this time. "I wish that was the case, but it's not. We're true mates, Kynlee, and I put a spell on him soon after I met him to suppress the bond so he wouldn't discover who I was."

Kynlee pulled back, and the expression of horror on her face said it all.

Fia had committed a cardinal sin among shifters, and she couldn't expect anyone to understand. But then she wasn't sure she herself understood anymore either. Why hadn't she put more effort into finding out what a mating bond actually meant? She still didn't know, and that said it all.

She had been terrified of being tied to a man who would treat her like a possession and betray her constantly. But instead of trying to find out whether her assumption was correct, she had just shut down the whole issue and gone about her daily life like nothing was different.

"Why would you do something like that?" Kynlee's voice was soft and measured.

Fia pulled in a shaky breath. "You have heard about all his women, haven't you? I was scared of being tied to someone who was going to betray me constantly. I just couldn't face it."

Kynlee frowned. "But he wouldn't. No shifter in his right mind would be able to betray his mate like that. I can't say it's never happened, but it's extremely rare. And among true mates I don't think it's possible."

"Why is that?" Fia studied Kynlee's face. "I'm starting to realize that I don't know enough about how the mating bond works."

Kynlee stood and reached out her hand to Fia. "Are you able to get up? I think this talk requires coffee. Let's go to the kitchen and make some, and I'll lock the doors so no one can disturb us."

To Fia's relief they didn't meet anyone on their way downstairs to the kitchen, and true to her word, Kynlee locked the doors after they entered the room.

"Have a seat at the table, and I'll get the coffee started." Kynlee busied herself by the counter.

"Thank you." Fia swallowed hard as fresh tears filled her eyes at the kindness Kynlee was showing her. The woman could have chosen to send her packing after what Fia had done to one of Kynlee's own kind, but she hadn't.

The blond woman shot her a glance with a small smile softening her features. "Don't thank me yet. Save it until we've sorted this mess out."

Fia chuckled through her tears. "And by this mess you mean me, I suppose."

Kynlee laughed. "You are part of the mess, yes. But not the only part. There's always a counterpart, isn't there? And he's partially at fault in this mess as well. But we'll deal with him later."

Fia nodded and took a seat before supporting her head in her hands. It was late, and she was tired, but she wasn't going to be able to sleep until Bry came back and she knew he was safe. And if he didn't come back on his own soon, she would go look for him.

A mug of coffee was placed in front of her, and Fia opened her eyes to look at Kynlee, who had taken a seat directly across the dining room table from her.

"Thank you." Forcing a smile she didn't feel, Fia lifted the cup and took a sip of the hot liquid. It was strong and exactly what she needed to regain her focus.

"So, tell me what you know about the mating bond." Kynlee looked at her over the rim of her own cup.

Fia shrugged. "It binds two people together and once sealed, it cannot be broken. A mated couple has to spend time together and have sex regularly. Most people choose a mate based on who they like, but true mates don't get that choice. Finding your true mate is rare, and it's revered among shifters, but to me it resembles an arranged marriage."

Kynlee's eyes widened while Fia spoke. "Damn, that sounds bleak indeed. If I had been presented with a prospect like that I would've opted out as well. But even though you've got some of the facts straight, you haven't mentioned anything about love."

"No, I haven't." Fia bit her lip for a second before she continued. "Are feelings part of the mating bond at all, or is love something which is expected to develop as you spend time together? I've never had anyone to ask questions about this except Bry and his panthers, and that would've been like discussing your escape plans with your jailer."

Chuckling, Kynlee tucked a stray lock of blond hair behind her ear. "Yes, that sounds about right." Then she frowned. "How did you even realize you and Bryson are true mates if you don't know much about the mating bond? Where did you even hear about the mating bond? Because it sounds like you knew what it was or at least had some idea before you even met him."

Fia nodded. "Magic runs in my family. Both my mother and my grandmother before her are witches. I found a book a few years ago, which had belonged to my grandmother, and it mentioned shifters and vampires. As part of the entry there were a couple of passages about mates and true mates. All I know about true mates, at least up until a few days ago, is from that book, and it didn't mention one word about feelings or love. It was all very clinical, perhaps even cynical, and I guess I didn't get a good impression. And then with

Bry's reputation…"

Breathing out heavily, Fia looked down at the black surface of her coffee. "I knew I would fall in love with him if I agreed to be more than friends. He snared my attention from the first time I saw him. But I would just be one insignificant woman among all the women who passed through his bedroom every year. How was I going to live like that without having it destroy me? It would be impossible. And that's why I put a spell on him to delay the inevitable for as long as I could. I knew the spell wouldn't last forever, but the longer it lasted, the more time I would have to come to terms with what was to come."

"Except, a true mate is the person best suited to you of everyone in the world." Kynlee had a warm smile on her face when Fia lifted her gaze. "Bryson is the one who can give you the most happiness, and the deepest love and friendship. True mates only have eyes for each other. Regular mates do, too, but the bond is even stronger between true mates, and that's why it's treated as sacred."

CHAPTER 16

Fia stared at Kynlee. "What does that mean exactly?"

Kynlee's smile widened. "It means Bryson would never stray. Just the thought of another woman than you in his bed would turn him off and might even make him physically ill. And from what I've heard, it works the same even if one of the mates is human."

Nodding slowly, Fia thought back to what Bry had told her. He hadn't wanted anyone else since he met her. Even under the influence of her spell, and not aware she was his true mate, it had still held true.

After squeezing her eyes closed for a few seconds, she opened them to stare at Kynlee. "I wish I'd known this two years ago. I might still have balked at the concept of true mates, particularly considering Bry's reputation, but I think I would've accepted it and learned to live with it."

"You haven't been completely unaffected by him these last couple of years, though, have you?" The blond woman lifted an eyebrow at her. "Has anyone else caught your eye since you met Bryson?"

"No. No one." Fia shook her head. "He's the only man I can think of. And I've thought about him a lot more than I should have, considering I've been trying to keep my distance as much as possible. But a spell like that must be maintained. It doesn't last unless you reinforce it regularly. Which means I've had to spend time with him to have the opportunity to maintain the spell."

Kynlee nodded. "So, I guess the real question is, are you ready to accept him now that you know more about how the mating bond works?"

"Yes." Fia nodded before lowering her gaze to the table. "But I'm not sure he'll accept me after everything I've done to him. I hid my true power from him, pretending I was just a low-level witch, until I had to reveal my true power yesterday to protect everyone from Amber's attack. And now he thinks I consider him unworthy because I spelled him to hide that we are true mates."

"I'm sure—" Kynlee suddenly spun her head around to look out the window toward the front yard.

Fia turned to look as well and saw the lights from a car seconds before she heard the purr of the engine. It drove up to the house before stopping next to Bry's car.

"That's Leith's car, isn't it?" Kynlee frowned. Her question was answered when the driver's side door opened, and Leith stepped out. "I hope nothing awful has happened to have them turning up at this time of night. It's past midnight."

Fia watched as Sabrina exited the vehicle just as another car drove up and parked next to her. Soon after, Trevor, Jennie, and Henry stepped out.

Rising from the table, Fia pulled in a deep breath. These people had been driving for hours to get there, so whatever had made them decide to leave Inverness had happened early in the evening.

Kynlee rose, and Fia followed her out of the kitchen and out onto the porch. Hugh was already there greeting the newcomers.

"I wasn't aware we were having a party." The red-haired panther alpha laughed and turned to look at his mate as she walked up next to him. "Is this your doing? You know I'm all for surprises, love, but after midnight? Damn, you are trying to wear me out."

"Oh, shut it." Kynlee chuckled and swatted his arm. "Come on in, all of you. You're all welcome no matter what time it is."

"Thank you, Kynlee." The corner of Leith's mouth pulled up into something resembling a smile as he put his arm around Sabrina. "Your hospitality is much appreciated."

Hugh's shoulders shook with his laughter. "Her hospitality, I like that."

They all moved into the living room, and Fia stood in the doorway while introductions were made. Hugh and Kynlee had never met Sabrina or Jennie, but to Fia's surprise they didn't know Henry either. Although, perhaps she shouldn't be surprised at all. It wasn't like she knew a lot of witches even though she was one.

"So why are you all here?" Hugh leaned forward in his seat with his eyes on Leith. They had all sat down on the couches. "Because I'm assuming this is not a social call."

Leith gave a short nod. "You would be right. And I

take it you have not watched the news."

Fia stood up straighter as apprehension stiffened her spine. She had been considering leaving to go look for Bry, but she needed to know what had happened first.

"We haven't." Hugh frowned. "We were back late from Erwin's cabin. The news hasn't been on our agenda, I'm afraid, with everything that has happened today."

"That is understandable." Leith took Sabrina's hand and put it on his thigh like he needed her touch. "There was an incident in Perth this afternoon. A woman ran screaming from a car. The other occupant of the car, also a woman, ran after her and dragged her back to the car before taking off. Nobody intervened. Callum was able to retrieve some footage from the area, and it confirms that the two women were Amber and her daughter, Mary."

"Which means they're on their way south." Kynlee scooted closer to her mate. "I hope they're not planning to come here. I don't particularly relish the prospect of seeing Amber again, particularly if we're not prepared to receive her. But then she doesn't have any reason to show up here, since she doesn't yet know we have retrieved Erwin. When she realizes that, though…"

Leith nodded. "I agree. But we still decided some of us should be here to support you just in case. Callum checked the license plate of the car, and it is registered to Erwin. It seems Amber had the car parked somewhere for her to retrieve when she needed it. Perhaps as a backup solution. Callum is currently performing some of his computer magic to try to identify where they are headed. He will contact us as soon as he discovers something relevant."

Fia's eyes widened as a chill settled in her bones. Bry was out there by himself. The chance of him crossing paths with Amber was slim, but if the witch was in the area, it could happen. And he wouldn't be able to put up a fight against her. She'd have him subdued in no time, and then she could do whatever she wanted with him including killing him. And Fia wouldn't be surprised if that was exactly what Amber chose to do if she recognized Bry as one of the shifters trying to take her down. Or just the fact that he was a shifter was enough for her to decide to kill him.

"Fia, where are you going?" Kynlee's question made her stop and turn back to look at the people still sitting on the couches. Fia hadn't even realized she had turned to leave until Kynlee said her name. All her thoughts had been on Bry and finding him before Amber did.

"Bry's out there. I have to find him. He's all alone, and if he meets that evil bitch…" Fia shuddered and turned to leave.

"Wait. I can help." Henry's words made Fia stop again and turn toward the alpha wolf, who had risen and was coming toward her.

"I would appreciate that." Fia nodded. "He ran off because I… I hurt him." Tears threatened to flood her eyes again, and she swallowed hard to keep them at bay. "But he's mine, and I need him back."

There was a gasp from one of the people still sitting around the low table, and someone murmured something. But Fia didn't really care what they thought of her.

Henry smiled softly and gave a small nod. "I have a good nose when I change. I should be able to follow his scent. Let's hope he hasn't run very far."

Fia nodded. "Thank you." Then she turned and headed toward the porch.

***

Henry followed the pretty red-haired witch down the hallway. It seemed Bryson had found his true mate as well. At least that was what he assumed Fia had meant when she called the panther hers. It had been like a veritable epidemic lately with all these shifters finding their true mates within the span of a few weeks. And it brought his hopes up that he would find his own soon as well. But it would be stupid of him to count on that when most shifters never did. It was still rare, and he had to keep that in mind, even when said mind was playing tricks on him like it had when he entered this house.

The most amazing scent had filled his nose and caused his cock to twitch in response, and Henry had looked around to find out who it was coming from. But there was no one within sight except their hosts, Fia, and the people he had arrived with, and the scent didn't originate from any of them.

The scent had diminished when they'd entered the living room, which made Henry dismiss it as something his mind had conjured. If the scent belonged to someone in the household, it should have been most pronounced in the common living areas. Anything else was illogical. Which meant it had originated in his mind as a result of wishful thinking.

Except when he reentered the hallway, the scent hit him with renewed strength, making him blink a couple of times to regain his focus. Fia needed him to help her find Bryson, and he couldn't let his strange mental state affect him.

Henry was just about to step outside, when he heard someone coming down the stairs behind him. He threw a glance over his shoulder and immediately froze at the vision descending the stairs.

Long chestnut ringlets framed a pale oval face. Large brown eyes were staring at him a bit wearily like she was uncertain of what he was going to do.

Turning toward her, he gave her a warm smile. Although it might have been a bit strained because he was suddenly realizing whom the heavenly scent belonged to. It hadn't been his imagination at all.

She stopped on the second step above the hallway floor. Her eyes narrowed slightly while she kept staring at him.

Henry had to swallow the thickness in his throat before he could say anything. "Hi." It was all he managed to say before his throat clogged up again.

"Hi." Her voice was melodic and sultry and caused a shiver to race through his body.

Taking a deep breath, he managed to unclog his throat enough to utter a few more words. "My name's Henry. It's a pleasure to meet you." And it certainly was judging by his hardening cock. It was an odd reaction to have to someone he had just met, but her scent, voice, and looks were having a more profound impact on him than he had ever experienced before with anyone.

Perhaps she's... No, you idiot. That would be too much of a coincidence. Even though she had made an impression, there was no indication she was his mate. Henry would have felt it immediately if she was, and he didn't. He only felt this profound attraction. Which was nice but not really what he had been dreaming of.

A lover would be great, but he was afraid it would cloud his vision and somehow prevent him from recognizing his true mate if he ever met her. And that was a risk he wasn't willing to take. So, this woman, however lovely she was, wasn't for him. Just a few years ago, he would have given in to the temptation but not anymore. He had his sights firmly set on his goal to find his true mate, and nothing was going to make him waver.

"I'm Eleanor." The woman descended the last two steps before coming to a stop at the bottom of the stairs. "You're a wolf, but this residence smells predominantly of panthers."

A gasp sounded behind him right before Fia pushed past him and placed herself between him and the woman standing a few yards away. "You're out walking. Are you…feeling okay?"

Nodding slowly, Eleanor cocked her head as her gaze moved to Fia. "Yes. And thank you for feeding me. Were you one of the people who rescued me?"

Shock suddenly reverberated through Henry's frame. No wonder he had been struggling to place the woman's scent in this house. She was the vampire Bryson and Fia had helped rescue from Amber's cabin. Leith had told him what Bryson had said on the phone, and this was apparently her, the vampire who had been left to starve by Amber and had attacked Fia.

"I didn't exactly volunteer to feed you." Fia's voice was calm, but her body seemed tense.

Eleanor's eyes widened a fraction before she

frowned. "So, I attacked you then. I'm sorry. I do not remember. The only reason I know you fed me is due to your scent. But I can see you are okay, and for that I'm thankful. Did I hurt anyone else?"

"No." Fia shook her head. "At least none of the rescue team. But I can't tell you what happened before we arrived at the cabin and found you and Erwin."

Eleanor's lips suddenly curled in distaste. "What happened to Amber? I hope the bitch is dead."

"Unfortunately, no. But hopefully she will be soon." Fia's voice was hard and cold. Then, she took a deep breath before turning to Henry. "We need to leave. Now. We have to find Bry before something happens to him."

Henry nodded, but his gaze was still firmly on Eleanor. He wanted to stay and talk to her, but he had already promised Fia to help her find Bryson, and he wouldn't break his promise. Besides, it was probably best to leave anyway, considering he didn't want his attraction to the vampire to grow, and he was certain that was exactly what would happen if he spent more time with her.

Tearing his gaze away from Eleanor, he turned and followed Fia out onto the porch, where he quickly stripped and changed into his wolf form.

But he couldn't resist throwing a last glance toward the bottom of the stairs before leaving. The vampire was still standing exactly where they had left her, but her eyes had a deep red glow when their gazes met.

CHAPTER 17

Fia ran beside Henry across the grassy field. He had easily caught Bry's scent, which made Fia breathe out a sigh of relief, even though it in no way guaranteed a positive outcome. But they would find her mate. They had to. She had to believe that instead of her anxiety, which was trying to convince her Bry was gone for good.

Henry was running fast but not too fast for her to keep up. Perhaps the wolf would have been able to track faster if he didn't have to adjust his speed to her human pace. But telling him to go searching without her wasn't an option. She wanted to be right there when they caught up with Bry to persuade him to come back with them. Henry's words of assurance might not be enough, particularly since Henry didn't even know the full story of what had happened between her and Bry.

They passed through a belt of trees before emerging in another field. Henry kept running in a straight line away from the farmhouse directly across the open field, and Fia got the feeling Bry had been too busy trying to get away from her to even consider where he was going. Which was understandable, but it worried her since it might mean he wasn't paying attention to his surroundings or people in the area. Shifters weren't supposed to exist in the real world, and black panthers weren't native to Scotland, so running around in the open was the same as asking for trouble.

When they reached another line of trees, Henry stopped and sniffed around the tree legs. Fia was dying to know why he had stopped, but he couldn't talk in his wolf form. She would just have to wait to see if it was important enough for him to change and tell her. For all she knew, he was just double-checking that they were heading in the right direction.

When he finally made his way past the trees, she hurried after him. Another field waited for them on the other side, but this time Henry followed the line of trees toward the right instead of running into the open field. It was almost like Bry had come to his senses and decided to be more careful. Or not. It might just be instinct driving him, and who knew where that would take him.

Tears filled her eyes as she recalled the pain and disappointment in his gaze. She hadn't been sure of his feelings for her earlier, having difficulty determining how much of his focus on her was due to instinct and how much was him actually caring. But it had been all there in his eyes when he realized what she had done, proving to her that he genuinely cared.

Now if she could only find him and tell him how

sorry she was for what she had done to him. Hopefully, he would listen to her this time and give her another chance. She was even prepared to go down on her knees and beg if that was what it took to get him back.

Henry stopped again, just a few yards away from a road. It wasn't a main road but a narrow country lane snaking its way through the landscape.

The wolf stared at her before looking behind her, and after he repeated the action a couple of times, she finally realized what Henry was trying to convey. Fia took a few steps back until she was hidden amongst the trees. "Okay, I'll stay here waiting while you do whatever you need to do. But don't you go running away from me."

The wolf shook his head, which looked strange, but she got the point. Henry wasn't going to take off and leave her there by herself.

He crept forward while using his nose. After investigating along the side of the road for about fifty yards in each direction, he crossed the road and did the same on the other side.

Fia fisted her hands at her sides as she stared at him. She couldn't be sure what he was doing, but his actions were making her anxiety spike. It looked like Henry had lost Bry's scent, and losing his scent by a road could only mean one thing. Bry had gotten into a car and been taken away.

It didn't have to mean something bad had happened to him, though. There was a good chance he had been hitching a ride just to be able to get farther away faster. But unfortunately, it wasn't the only explanation, and it was the alternative explanation that had Fia's body tense with fear.

Henry came back across the road and walked past her until he stood with his head facing away from her. His change was quick and looked effortless. Within a couple of seconds Henry the man was standing with his back to her where his wolf had been standing before.

He was naked, so she made sure to avert her eyes before she spoke. "What did you discover? Did he get into a car?"

Henry turned a little so he could look at her comfortably over his shoulder without showing her his front. "Yes. His scent stops here, and cars have passed recently. It's the logical explanation."

Fia squeezed her eyes shut and sucked in a deep breath to try to calm her anxiety. "Did you catch the scent of anyone else around here, like Amber?"

"A human, yes." His voice was firm yet warm. "But not Amber. A human has been here recently. And I mean right there and nowhere else."

Fia opened her eyes and looked at the spot at which Henry was pointing. It was close to the edge of the road only a few yards away, and it was consistent with someone opening their car door and stepping outside only to get back into the car and drive away. Most likely after exchanging a few words with a naked hitchhiker.

It was discouraging and frustrating, but at least Bry hadn't been picked up by Amber. Which meant that wherever he was, he was most likely safe.

But she was no closer to finding him and begging his forgiveness. And it was impossible to predict what he would do next. Would he go back to his clan? But if that had been his intention, he would have taken his car. Unless of course he had been too devastated to even think. It was a good chance he had been driven by an instinct to get away.

But at least he seemed to have come to his senses by the time he reached the narrow road, since he had changed and hitched a ride with someone. Or she assumed he had changed.

"Henry. Did Bry change when he reached the road?" The implications of someone meeting him in his panther form was threatening to send her to her knees. What if he ended up a test subject in a lab somewhere? *What if...*

"His scent is the same in both forms, but it's unlikely he caught a ride with someone as a panther. I don't think a human in their right mind would let a huge panther into their car." There was a smile in Henry's voice, and Fia's shoulders sagged in relief when she realized he was probably right.

But she couldn't stop the tears that started flowing again. This was all her fault, and she didn't even know how to make it right. How was she supposed to find her mate when he was so desperate to get away from her that he chose to flag down a car naked? And who would stop and agree to give a big naked guy a ride? The last question was a different topic altogether, though.

It was reasonable to assume Bry would eventually go back to his clan. He was their alpha, after all. But it was impossible to predict how long it would take him to do so. And even when he chose to go back, there was no guarantee he would agree to meet her. It wouldn't surprise her if he decided to declare her persona non grata and have his panthers turn her away if she ever showed up.

"I think we'd better head back." Henry's voice made her turn to meet his gaze. He had a warm and caring smile on his face.

Nodding, she turned slowly until she faced the direction they had come. Henry changed back into his wolf, probably feeling more comfortable moving in his animal form instead of walking beside her naked.

Fia couldn't muster the strength to run this time, but she moved fast as she followed Henry's loping form. Why couldn't she have fallen in love with someone like Henry? She had only met him a couple of times at Bry's, but from what she had heard, he was one of the most decent and no-nonsense alphas around.

But the truth was she didn't want a Henry, she wanted a Bryson. She had been attracted to Bry from the first time she met him, with his tall, dark, muscular gorgeousness. Some of it might have been the result of the mating bond, but she had always had a thing for the bad boy persona, and Bry checked all the boxes in that respect. If it hadn't been for all the women he'd entertained, she would have given in to his attention easily. And if she hadn't already been burned by a cheater, she might have been open to explore the pull of the mating bond despite his reputation.

But there was no point dwelling on any of that. Instead of acting like an adult and talking to Bry about her concerns, she had spelled him and tried to pretend she could live a life without him and be happy. Except she hadn't been happy in the last two years. He had constantly occupied her mind and been a source of longing, hopelessness, fear, and frustrated desire.

∞∞∞

Bryson thanked the old man again for his help before closing the door to the SUV behind him. The man was probably still wondering why he wanted to be let off in the middle of nowhere, and Bryson wasn't even sure himself if he was making the right choice. But he needed time alone for a while to come to terms with the fact that his true mate had lied to him.

His whole body tensed when pain shot through his chest again at the thought. Actually, lied was too mild a term for what Fia had done. It couldn't be called anything less than manipulation, and all to avoid being mated to him. She must really hate him to do something like that, unless using her magic to manipulate people was second nature to her. But he didn't think so. From what he had witnessed over the last two years, she cared about people. Hurting someone deliberately didn't seem to be in her nature.

Bryson moved off the road and into the trees, discarding the blanket the man had given him to cover himself. The old man had wanted to know why he had been out running naked in the middle of the night, and Bryson had answered vaguely, giving the impression it was due to a lover's tiff. Which was close enough to the truth, except Fia had never agreed to be his lover. She had given in to him after everything that had happened the day before, but it didn't prove she accepted him. It might have been a one-off occurrence for her, a weak moment brought on by him coming to her rescue twice in one day.

Both incidents had been due to his carelessness, but despite that she had been grateful and didn't blame him for what had happened. Or so she had said. Perhaps she did and was just excellent at hiding it. Bryson didn't know what to believe anymore. He had thought he knew Fia quite well, but he obviously didn't.

Tipping his head back, he squeezed his eyes shut and just stood there, breathing through the pulsing pain in his chest. There was no denying the fact he was partially to blame for all this. Partially to blame for what Fia had done to him. If he hadn't kept pretending he was still entertaining a new woman every few nights, he might have appeared a more worthy mate. But it was impossible to know whether it would have been enough to prevent her from spelling him. Although with how she called him a fuckboy, it was a possibility. Unless she had other reasons for messing with the mating bond that had nothing to do with his lifestyle.

But Fia had specifically mentioned his multitude of women as one of the main reasons for turning him down. And he should have guessed it would be repulsive to a sensible woman like her, but the truth was he hadn't really stopped to think about his behavior and the impression he was making. He had been more concerned with pretending everything was normal to hide what he had considered a weakness.

"Fuck, I'm such an idiot." It hadn't been a weakness at all but a sign he had found his true mate. Fia's spell had hidden some of the effects of the mating bond from him but not all of them. And if he had been man enough to talk to someone about what was happening to him, he might have realized what was going on with him sooner. Spell or no spell, his pride was the real cause of his downfall.

Bryson opened his eyes and let his gaze glide down his body. He was a big and powerful alpha, with muscles and tattoos to entice and intimidate. He was respected for his power, ruthlessness, and care for his clan. But none of it mattered anymore. Because without his true mate, he was nothing. He was going to die without her, and he didn't even care. His only hope was that it would happen soon, because knowing Fia didn't want him was like having his heart slowly gouged out of his chest.

He suddenly froze. Pride. Power. Ruthlessness. And apparently stupidity. He was running away instead of confronting Fia about what she had done and why, and most importantly trying to find out what he could do to change her opinion of him and gain her affection. This wasn't him. He had never given up before. "And I'm damn well not going to start now."

Bryson spun and started running back toward the road. He knew what he wanted, or rather who he wanted, and running away wasn't conducive to making that happen. Confronting Fia would most likely mean revealing to other people that she found him undesirable as a mate, but if that was what it took to have a long life with his true mate, it was worth it. His pride would take a knock, but it was probably a life lesson he was due in any case. He could practically hear his parents tell him *about time*. They had always considered him too proud and told him his attitude would end up biting him in the ass one day. Well, it had.

CHAPTER 18

Henry was itching to get back to see Eleanor again. He had hoped the search for Bryson would push the image of her out of his mind, but that hadn't happened. If anything, the urge to return to her had gotten stronger, and as soon as he saw the house in the distance, he wanted to speed up and leave Fia behind. But he didn't. It would be disrespectful, and it was the type of behavior he didn't approve of. He was an alpha, which to him meant a protector and a provider. And you couldn't be any of those things without respecting people.

As soon as they reached the porch where his clothes were still lying in a pile, he quickly changed into his human form and got dressed.

They found the others, including Eleanor, in the living room. She was sitting at the end of the table and didn't move when they entered the room, except for lifting her gaze to his. A shiver raced through him when their eyes met. Her eye color was back to its usual brown, but a red tint developed as they stared at each other, and his cock took that as a perfect incentive to start hardening.

Fuck. No woman had had this kind of effect on him for a long time—if ever. As far as he could recall, he had never experienced this kind of intensity before.

Taking a deep breath, he yanked his gaze away from Eleanor's and turned to look at Fia. She was telling the others what they had discovered about Bryson, and everyone seated around the table was focused on her.

Hugh frowned. "It doesn't sound like he wants to be found, so I'm not sure there's a lot we can do to help you."

Fia sighed and nodded, tears shining in her eyes. "I know, but there's a chance he'll be heading back to his clan, so I'll call G, his second in command, and explain what has happened. At least he'll be prepared if Bry turns up." She turned before anyone could respond and disappeared out into the hallway.

"He won't be able to stay away for long." Kynlee's lips curved into a small smile. "True mates never can. He'll be back in a few days at the most, and they'll sort this out." Her smile faded. "I can't imagine the hell they're both going through at the moment, though."

"Hell. That's the correct term for it." Jennie shuddered and turned to look at Trevor sitting next to her. "I still remember the horrible feeling when I thought I'd lost you. I don't think I'll ever forget it."

Trevor's arm tightened around his mate. "Don't remind me. And when I thought you might be hurt…" His hand cupped Jennie's neck a second before he leaned in and gave her a hard kiss. The tension in his body and face told of the fear and hurt he had suffered, and Jennie's body language mirrored her mate's.

Eleanor gracefully rose from her seat and looked at Hugh. "Please excuse me."

Henry froze when her gaze swung to his, and she glided over the floor toward him, her hips swaying gently and alluringly, causing his cock to twitch.

She stopped right in front of him with her lips curled into a small smile and a hint of amusement in her eyes. His admiration had obviously not gone unnoticed. "Henry, would you please follow me? I would like a word."

His tongue didn't work, so he ended up nodding his agreement before following her out of the room.

She led him into the empty kitchen before turning around and closing the door behind them.

Henry stopped in the middle of the room and turned toward her. His heart was racing. He shouldn't be there. With her. Nothing good would come from talking to her, just a whole lot of complications. And he didn't want any more complications. He had more than enough on his plate already with a pack that was still in a transition phase adjusting to his rules, and Amber killing shifters and putting everyone on edge.

Eleanor sauntered over until she was so close he wanted to take a step back to maintain a safe distance to her and her amazing scent. Her enticing fragrance was almost overpowering when standing this close to her, and he felt an urge to lean forward and let it suffuse his lungs and mind.

When she smiled up at him, he noticed her teeth were longer and sharper than they had been just a minute ago. And when she took another step toward him, he automatically took a step back. But it wasn't because he was scared of her sharp teeth. Quite the opposite, in fact. It had everything to do with how much he wanted to feel her teeth sink into his skin.

"Are you scared of me?" She cocked her head and raised an eyebrow. "Or are you feeling the draw between us like I do?"

He sucked in a breath at her words. She was feeling it, too, which was more than a little disturbing. "Please don't come any closer. I think it's better if we keep a safe distance between us."

"Why?" Her lips twitched like she was finding this whole situation amusing.

Henry wasn't, though. He didn't need this kind of temptation, and he would do his best to fight it. Even though his body was conspiring against him. His cock was almost painfully hard. "Because whatever this is, I don't think we should give in to it. I'm sure you have a life to get back to, and so do I."

In less time than it would have taken him to blink, she had his shoulders locked in an iron grip and the tip of her nose brushed against his throat as she inhaled deeply.

A shudder of pure lust tore through him so violently his knees almost buckled. "Eleanor, please." His voice was shaky and breathless. He wanted to wrap his arms around her and kiss her hard, but he resisted the urge—barely.

"Please what?" Her husky voice made him shudder a second time. Then she kissed his jugular, and he gasped and tightened his glutes as he just about exploded in his pants.

"Let me go. This is…not a good idea." He almost

choked on his words, as blinding lust pulsed through his body, trying to tear down his resolve to not give in to the attraction between them. They had just met, and this wasn't the time to get intimate with anyone.

At least not until they had caught and dealt with Amber. He had seen the strain her threat was putting on the mated couples. They had more to lose than the rest of them, and they knew it.

"Why are you resisting this when there is so much pleasure to be had?" Eleanor's lips were a hair's breadth from his jugular, and he just knew her fangs were fully extended and ready to pierce his flesh. "Chemistry like this doesn't come around often, I can tell you. It's unique and should be treasured. Please let me give you a little taste of what we can have." The tip of her tongue touched his skin just above his jugular, and all he could do was groan. His vocal cords were no longer working well enough to help form words.

She must have taken his silence as consent because a few seconds later, her fangs breached his skin, and he was swallowed by the most mind-blowing orgasm he had ever had. Pleasure enveloped his body, mind, and soul, and he lost himself in it. The only thing he could feel through it was her soft lips on his skin and her hard teeth embedded in his flesh.

He barely registered when all hell broke loose around him. Eleanor suddenly let go of him, and with her not holding him up anymore, he sank to his knees as the orgasm still held him firmly in its grip, making his body vibrate with pleasure. But it soon faded, and he became aware of the people and noise surrounding him.

A loud crash and the sound of glass hitting the

floor made him jerk his head toward the kitchen window. Most of the glass pane was gone, leaving a gaping hole.

"Are you all right?" Trevor's voice made Henry turn his head to look at the big man. He was crouching in front of Henry, studying him with concern lining his features.

Henry nodded and frowned, not sure what had just happened. But there was a likely cause. "Did Amber attack? Is everyone okay?"

Trevor's eyes seemed to darken with worry. "Don't you remember what just happened? Eleanor fed from you and hurt you. She must've made you forget, and—"

"No." Henry shook his head as his frown deepened. "That's not what happened." He scanned the people in the room, but the woman in question was nowhere to be seen, and he suddenly got a bad feeling and started to rise. "Where is she? What did you do to her?"

Trevor's hand landed on Henry's shoulder, keeping him from getting up. "She managed to escape after we pulled her off you. Which means we have two people to hunt down and neutralize. She's obviously more dangerous than she led us to believe."

Henry blinked a couple of times while staring at Trevor. Dangerous? Perhaps she was, considering she was a vampire, but the same could be said for shifters, or even humans for that matter. They could be lethal if they wanted to be. "You've got this all wrong. Eleanor didn't hurt me. If I made any sounds at all it was for an entirely different reason."

Trevor's eyes widened, and his jaw dropped open,

before he suddenly threw his head back and laughed.

Frowning, Henry got to his feet. "I fail to find this situation funny. What did you do to her to make her take off through the window, because I assume she's the one who smashed it? Did you hurt her?"

"We didn't hurt her." Hugh came to stand next to Henry. "But we did threaten her and accuse her of hurting you. I'm sorry we completely misread the situation, but it has not been that many hours since she attacked Fia."

"As a result of starvation." Henry glared at the big panther alpha. "That's not the same thing."

Hugh sighed. "I realize that, but the way you were roaring like someone was killing you... Well, that's exactly what we thought was happening." A smirk stole across the man's face. "I'm sorry we destroyed your romantic moment, but you should've warned us what was going on. How were we supposed to know—"

"I didn't exactly plan to..." Henry's voice faltered when he realized what he was saying. "I'll have a look outside to see if she's still nearby." He turned away and headed out of the kitchen, but he already knew he wouldn't find Eleanor out there. She was long gone. He could feel it like she had been fitted with a GPS linked directly to his brain. She was already close to a mile away, heading in a north-westerly direction.

Stopping on the porch, he stared in the direction she had gone. How he could be so sure where she was, he had no idea, but he trusted the feeling. Perhaps it was a side effect of her bite, but if that was a common consequence of a vampire bite, he would have heard about it. To be able to home in on someone's location was such a special ability that it would have been hard to keep a secret in the supernatural world.

Ironically, he had gotten his wish. Eleanor had left him alone like he had asked her to. He wasn't so sure that was what he wanted anymore, though. But then perhaps he wasn't thinking straight after what had happened. She had blown his mind with what she had done to him, and he wasn't yet sure how he felt about her method of seducing him. But one thing he was sure of, she hadn't hurt him, and there had been a real attraction between them. For him it had started as soon as he had picked up her scent.

His biggest regret was that he hadn't had a chance to do anything for her in return. He hoped she had felt the kind of pleasure he had, but he had been too deep into his own orgasm to tell. And that didn't feel right. She might have been left wanting after giving him such an amazing experience. An experience he didn't think he would ever forget.

Henry raked his fingers through his hair in frustration. What if he never saw her again? The thought was unnerving. But if the GPS effect lasted, he should be able to track her down. Unless the range was limited, and he had to be within a certain distance for it to work. He would have liked to be able to ask someone about that, but he didn't know whom to ask. And even if he did, he wasn't sure he was ready to know the answer.

***

Fia stood in the hallway, watching Henry's dejected posture. Even from behind he looked like he had just lost something valuable and wasn't sure what to do about it. But she might be wrong. She didn't know him very well.

Fia had just hung up after talking to G upstairs when there was a loud crash, and she had run downstairs while preparing to fight Amber. But she had soon realized the crash had nothing to do with the evil bitch and everything to do with some kind of development between Henry and the vampire.

There was nothing she could do to help Henry, and God only knew she had enough to worry about at the moment. But she still felt bad for the wolf alpha. He had been quick to offer his help when she had been about to go out looking for Bry on her own. And he hadn't even lifted an eyebrow in disapproval when she told him she had hurt her mate. He had shown her nothing but support and goodness, and she would do the same for him if he needed it.

She wasn't sure how a relationship with a vampire was viewed in the shifter community. But she wouldn't be surprised if there was a level of condemnation. Interspecies or interracial relationships seemed to annoy some people for some reason.

Her conversation with G came back to her. He hadn't been nearly as supportive as Henry, not that she had expected him to be. She hadn't even been halfway through explaining what had happened between her and Bry when G told her in no uncertain terms that she was worth less than the dirt under his alpha's feet.

It was no secret the second in command looked up to his alpha, but she had never heard him express it quite so harshly. Apparently Bry was raised above even the possibility of doing something wrong, and the fact that she had hurt him was on par with a mortal sin.

She had no trouble agreeing that what she had done

was despicable, but treating Bry like something akin to a god was on the extreme side.

Fia approached the kitchen where everyone except Henry was still gathered. Sabrina was standing next to her mate, and she turned to look at Fia when she entered the room.

"Do you want me to help you locate Bryson?" The blond woman gave her a warm smile. "Even if he needs some time alone and doesn't want to be found, it might help you relax if you know where he is."

Fia nodded. "That would be great. I'm not so sure it will help me relax, but I'd like to know anyway. I can't help hoping he's still close and will return soon."

"Let's hope so." Sabrina put her hand on Leith's arm, and he gave his mate a small nod. "Is there a room we can use?" The blond witch turned to look at Kynlee. "I try not to use magic close to people unless it's strictly necessary. There's always a risk of injury."

Fia spoke before Kynlee could say anything. "I'm sure we can use the bedroom we used earlier upstairs."

Kynlee nodded, and Fia headed up the stairs with Sabrina following.

"How can I help you?" Fia turned to Sabrina after closing the door.

"Just let me draw on some of your power. I can do it myself using only my own, but it's faster when I can pull on someone else's." The blond witch sat down on the floor in a Lotus position, and indicated for Fia to sit down in front of her.

"Okay." Fia sat down and clasped Sabrina's outstretched hands.

The blond woman closed her eyes and pulled in a deep breath, and Fia did the same to try to alleviate some of the tension in her body. The last couple of days had been draining, and the time since Bry left had been the worst. Worrying about him was taking its toll, but perhaps it would help if she knew where he was.

Sabrina started pulling Fia's power to her, and Fia let her take what she needed for the spell. It was a strange feeling having someone else pull on her power, and not something she was used to. Fia had worked with her mother many times, but they had always worked side by side and never combined their magic like this. There had been no need for it.

A few minutes went by before Sabrina stopped pulling on Fia's power and let go of her hands. "He's almost directly north of here. I'd say less than ten miles, but I would have to pull up a map to give you the precise location."

Fia nodded and forced a small smile that didn't reach her eyes. "Is he stationary or moving?"

Sabrina chuckled. "The only way I would be able to tell you that would be to check again in a little while and see if he has moved. I only get the position at the moment I connect."

"Okay." Fia nodded again. "And thank you. It's much more than anything I can do."

Smiling, Sabrina pulled her phone out of her pocket. "Give me a second, and I'll find his position." She enlarged the image several times until she pointed at a road in the middle of a forest. "Right here in Queen Elizabeth Forest Park. But I can't tell you whether he's resting on the side of the road or running along it. Chances are he's heading north, or perhaps northeast."

Fia breathed a sigh of relief. "At least he's not

wandering the main road. Which means he should be safe for now unless Amber has the same ability as you've got to locate people. I hope not."

Sabrina nodded slowly. "Me too. But she has an uncanny ability to find people, so I wouldn't put it past her. How would she otherwise have found Callum? Unless, of course, she was the one who caused his accident. He can't remember what happened, so we don't know. All we know is that she was there with him soon after the accident, and the wreck wasn't visible from the road."

Fia fisted her hands, and her whole body tensed as fear sank its icy claws into her upper back right between her shoulder blades. The urge to find Bry and bring him back was so strong she was halfway to the door before she realized what she was doing.

Pulling in a deep breath, she turned to look at Sabrina. "I want to go get him, but if I turn up when he clearly doesn't want to be near me, it might make him careless in his haste to get away from me. But I'm terrified Amber will find him first. We all know what she's capable of."

Sabrina got up off the floor before closing the distance between them. "We do. But Bryson isn't stupid, and he's powerful. Perhaps all you can do is trust him right now. I agree this wasn't the best time for him to run off and be on his own, but shit tends to happen at the least opportune times. That's just life."

Fia chuckled despite her anxiety. "Yes, that's one way to look at it. Thank you for your support. I know this is all my fault, but you've all been so good about it."

"Well, I pushed Leith away in the beginning too.

My reasons weren't the same as yours, but he was hurt regardless. It worked out in the end, though, and it will for you too."

Swallowing down the tears that were threatening to take over again, Fia nodded. "I hope so. Because I love him. I think I have for a long time, and I can't face a life without him."

"That wouldn't be possible anyway. You do know that, don't you?" Sabrina's eyebrows pushed together. "True mates can't be apart."

Fia nodded. "I know, but we haven't mated yet, so—"

"That doesn't matter." Sabrina studied her face. "True mates have a bond even before they mate, and it will force you to claim each other within a few days. At least that's the norm without a spell to suppress it. Staying apart isn't an option unless you want to die. The bond doesn't care."

CHAPTER 19

Fia felt herself pale. She had known all along she would eventually give in to Bry because of how she was drawn to him, as well as the fact that he would expect it when he eventually found out the truth. To deny a true mate claim just wasn't done. But Fia had thought Bry could refuse to mate her if he wanted to and go on to mate someone else of his choice. She just hadn't thought he would.

"Die. I didn't know that." Fia's head tipped forward and she stared at the floor. "Which means he doesn't have a choice other than to come back to me or perish, and he knows it." Lifting her gaze back up to Sabrina, she winced. "I don't know which is worse, losing him because he doesn't want to mate me anymore or having him come back to mate me even though he hates me."

Sabrina gave her a gentle smile. "Forgive my directness before. It tends to come out a bit harsh. It's true you'll have to stay together, and Bryson will come back. But he doesn't hate you. He might be hurt right now, but he'll get over it and you'll be happy together. You wouldn't be true mates if you weren't perfect for each other."

Fia wasn't sure she believed that, even though Sabrina sounded convinced. But then the woman was newly mated, so why wouldn't she be?

It was obvious these true mated couples were all deliriously happy, but that could be coincidence and didn't mean every true mated couple were as happy or well suited. Nature just wasn't that perfect in her experience. Mistakes could be made and were made. And she and Bry might just be one of them.

"Don't let your doubts get the better of you now." Sabrina shook her head slowly with a small smile curling her lips. "I can see those cogs working from here, and from the look on your face, they are spinning doubts and misery. Don't listen to them. I've seen you and Bryson together, and trust me when I say you will be dynamite once you accept each other."

Fia nodded even though she wasn't ready to accept that. Her relationship with Bry wasn't important at the moment. What was important was that he was safe, and she wasn't convinced he was.

Perhaps she should go after him after all. His car was still outside, and the keys were probably in the pocket of his pants. His clothes were on the bed where she had put them earlier. But what if he ran? Or even worse, what if he told her to stay away from him and never approach him again? Sabrina had said they would both die if they didn't mate. But what if Bry chose death over mating her?

"Fia. Let's go downstairs to the others. You look

like you need some moral support." Smiling, Sabrina moved over to the door and opened it before indicating to Fia to walk out ahead of her.

Fia could, of course, say no and stay behind in the room alone, but the truth was she needed the distraction to cope. Being alone would only allow her mind to drag her down into the ditch, and even though she felt like she deserved that, it wouldn't solve anything.

"Okay." She could feel the smile she gave Sabrina was more a display of teeth than a pleasant expression.

Everyone was in the living room when she arrived downstairs. It was still dark outside, but it wouldn't be long before dawn started to lighten the skies. Getting some sleep would be the prudent thing to do, considering they didn't know what Amber would do next. But Fia couldn't even contemplate sleeping. It would be impossible until Bry came back or returned to his clan. G was pissed off with her for hurting Bry, but at least he had promised to send her a text if his alpha turned up at home.

∞∞∞∞

Fia got up and walked out of the living room without meeting anyone's gaze. She couldn't take it anymore. It had been more than an hour since she sat down with the others in there. They had been discussing what to do about Amber if she turned up at the farm, but Fia couldn't concentrate on what people were saying. Some sort of plan had been made, but she couldn't for the life of her recount the details.

Hurrying up the stairs, she recalled the place

Sabrina had pointed to on the map. Hopefully, Bry was still there, but if he wasn't, Fia would keep driving until she found him. It was reasonable to believe he was on his way home, and she would go after him. Staying away from him wasn't an option anymore. She needed him more than her next breath, and she would pursue him until he physically pushed her away. He had pursued her tirelessly for two years, and now it was her turn.

She could have asked Sabrina to check if Bry had moved in the last hour, but Fia got the impression the blond witch thought it was better to wait until Bry returned or contacted her of his own free will, and she might have been right. Besides, everyone in the living room was deeply engaged in coming up with a plan B and C to make sure they had covered all eventualities when it came to Amber, and Fia didn't really want to disturb them just because she was too impatient to wait.

The car key was in Bry's pants pocket like Fia had expected, and after grabbing it, she quickly ran downstairs and headed outside.

"Would you like me to join you?" Henry's voice startled her when Fia stepped out onto the porch.

Frowning, she turned to look at him where he was standing just to the right of the entrance. There was a tension in his jaw that hadn't been there earlier, and she had a feeling it had something to do with Eleanor.

She nodded. "If you want. I can't stay here doing nothing anymore. I have to find Bry."

"I thought that's why you stormed off." The corner of Henry's mouth lifted, but his expression looked more like a grimace than a smile. She couldn't remember having seen him so grim before. He usually had an easy smile for everyone.

Showing Henry the key, she nodded toward Bry's car. "Would you mind driving? Then I can keep an eye out for Bry."

Henry nodded, and she handed him the key before heading toward the passenger side of the vehicle. "You have to tell me where to go, though."

"I will."

They got in the car and were soon headed down the long driveway toward the road. The sun was just creeping above the horizon, signaling the start of another sunny day. But the brightness certainly didn't match Fia's mood. She was anxious to find Bry and pissed off with herself for hurting him in the first place.

The dirt roads crisscrossing Queen Elizabeth Forest Park weren't really made for a sports car, and Fia wasn't in a position to pay for any damage, but she'd worry about that another day. Whatever happened she would deal with it after she had found Bry.

They were close to the position Sabrina had shown her on the map when Fia's phone rang. "Hi, Sabrina."

"Fia. If you're looking for Bryson, he's located a little further north now. But no more than about half a mile. I'll send you his position. But be careful and approach slowly just in case." Worry laced Sabrina's voice.

Fia nodded, even though the blond woman couldn't see her. "I'll be careful. And thank you."

"My pleasure. Now go get your man and hurry back. We have work to do." There was a smile in Sabrina's voice.

"I really hope it's going to be that simple." Fia didn't feel nearly as optimistic as Sabrina sounded. "But I don't think it will be. He's more likely to run from me than to me."

"Well, if he tries to run away, you just undress in front of him. He's sure to react to that. Particularly if Henry's there. Men are simple that way." Sabrina's words ended with a smack and a squeal before Leith's grumbling voice took over.

"And so are women. I know a beautiful woman who practically drools whenever I take my shirt off. Do you know who that is, my angel?"

Envy made Fia squeeze her eyes shut. What she wouldn't give to have that kind of relationship with Bry. "Thank you for the advice. I'll talk to you later." She ended the call before she could hear any more of their teasing banter.

A few seconds later, her phone chimed with an incoming message, and Fia opened it to find a section of a map with a circle marking what looked like a building not far from the road.

"We're almost there." She glanced over at Henry, who was staring straight ahead. "Just follow this road for another couple of minutes or so. Then we'll park the car and walk. The building isn't far from the road. We should be able to see it through the trees."

"Okay." The wolf alpha nodded without looking at her, his power filling the car like he was upset about something. "You just tell me when to stop."

Fia stared into the forest, until she spotted a gray stone building. Thankfully, this section of the forest wasn't dense enough to hide it from the road. The cottage was small and in need of some serious renovations. Moss covered the roof in patches, and a few of the visible slates were missing. The only window facing the road was missing a pane, and the door looked to be ajar.

After parking the car on the side of the road, they got out. Fia wanted to run up to the cottage and throw the door wide open to see if Bry was there. But instead she took a deep breath and steeled herself for his reaction to her arrival as they moved slowly toward the decrepit building. It wasn't a place she would have taken refuge in even if it had been pouring rain. She would have felt safer beneath a large tree than inside that building.

They crept closer while keeping an eye out for anything moving in or around the building. But it was quiet, eerily so. When they got closer, she reached out with her power to check inside, and she came to an abrupt stop when instead of one power signature, she felt two. And she knew both of them.

She didn't know whether to take it as a good or a bad sign. Amber wasn't one of the people inside, which was a good thing. But Eleanor was in that building with Bry, and that could be good or bad depending on why she was there.

Fia reached out and put a hand on Henry's arm to get his attention. He had stopped when she had and might have been wondering why she had stopped so abruptly. "Eleanor is in there with Bry." Her voice was no more than a whisper.

He gave a sharp nod but didn't say anything, just stared at the door of the cottage. His body seemed to have gone tight like a spring, confirming her suspicions that Eleanor meant something to him.

Fia started toward the cottage again and didn't stop until she reached the door. The narrow opening didn't allow her to see any of the people inside, and she put her hand on the door and pushed. It creaked as it moved, and the sound made her stop and listen, but there was no response from inside.

Her heart sped up as she gave the door a hard push, and it opened to reveal the room inside. A strange whine came from Henry behind her, but Fia was straining her eyes to try to make out the shape on the floor in the dark room. The windows were dirty, and even with the missing pane and the door open, it wasn't enough light for her to see clearly.

She took a step inside, and suddenly she could see. But she immediately wished she couldn't. Closing her eyes, she quickly backed out of the cottage, not even caring that she didn't know where she was stepping. All she wanted was to get as far away from there as possible.

Pain exploded through her chest as the image burned itself into her mind forever. It would stay there until she died, but from what she had heard that might not be long. Because there would be no mating and no happily ever after for her and Bry. Sabrina had been wrong. Having a true mate didn't stop someone from fucking around. At least it hadn't stopped her mate.

She ran back to the car, only to swear when she realized Henry had the key, and he was still back at the cottage. But then what did she want with Bry's car, anyway? She didn't want any reminders of him.

It was time to move on in every sense of the word. Time to leave this place, and time to get her mother and move to another part of Scotland or perhaps even farther away. She didn't know whether Sabrina had been right that Fia would die without her true mate, and she couldn't seem to care at the moment. But one thing was certain. For as long as she had left, she never wanted to see Bry again.

CHAPTER 20

Henry couldn't tear his eyes away from the two people on the floor. He had been aware of Eleanor's location as they drove toward this place, and it had alarmed him to realize she was in the same location as Bryson. But he still hadn't been prepared for seeing her like this. Naked, with an equally naked panther alpha spooning her stunning form with one arm curved around her narrow waist.

The scene was threatening to choke him, bile rising in his throat. But even if he turned away, he wasn't going to unsee this no matter what he did. It had happened, and it was threatening to tear his guts out.

Henry didn't know how long he had been standing there, when some kind of sense found its way through the devastation he was feeling. Why hadn't they moved? They should have woken up when the door creaked open, but they hadn't. In fact, they were lying so still they looked…

He narrowed his eyes as he closed the distance to

the couple before sinking down to the floor in front of Eleanor's naked body. Vampires didn't need to breathe, and they didn't have a heartbeat, so checking Eleanor's pulse or breathing was pointless. But if she had been truly dead, she should have turned to dust by now.

Bryson was breathing, but it was shallow like his lungs weren't working properly. It wasn't consistent with normal sleep.

"Eleanor?" Henry put his hand on her shoulder and shook her gently, but there was no response. But the movement was enough to make Bryson roll onto his back with no resistance and without waking up.

Henry reached over and slapped the big man's cheek hard, but there was no response. Still, it had felt good slapping the asshole, even though Henry already knew the image of Eleanor and Bryson together was wrong.

After pulling out his phone, he called Leith. The man answered on the second ring. "Henry. Have you found him?"

"Yes, but I think we have a problem. He seems to be unconscious or in some kind of trance, and he won't wake up. Eleanor is here as well, and she's the same."

"We will be there shortly." There was concern in Leith's voice. "Did you find them where Sabrina indicated?"

"Yes. I don't know what's happened to them. They have been positioned to look like they've had sex, but their scents tell me they haven't." Which was a relief. But Henry still wanted to know what had happened before they fell unconscious. This could be Amber's work, but why would she leave them alive? Unless she knew Bryson was Fia's mate, and the evil bitch wanted to destroy them both by making it seem like the panther was cheating.

"Okay. We'll be there soon." Leith ended the call.

Henry rose and had a quick look around, but he couldn't find Eleanor's clothes, which was another strange thing about this situation. Even if Eleanor hadn't undressed herself, her clothes should still be there. Why would someone take her clothes? Unless, of course, she had undressed or been undressed somewhere else.

After taking off his T-shirt, Henry gently dressed the beautiful woman on the floor while trying not to touch her naked form more than necessary. But he couldn't help letting his gaze glide over her stunning body, and he enjoyed it entirely too much as evidenced by the rigid bar in his pants. What was it about this woman that had him practically salivating after just one look? Not to mention her scent.

He rose to distance himself from her and turned to look out the door. Fia had run toward the car, and he should probably go after her and tell her she had misunderstood the situation, but he was reluctant to leave the two unconscious people alone. And he couldn't call her since he didn't have her number. Fia was probably distraught, but at least she wouldn't be able to leave since he had the key to the car.

The sun suddenly spilled through the trees, having risen high enough to reach the forest floor. His eyes widened when he realized what it meant, and he spun to stare at Eleanor.

He hadn't been in the company of many vampires,

since they tended to keep to themselves, but he knew the basics about them. And the first and most important rule was that they needed to stay out of the sun.

The sun hadn't yet reached through the windows, and he wasn't even sure it would penetrate them with how dirty they were. But that wasn't something he could rely on.

After clearing a space in the debris in the southeastern corner, he placed Eleanor close to the wall. The spot would allow her to stay out of the sun at least until the afternoon, and he would stay with her and make sure to move her before then. But hopefully, she would be awake by that time and could move around to where she felt the safest.

It didn't take long before Leith and Sabrina turned up, and Trevor and Jennie had obviously decided to join them.

"They're in here." With a nod, Henry took a couple of steps back to let them all inside. But as soon as Leith and Trevor caught sight of Bryson's naked form, the women were quickly rushed back outside.

"How am I going to be able to check any of them if you won't allow me inside?" Sabrina's arms crossed over her chest as she stared up at Leith with one eyebrow raised. "I can't do it from here."

Leith grumbled something low that Henry couldn't decipher before pulling off his shirt. Turning to Henry, the man threw his shirt at him. "Please cover Bryson before I am forced to kill him when my stubborn mate puts her hands on his naked ass."

"I'm not going to touch his ass." Sabrina's eyes widened with her outrage. "What the fuck are you—"

"I know." Leith sighed and took a step toward her, wrapping his hands around her upper arms. "But the animal side of me will not be able to tell the difference when he is naked. Please trust me when I say I will not be able to handle that in a gentlemanly fashion. I will want to kill him. Perhaps even try to."

Sabrina's blue eyes lit with unmistakable desire, and Henry turned away to head back to Bryson. "That would be...interesting to watch."

Henry wasn't sure why Sabrina seemed to like the idea of Leith fighting Bryson, but he knew he wanted a mate who looked at him like Sabrina looked at Leith.

Kneeling next to the panther alpha, he spread Leith's T-shirt over the man's middle. Bryson hadn't moved a finger since Henry first arrived, and his breathing was still showing no sign of improvement.

"He's covered," Henry called and turned to look out through the door at Leith. "Sabrina can enter now."

Leith's mate hurried inside and let her gaze swing around the room before settling on Henry. "Where's Fia? I thought she was here with you."

"She went back to the car after seeing these two spooning." Henry indicated Bryson and Eleanor. "Didn't you see her when you arrived?"

Sabrina shook her head, and her brows pushed together in concern. "There was no one in the car when we arrived or on the road for that matter. Are you sure that's where she went?"

Henry rose and looked at Leith, who was standing in the doorway. "She ran toward the car, but I didn't go look for her since I didn't want to leave these two alone. She was upset by what she saw, and I assumed she went to sit in the car. I have the key, so I wasn't worried about her leaving. But that seems to have been a mistake."

"Shit." Sabrina closed her eyes for a second before opening them to stare at him with a piercing gaze. "Fia still thinks they fucked, doesn't she? She's his true mate, Henry. What do you think seeing Bryson like that did to her? Particularly considering his reputation."

"Fuck!" Running his fingers through his hair, Henry moved his gaze to the man in question. "I should've gone after her. Of course, I should've." As soon as he realized nothing had happened between the panther and Eleanor, he should have told Fia.

"Leith." Sabrina turned to her mate. "Can you go look for Fia? Take Trevor and Jennie with you. I'll stay here."

Leith frowned. "I do not want to leave you here with…" His eyes dropped to the mostly naked man on the floor. "Particularly when we do not yet know why neither of them have woken up."

After closing the distance to her mate, Sabrina rose on her toes and kissed him. "I can take care of myself. And you know there's only one man I want. I'm not susceptible to that." She waved her hand in Bryson's general direction.

Leith studied her face for a few seconds before he nodded. "Fine. But I will stay close. Leaving you here to fend for yourself is not an option. If Fia is more than a few hundred yards away, we will have to look for her after we have dealt with these two."

"Okay." Sabrina took a step back and turned away from her mate. "Now go and leave me to try to find out what's going on here. But I think Fia is better at this than I am, which is another reason to find her and bring her back here."

Sabrina knelt beside Bryson just as Leith disappeared from the doorway. She put her hand on the panther's chest, and her brows wrinkled in concentration.

Henry stayed still, not wanting to disturb her. He had nothing to offer in the way of help. All his efforts to wake Eleanor and Bryson had done nothing.

He turned to look at the beautiful woman in the corner. Everyone else was weary of her, particularly after what she had done to him in the kitchen. But he hoped Sabrina would try to help Eleanor anyway.

"Amber has been here."

Sabrina's statement brought Henry's gaze back to her. "Are you sure?"

The blond woman nodded and lifted her gaze to his. "Yes, I recognize her power. She put a spell on Bryson, and I would think on Eleanor as well. I think I've managed to remove it, but this is not my specialty, so there might still be traces remaining."

"Will you help Eleanor as well?" Henry's spine tensed as he braced for her refusal.

"Of course." Sabrina stood and moved over to the woman in the corner, and Henry breathed a sigh of relief.

He didn't know why he had expected anything less from Sabrina. Perhaps the bad elements in his pack were lowering his general expectations of people.

The blond witch repeated the process with Eleanor before pulling her hand away and looking up at him. "I've done what I can. Hopefully, they'll wake up soon so we can talk to them and make sure they're okay."

"Fuck!" The exclamation made them turn to Bryson. He looked a bit bleary-eyed but at least he was awake.

***

Bryson blinked to make his eyes focus. His head was spinning, and he couldn't remember where he was or how he had ended up there. But at least he recognized Henry and Sabrina, who were in the room with him.

There was someone lying in the corner. A woman judging by the shape of her legs. But her head was hidden behind Sabrina, so he couldn't tell who it was.

Fia. Her name rang in his head and resonated like a bell through his frame, and he tried to get to his feet. But he only managed to sit up before dizziness hit him with such force that he had to plant his hands on the floor behind him not to fall back down on his back. "Fia." His voice was rough like he hadn't used it for days.

"Leith is looking for her." Sabrina gave him a small smile. "How are you feeling?"

"Like shit. So that's not Fia then?" He nodded at the woman in the corner.

"No." Sabrina rose and moved toward him.

The woman's face was revealed, and there was something familiar about her, but he couldn't remember where he had seen her before.

"Who is she?" Bryson studied the woman's face, trying to make the connection.

"Her name's Eleanor." Henry stared at him from where he was still standing close to the woman. "She's a vampire. Don't you remember rescuing her from

Amber's cabin?"

Bryson shuddered as an image of the vampire latched onto Fia's wrist slammed into his mind. "She hurt Fia. What's she doing here, and where's here, anyway?" He frowned as his brain drew a blank. "The last thing I remember is having dinner with Fia, Hugh, and Kynlee after we had returned from Amber's cabin."

Henry's gaze dropped to the floor, and Sabrina bit her lip and winced like she had a bad taste in her mouth.

Bryson's shoulders tensed. "What happened? Tell me! I don't care how bad it is. I want to know." *Fia, Fia, Fia.* Her name rang in his head again, and he knew their silence had something to do with her.

Sabrina took a deep breath before she spoke. "She loves you, Bryson."

His eyes widened in surprise and confusion. He really hoped that was the case, but how would Sabrina know when he didn't? And Fia loving him wouldn't have caused their silence. "Is she all right?"

"I think so." Sabrina didn't look convinced, though. "As I said, Leith is looking for her. Hopefully, he'll find her, and they'll be here soon."

His heart sped up when he realized the implications. "How long has she been missing? And who took her?" He didn't even want to consider the most likely culprit, but he couldn't come up with another likely candidate.

"She ran off. As far as we know no one has taken her." Sabrina's small smile looked forced. "She found you and Eleanor in a compromising position, and she probably assumed you'd had sex. I don't think she understands what true mates really means."

"True mates." The words sent a shockwave through his system, and his chest erupted with pain when everything came flooding back to him. Fia's spell, her deception, and her rejection. And him running away from her. Breathing became difficult, and he hunched forward as he strained to pull air into his lungs.

It didn't make sense, though. Why had she come after him if she didn't care about him? And why would finding him with another woman affect her if she didn't want him?

He opened his eyes and stared down at himself. A T-shirt that wasn't his was strategically draped over his middle. Looking at Eleanor, he saw she was wearing a T-shirt too big to be her own. Fia had obviously found them naked together, but he had no idea how that had come to be. He couldn't remember seeing Eleanor at all after he put her in Hugh and Kynlee's car after they had hiked back from Amber's cabin.

"I never fucked Eleanor." He stared at Sabrina before moving his gaze to Henry. "I don't know how we ended up here together, but I do know we didn't fuck."

Henry gave a sharp nod. "I know. When I leaned over you, your scent confirmed it. But Fia had already run off by then, after taking one look at you spooning naked on the floor."

Bryson frowned. "Why didn't you go after her and tell her nothing happened?"

The wolf alpha sighed and looked away. "I should've. I realize that now, but I didn't know what was wrong with you two, so I didn't want to leave you.

And I assumed Fia only went back to the car. The others hadn't arrived yet."

Bryson wanted to shout at the wolf for letting Fia run off with an image of him cheating on her retinas. But he didn't. If anyone was to blame for all this, it was him. He was the one who had pretended he was still fucking other women every few days after he met Fia. If he had been honest, she might have realized he wouldn't fuck Eleanor.

He had a lot to answer for and one thing was causing his mate to run off alone when Amber might still be close by. Because there was no doubt who had set this up. But he wasn't going to spend any time pondering why before he found Fia.

Bryson struggled to his feet, still dizzy, while holding on to the T-shirt that was the only thing protecting his modesty. He needed to find Fia immediately before something happened to her. Staggering toward the door, he glanced at Henry. "When did Fia run off?"

"Less than an hour ago. I can't tell you exactly, though." Henry frowned. "Perhaps you should stay here. You look—"

"No. I need to find her." Bryson exited the cottage and looked around. He was in the middle of a forest, but three cars were visible through the trees. They were all parked on a dirt road not far from the cottage, and one of them was his.

His balance improved as he made his way toward the road, his dizziness slowly fading. Hopefully, that meant he would soon be one hundred percent again, because he needed his strength to find and convince Fia to accept him. He could vaguely remember deciding to go back to her instead of running, but after that everything went black.

Bryson reached the road just as Leith, Trevor, and Jennie walked out of the forest on the opposite side of the road. But Fia wasn't with them, and the worried expressions on their faces told him everything he needed to know.

"Did you change and try to follow her scent?" Bryson stared at Trevor, but he already knew the answer.

Trevor shook his head. "It's too risky. I don't know this area, so running around as a wolf isn't an option, at least not during the day."

Bryson gave a short nod of acknowledgement. "Well, I don't have your qualms, but I don't have your nose either. I'm not sure I could follow her scent even if I wanted to, but I'll give it a try anyway. I'll do anything to find her. Being spotted is the least of my concerns. I'll pay someone to make sure any video evidence is discredited."

Raising an eyebrow, Trevor turned his head and looked at Leith.

The long-haired man nodded slowly as he met Trevor's gaze. "I would do it if I could. She is his true mate, after all."

"She is." Trevor's eyes landed on Bryson. "I'll change and help you find her, but we'll have to be careful. I don't want to end up an Internet celebrity."

CHAPTER 21

Fia didn't look away and maintained her position as Amber walked into the clearing. Ready for an inevitable attack, Fia let her magic swirl inside her in preparation. She had felt the bitch's power as soon as she walked into the clearing, and there was no point trying to flee. It was too late for that. She would have to stay and face the evil witch.

"How's your mate?" The smile curling Amber's lips was nothing short of evil. "He just can't seem to help himself around women, can he? But you already knew that. What will you do when he comes back and expects you to mate him?"

Every word was like having a new knife stabbed into her heart, and Fia had to fist her hands at her sides and lock her knees just to keep standing. Amber was baiting her, of course, clearly having had something to do with Bryson and Eleanor ending up in that cottage together. But it didn't change the simple fact that they had fucked, and Fia didn't want to see any of them again. She didn't even know how she was going to go on living after witnessing that.

"Aw, nothing to say?" Amber chuckled. "That much of a shock, was it?" Her mouth twisted into a disgusted sneer. "I don't know why, considering his reputation. You already knew what he was, and you're better off without him. You're a strong woman, Fia, and a capable witch. Why don't you embrace that side of yourself and join me in my quest to rid the world of people like him? Humanity will be better off without supernaturals like that preying on them."

Fia blinked when Amber's words sank in. Was the bitch really trying to win Fia over to her horrible mission? She wanted to laugh in the woman's face, but instead she kept her expression neutral. This might be an opportunity to end Amber once and for all, and Fia wasn't going to waste that chance.

"There are millions of shifters in the world. How are you going to kill them all?" Fia cocked her head and made her body relax to look like she was actually considering Amber's offer to join her.

Amber's eyes narrowed into slits. "I'm not stupid. I'll tell you that once you've proven your loyalty and willingness to kill." She raised her right arm to the side and made a come-hither motion with her hand toward the dense tree line. "Please welcome your first victim. I expect you to kill him quickly and efficiently, and without having to touch him to do so."

Fia saw a figure emerging from the trees out of the corner of her eye, but instead of looking at him directly she kept her eyes trained on Amber. "Who is he?"

His power had the lightest shade of color she had

ever observed in a person. A light rosy shade, indicating a person with considerably more good intentions than bad. Whoever he was he had done nothing to deserve to die.

"Does it matter?" Amber lifted an eyebrow and crossed her arms over her chest. "He's a supernatural and capable of massive destruction. That's all you need to know."

Fia lifted her hand and tapped her chin with one finger like she was thinking it over. The man had stopped a couple of yards away from Amber, and Fia glanced at him while keeping the evil bitch in her peripheral vision.

His looks matched his power with kindness seeming to radiate from his features, making his skin glow. At least it looked that way to her, but perhaps it was just a result of how she sensed the color of his power. His hair was so light it could be considered white, and his eyes were a brilliant ocean blue.

But what was more surprising about the man than his looks and his power was the lack of fear or pleading in his eyes. Either he didn't understand what Amber had asked Fia to do, or he counted on his own power to be strong enough to protect himself.

Fia nodded slowly as she moved her gaze back to Amber. "Okay. But I expect you to tell me how you're planning to pull this off after I've killed him. Deal?"

A few seconds went by while Amber stared at her. "Fine. After you've killed him, I'll tell you. But not here. We'll go somewhere else where I know no one is listening."

"Deal." Fia let her power increase and instead of hiding its potency she magnified it until it pulsed around her. She almost smiled when Amber's lips tightened into a hard line, and the woman took a step back like she was struggling to keep her footing. It was exactly what Fia was going for, making a show of the power she had seemingly without effort, like she was using only a fraction of the magic she possessed.

Fia kept some of the magic as a shield around herself while she sent the rest in one burst directly at Amber.

Unfortunately, the evil bitch had put up a similar shield. Amber stumbled back a couple of steps, but she stayed on her feet and was unharmed.

Fia didn't pause her attack but kept hammering Amber's shield with magic, hoping the woman would tire and let her shield drop long enough for Fia's magic to reach her and take her down.

Amber screamed in rage and started retaliating. Powerful magic hit Fia's shield with enough force to push her back a step, but she kept up her own attack.

It was hard to tell whether Amber was using all the power she had or if she was waiting for an opportunity to reach Fia before leveling up her attack.

Fia was using enough magic to keep Amber occupied, and if the woman's shield fell, she would be incapacitated in seconds. Using more would be a waste of power against Amber's shield. It was a possibility that a massive burst of magic would break through the shield and kill the bitch, but if it didn't, Fia would have tired herself out and rendered herself defenseless against the other woman's magic.

Amber's gaze suddenly moving to the man still standing in the clearing was the only warning Fia got before he moaned in pain and sank to his knees.

Fia immediately put a shield around the man to protect him, but in doing so she wasn't careful enough to maintain her own shield. It wavered for a fraction of a second, but it was enough for Amber's magic to reach her.

Fire seared through Fia's chest and sent her to the ground, but by sheer will she managed to hold on to her magic and push more power into the shields protecting herself and the man. Attacking was beyond her capacity, though.

A snarl loud enough to resonate through her made her force her eyes open. It had sounded from somewhere behind her, and she immediately knew who it was. Both the snarl and the power accompanying it wrapped around her like a warm blanket, and tears sprang to her eyes. But the warmth was soon replaced with an icy fear sinking into her bones. Bry was there in his panther form, perhaps to rescue her or perhaps to fight Amber, but no matter the reason the evil bitch would kill him without hesitation.

Using all the remaining power she could muster, Fia reached out and put a shield around him as well. It reduced the strength of her own shield, which wouldn't keep her safe for long, but it didn't really matter anymore. The hit she had taken to her chest was fatal, and her strength was already fading. But she would fight to keep Bry's shield in place for as long as she could, and hopefully, it would be enough for him to take the bitch down with claws and teeth.

***

The agony that ripped through him would have sent Bryson to his belly if it weren't for his instinct to protect his mate until the bitter end. The snarl that tore from him caused Amber's focus to shift from Fia to him, and he welcomed the challenge in her gaze. He was going to tear her apart if it was the last thing he did. And it probably would be, considering Fia was unlikely to survive with a wound like that.

Bryson would never forget the way Fia's shirt had sizzled and burned away, revealing the charred flesh in the center of her chest. He knew a mortal wound when he saw one, even though his battle experience was limited. And losing his mate left him nothing to live for except revenge. The evil bitch would die this day and allow him to die with his mate is in his arms. At least in death they would finally be together.

Fia's magic wrapped around him, making him realize she wasn't gone yet. She was protecting him. With one foot in the grave, she was using her magic to keep him safe. She had known all along they were true mates, and he could only assume she knew the implications of that. He would die with her, so the only reason to protect him was to enable him to fight. And by God he would.

Without wasting any more time, he bounded toward Amber. His powerful panther body ate the distance between them in no time, and a few yards before he reached her, he leapt.

Amber's magic hit the protective barrier surrounding him repeatedly, but he barely felt the impact. He didn't know how long Fia would be able to keep the barrier in place, but he would have to make the most of the time he had.

Amber threw herself to the side, but he was already on her, sinking his teeth into her shoulder. Screaming, she put her hand on his head, but whatever magic she was trying to push into him didn't penetrate the barrier.

He let go of her shoulder and turned his head to rip out her throat, but before he could latch on, she put a hand on his chest and pushed him hard enough to send him flying backward several yards. She must have realized her magic didn't hurt him, so she had used it to increase her own physical strength instead.

Bryson twisted in the air and landed on his feet before immediately spinning around to face her again. But she was gone. Vanished. And there was no trace left to tell him how or where. He screamed his rage before meeting Trevor's gaze. The wolf had been about to attack Amber from behind.

The wolf alpha shook his head at him, but Bryson had no idea what that meant. Had Trevor seen how she disappeared and was trying to tell him there was no point looking for her? Or the wolf didn't know what had happened either.

No matter what it meant, Bryson was done fighting. His place was with his dying mate. She was still hanging on, the protective barrier around him weak but still present.

The unknown man had moved to kneel at Fia's side. As Bryson started running toward them, the man put a hand on her shoulder, and his skin started glowing like a fire had just ignited inside him. Fia's body tensed, and she wailed in pain in response to whatever the man was doing to her.

Bryson was close and ready to tear the man apart, but the man lifted a hand toward him, and Bryson's body froze. As he watched, unable to move so much as a whisker, Fia pulled in a deep breath, and the wound in her chest closed and disappeared, leaving just flawless skin behind. The man, whoever he was, had just healed Bryson's mate, and at a much faster rate than a shifter would have been able to heal themself.

Bryson stopped struggling against the force holding him motionless and stared at Fia as her breathing settled, and a smile spread across her face. He had never seen a more beautiful sight in his life than his mate returning from death's door.

"You will forever have my allegiance, my lady." The man tipped his head forward in deference. "Please let me offer myself as your mate and consort. I will care for you always and give you whatever you ask of me."

No! Fear and rage caused Bryson's power to spike, and he tore from the man's magical hold on him, making the man snap his head around to stare at Bryson with an astonished look on his face.

Bryson wanted to rip the man's head off, but he quickly realized that killing the man who had healed her wouldn't support his case with Fia. After changing into his human form, Bryson knelt at his mate's side directly across from the still-glowing man. "Please forgive me for all the hurt I've caused you, redbird. I love you with everything I am and will cherish you for the rest of my life." He wanted to give her all the reasons why the other man wasn't good enough for her, but it wasn't the way to win Fia. She wanted love and devotion, not to listen to him humiliate another person.

Fia's expression was guarded when she met Bryson's gaze, and he knew at least one of the reasons why. She still thought he had fucked another woman, something he had told her he hadn't done since he met her and wouldn't do if she agreed to be with him. But at least that was one thing he could prove hadn't happened. None of that would matter, though, if she didn't care about him at all.

She lifted her hand and put it lightly on top of his, her thumb caressing the back of his hand in small circles. The gentle touch was enough to make his whole body tighten with hope and need.

"I'm sorry, Bry." Her eyes grew shiny with tears. "I'm so sorry for what I've put you through in the last two years. You didn't deserve that."

He wanted to protest, but his throat had clogged up, choking him. Fia was telling him goodbye. He was losing her for good this time. His muscles tensed until they vibrated with pain and despair, a burning pain settling deep in his chest.

Her hand suddenly tightened on his, making him frown as he stared down at it, not sure why she hadn't let go of him yet.

Then she moved. Sitting up on her knees in front of him, she grabbed his head with both hands, so he had no choice but to look into her eyes. "Bry. Are you okay? Did the bitch hurt you? Tell me! I need to know you're all right. You're mine, remember? And I'm not letting you go again. You'll just have to learn to behave, or I'll keep you tied up in bed until you do."

He blinked, his mind trying to make sense of what she was saying. Those weren't words of rejection. They were words of commitment, of wanting him, of staying with him.

Swallowing, he kept staring into her eyes, not able

to say anything. His eyes pricked and his vision became blurry, and he had to blink again to keep staring into her beautiful hazel eyes.

"Bry, please say something. Anything." A deep crease developed between her brows as her grip on his head tightened. "You're crying. Why are you crying?"

"I love you." His words were choked and barely comprehensible.

"Oh, Bry, I love you too." Her lips stretched into a wide, happy smile. "I think I have since the first time I met you."

"What I told you earlier is still true. I haven't fucked anyone since I met you. Amber set it up to destroy us, but Henry can verify that I'm telling you the truth. He smelled that nothing had happened between me and the vampire." His words were rushed and desperate, but he needed her to know he hadn't cheated on her.

Fia nodded with a smile so wide it threatened to split her face. "I believe you, and I know why the bitch did it. Amber wanted me to join her, and she wanted me to prove myself to her by killing him." She nodded at the man still kneeling behind her without looking at him.

Bryson glanced at the man, who was staring at them with a frown on his face and his head tilted to one side.

"I take it my offer to you is rejected, then?" The man sounded like he had trouble believing it.

Fia nodded while staring into Bryson's eyes. "Yes. I made my choice a long time ago, even though I was too scared to accept it. There's only one man I want, and he's right in front of me."

Bryson threw his arms around Fia and crushed his lips to hers. The kiss was messy with their teeth clanking together and noses bumping, but it was the best kiss he'd ever had.

They broke apart when the need for oxygen became urgent, but Bryson didn't let her go, and she still had her arms around his neck.

"I think it's time we head back." He kissed the corner of her mouth. If it had been up to him, he would have sent the others away and not left the clearing until Fia was irreversibly his. "The others need to know what happened here and that you are okay."

Bryson lifted his gaze to the man who had risen and was standing a few yards away. The man's stare made Bryson tighten his grip on his mate. "Thank you for saving my mate. I can never repay you. But if you ever need anything I'm there." *Unless you try to take her from me. Then I'll end you.* He didn't say it, but he hoped the man could see it in his eyes.

The man nodded, but it seemed like an automatic reaction and not like a true response to what Bryson had said.

"Shall we go?" Smiling at Fia, Bryson put a hand on her cheek. "I need some time alone with you, and I'm sure we can have that at Hugh's house."

She suddenly narrowed her eyes at him, and apprehension raked its fingernails down his spine, making him tense. "You're naked."

He nodded slowly, not sure why she was stating the obvious. "Yes, my clothes don't fit my panther."

Her eyes narrowed into slits. "That's not funny. You refused to show me your cock, but you have no qualms about showing it to everyone else?"

He would have laughed if not for the anger burning in her eyes. His mate clearly wasn't amused, but he loved the possessiveness she was showing. "I'm sorry, redbird, but I didn't bring any clothes with me, so I have nothing to put on to cover myself. I'm not ecstatic about you almost showing your nipples to everyone either, but your shirt is ruined and there's not much I can do about that right now."

Her eyes widened, and she pushed at his chest while looking down at herself. He loosened his hold on her to allow a gap between their bodies. There was a gaping charred hole in her shirt between her breasts, but the ruined fabric still covered her nipples. But they might easily show when she started moving around.

Fia gasped and pulled a little farther away from him. But she was no longer staring down at herself. Her gaze was firmly locked on his hard cock. "That's not one piercing. It's a full ladder." Her hand reached toward him but stopped an inch away from his straining member.

"It is. I hope you like it." He studied her astonished face, but there was no sign of disgust or disapproval.

Nodding slowly, she lifted her gaze to his. "I do. It's…" She bit her lip for a second, and color crept into her cheeks. "Interesting."

Chuckling, he shook his head. "That's not exactly what I was going for. Enticing, sexy, a turn on, or anything similar would be better. But perhaps that will come once you try it."

Fia burst out laughing. "I'm sure *that* will come."

He grinned. "And I'll make sure you do too."

A bark sounded from behind him, and Bryson turned his head to look at Trevor. Even in wolf form, he managed to look impatient and exasperated, and Bryson had no trouble understanding why. Watching him and Fia flirting wasn't what Trevor had signed up for, and the wolf was probably eager to get back to his own mate. Particularly considering Amber was most likely still in the area, and it was impossible to know what she would do next. Although it was almost certainly something bad.

"Who's that? Henry?" Fia was studying Trevor like she was trying to find a clue as to who the wolf was.

"Trevor. I wouldn't have found you without him." Fia's hair was messy and had leaves and pieces of straw stuck in it, but he couldn't remember her ever looking more beautiful. "He has a better sense of smell than I have as a panther and is far better at tracking. And he'll have to help us get back to the others. I was too worried about you to pay attention to where we went."

"Okay." Fia met his gaze. "But I want him to give me a sign before we reach the others, so I can go get you something to cover up with. I won't allow any other woman to see what you're packing. Not anymore. That's mine and mine alone."

Happiness sang through him at his mate's possessive behavior, making him chuckle. "Good. I wouldn't have it any other way. All I want is you."

CHAPTER 22

Fia couldn't take her eyes off her mate as they drove back toward the farm. He was still naked with only a T-shirt draped strategically over his lap. But it didn't hide the outline of his huge, rigid cock.

She had known he was big, but seeing him fully erect with no clothes to hide his true size had been a shock. And his piercings. *Damn.* It was enough to make a woman's vagina clench with a burning need to be filled.

But if she was going to be honest with herself, his size was also a bit intimidating, and she couldn't help wondering if he would actually fit inside her. None of the men she'd had sex with had been close to Bry's size, and none of them had been pierced down there.

"Should I be scared by how you're staring at me like you don't know whether to jump me or run from me?" Bry's eyes crinkled at the corners when he glanced at her. "Please tell me what you're thinking, redbird. I want our relationship to be the best it can be, and to achieve that we need to communicate openly with each other. If you're worried about something or just curious, please ask."

Fia couldn't help laughing at his logic. It was flawless yet so funny hearing him tell her that while driving naked with an erection.

Licking her lips, she reached out and yanked the T-shirt away from Bry's lap.

"Hey." His eyes widened. "I thought you didn't want anyone to see—" His words cut off on a groan when she wrapped her fingers around his hard length.

"There's no one here but me." Letting her hand glide up his silky skin, she enjoyed the feel of his piercings sliding against her fingers. She couldn't wait to feel those inside her, massaging her internal walls. Would that help her come without having her clit stimulated at the same time? Perhaps, but even if it didn't, she was convinced it would feel amazing. *If* he fit inside her. She still wasn't certain about that.

"Fia. Fuck." He swerved into the middle of the road before slowing down and stopping on the side of the road. Putting a hand on hers to stop her, he faced her with need turning his eyes almost black. "I'm going to paint the inside of my car with cum. It'll be a mess."

Fia wasn't ready to let him go, though. She wanted to hear him enjoy himself when he came. But he had a point about his car. There were ways to avoid that, though.

"That won't be a problem." Grinning at him, she released her seatbelt and bent over his lap. "But you have to remove your hand."

A few seconds went by without him responding, and she was starting to think he wasn't going to when he suddenly pulled his hand away from hers.

Fia didn't let the opportunity go to waste. Sliding her hand down to the base of his thick length, she sucked the head of his cock into her mouth.

His reaction was immediate. "Fuck! Oh, fuck." His already tense thigh muscles bunched, and from how he lifted in his seat, she could tell his glutes tightened as well.

She moaned when the taste of him hit her tongue and made her channel clench and wetness soak into her panties. Why did he taste so good? She hadn't expected him to taste this good. Using her tongue, she played with his piercings as she lowered her head and took as much of him as she could into her mouth.

"Is everything all right?" The muffled male voice came from outside the car, and Fia thought she recognized Leith's voice. *Shit.* She hadn't even thought about the others following them in their own vehicles but letting go of Bry wasn't an option. Leith probably already realized what was going on, or he would in the next few seconds. And lifting her head to look at the man would only make this more awkward.

"Yes." The word sounded like it was forced between Bry's clenched teeth, and she would have laughed if her mouth wasn't full. "Leave."

A low chuckle sounded from outside the car. "Very well. I guess we will see you later."

The whole incident should have made her cringe with embarrassment and run a mile to get away from the situation, but for some reason it didn't bother her that much. She knew the other couples were all over each other whenever they had the chance, some of them more careless in public than others.

Bry groaned and buried his hands in her hair, but without restricting her movement. "Fuck, Fia. I'm going to come. Your mouth is heaven."

Tightening her lips around him, she increased the suction and swirled her tongue around the rim of his cock head.

She reached between his thighs, and he widened his legs. Cupping his balls, she massaged them gently, enjoying the velvety skin in her hand.

And apparently he enjoyed it as well. Bry roared her name as he started coming, shooting his hot cum down her throat. She swallowed down everything he gave her, while savoring the way his body jerked and vibrated with ecstasy—ecstasy she had given him.

He was breathing hard by the time the tension in his body eased, and he sagged in his seat. His hands were still in her hair, his fingers slowly massaging her scalp.

Fia let his cock slip from her mouth and sat up while making a show of licking her lips. She had expected his hard shaft to soften, but it was still straining from between his legs like he hadn't just come.

Bry's eyes were hooded, and his lips parted as his gaze followed the movement of her tongue. "Redbird, I'm in awe and fucking pissed off with you."

Her eyes widened; she wasn't quite sure what she had done to make him angry. Was he talking about the spell she'd put on him? He probably was. It was a horrible thing to do to a shifter, and it would probably take some time for him to forgive her. But she had hope that he would. He loved her. Warmth spread through her chest, making her smile.

"Come here." One of his hands curled around her neck and the other slipped beneath the ruined fabric of her shirt and pinched her nipple.

She gasped as need zinged through her and made her clit throb.

He pulled her closer until his lips covered hers. His hand was on her breast, massaging it while he kissed her slowly, gently exploring her mouth with his tongue like he wanted to savor the moment. Or drive her crazy.

Her body was hot and tense from how much she wanted to feel him inside her, but he didn't seem to be in any rush to make that happen. But, he had just had an orgasm, so he might be sated for a while.

Bry ended the kiss and pulled back with a grin on his face. "Are you ready to be fucked?" He reached between her legs and scraped his nails along the fabric of her jeans right across her clit.

She shuddered and widened her legs to give him better access. Skin-to-skin contact would be so much better, but anything was better than nothing. And her clit was so sensitive, she would probably explode if he kept going just doing what he was doing.

"Oh no, you won't." His hand disappeared, and she couldn't help her whine of disappointment. "This is why I'm pissed off with you. I can't make you come here. It's too public, and I don't want anyone else to see you when you come. That show is all for me."

Squeezing her eyes closed, Fia squirmed in her seat. Her whole lower body was on fire with how turned on she was, and if he wasn't going to do anything about it, then perhaps she had to take matters into her own hands.

But she had barely touched the button of her jeans before his hand closed around her wrist and pulled her hand away. "Look at me, redbird."

Opening her eyes, she turned to look at him. His eyes were practically glowing with desire, and her gaze automatically dropped to his lap to see his hard length standing proud with a pearl of precum gathered at the tip. She didn't know how to feel about that. He had seemed to come hard, but if he was still this hard, it might not have been that good.

His hand cupped her cheek, making her gaze rise back up to his. "Your mouth is magic, and I'm going to beg you to suck my dick again. But not before I've seen you come on my cock so hard you can't breathe. Your pussy is mine, and it won't get a lot of rest with me around. That's a warning and a promise."

Fia snapped her mouth shut when she felt drool dripping from her bottom lip onto her bare chest. If he didn't make good on his promise soon, she was going to spontaneously combust.

"We're only a couple of minutes from the farm." His focus was suddenly on the road, and they shot forward when he pushed the accelerator. "Put your seatbelt on."

She absently did as she was told. All she could think about was being alone with him, close to him, and finally feeling him inside her. It was two years overdue, so in other words about fucking time.

They soon came to a stop in front of the farmhouse, and Bry glanced at her with a wide grin on his face before he grabbed the T-shirt and covered his cock. "Get out, and keep those breasts covered, or I'll have to spank you."

A shiver raced down her spine as her internal muscles tightened. He had smacked her ass the day before, and the pain had felt startlingly good. No one had ever spanked her before, and she had never thought she would be into it, but apparently she was into a lot more than she had thought. At least with Bry.

She wasn't about to flash her breasts to everyone, though, so she pulled on the burned edges of the fabric to cover as much of her chest as possible with what was left of her shirt.

Fia had just stepped out of the car when someone called her name. Kynlee hurried down the steps from the porch and headed directly for her with a huge smile on her face.

"Congratulations. I'm so happy for you. I knew it would sort itself out." The beautiful, curvy blonde enveloped Fia in a hug before letting go and taking a step back. "Here. The barn is ready for you." A keychain with one old-fashioned key hung from the woman's index finger.

"The barn?" Fia couldn't help her shocked expression. Kynlee expected them to stay in the barn? If that were the case, they might be better off finding a hotel or B&B.

Kynlee's laughter rang out. "I'm sorry. Bad assumption on my part. We have a guest suite in the barn, complete with a huge bed, bathroom, and kitchen area. But you didn't know that, did you? I've just been out there stocking the fridge with food and drinks for you. You can stay for as long as you like."

"Oh." Fia laughed, before glancing at Bry, who was standing in front of the car, grinning at her. "Thank you, Kynlee. That's very generous of you." Fia gave the woman a warm smile and accepted the key from her.

"Happy mating." Kynlee returned her warm smile before she spun and headed back to the house.

"I'll go get our bags from upstairs." Bry let his gaze slowly caress her body from her face to her toes before he raised it back up to meet hers. "You go get ready. I'll be there in less than a minute. But…" He narrowed his gaze at her with a wicked smile curving his lips. "No touching yourself."

"We'll see." Fia winked at him. "Depends on how fast you are. If you let me wait…" She spun and hurried toward the barn while she chuckled at the way his eyes had widened with her challenge.

CHAPTER 23

Bryson froze to the spot as all the blood going to his brain changed direction and headed south. She had winked at him. *Fucking winked.* Which meant he would have to spank her. And she would love it. Just the thought of being inside her when her channel clenched like it had around his fingers the day before had his balls pull up tighter.

The question was how long he was going to last with how insanely horny he was. Even the powerful orgasm she had given him minutes ago hadn't been enough to reduce his need to claim her. It was the mating bond talking but also the fact that he had wanted her for so long.

He finally managed to force his body to move, and he hurried up the stairs. After putting some pants on, he grabbed their bags before racing out to the barn.

Fia was standing by the huge bed with her back to him and her jeans and panties around her ankles when he yanked the door open to the guest suite.

Bryson slammed the door shut and dropped everything he was carrying on the floor. "I told you not to touch yourself."

She turned her head and grinned at him over her shoulder. "And I told you not to let me wait." She widened her legs and showed him her middle finger between them before shoving the finger inside herself.

Fuck me. He almost came right there and then. "Fia, I warned you." His voice was filled with a deep growl, making his words almost incomprehensible.

He closed the distance to her in a few long strides, and reaching around her from behind, he grabbed both her wrists. After leaning in, he nipped her earlobe before whispering in her ear. "Do you want my cock inside you?"

"Yes." Her voice was shaky, and she swallowed hard. "Please. I need you."

"Then get on the bed on your hands and knees, redbird." He nipped at her earlobe again before letting go of her wrists and taking a step back to take off his pants. "Now!"

She quickly turned toward the bed and crawled onto it, her movements a bit awkward with her jeans still restricting her legs.

Bryson quickly removed her socks, jeans, and panties, before getting on the bed behind her. "Spread your legs for me, Fia, nice and wide."

She did as she was told, and the scent of her arousal assailing him would have brought him to his knees if he wasn't already there. "Good girl. Do you want me to make you come?" His body was pushing him to enter her immediately, but he would end up spilling within seconds and be a huge disappointment to her if he didn't bring her close to coming before entering her.

"Yes, please fuck me. I've been dreaming of having you inside me for two years."

"You and me both, redbird." Bryson groaned when he reached between her legs and felt how dripping wet she was. "Fuck, you're wet. I'm sorry I had to make you wait, but I won't ever give you an orgasm in public. If someone sees you coming, I'll have to kill them."

Her eyes were wide when she turned her head to stare at him. "What?"

"You heard me." He drove two fingers inside her hot, wet sheath, making her moan and her eyes lose focus. "Your orgasms are mine." He slapped her ass, making her squeal and clench around his fingers so hard his breathing stuttered. He was going to be so fucked, in every sense of that word.

Pumping his fingers inside her, he reached around and slid a finger over her swollen nub.

"Bry." His name was uttered on a gasp, and she pushed her ass back against him. "I'm ready. I need your cock."

Chuckling, he pulled his fingers from her pussy and slapped her ass again, a little harder this time. "You do, do you? Have a little patience." But he knew she could hear the smile in his voice.

While continuing to slide his finger back and forth over her clit, he wrapped his hand around his cock and placed the tip at her entrance. Hopefully, he would last more than ten seconds, but even if he didn't, he would make sure she came hard. And it wouldn't take long before he was ready again. There was always that.

He pushed into her slowly, letting her adjust to his girth. There had been women who had taken one look at him and run, and even with the most eager ones he'd usually had to be careful. But hopefully, Fia would enjoy his size and adjust to it in time. Until then he would make sure to be gentle.

***

Fia's mouth was hanging open as Bry pushed into her slowly. He was stretching her to capacity and then some, but the pleasure far outweighed the pain. It was a good thing he was taking his time, though, because she needed it to adjust. He was by far the biggest man she had ever been with.

Grunting, he grabbed her hip before pulling out slowly until just the head of his long shaft was still inside her. He then pushed back in, his piercings sliding against her sensitive front wall, making her want to slam her legs closed and pull away at the almost overwhelming sensations. "I love…your…ladder."

"Good." His grip on her hip was bruising, and his breathing turned ragged as he pushed farther and farther inside her. Apparently she wasn't the only one barely holding on at the moment.

Biting her lip, she shuddered as pleasure started unfurling in her belly. She was already getting close, and he wasn't even fully inside her. His finger playing with her clit felt amazing, but the starting pleasure was somehow deeper and fuller than anything she had ever experienced before from having her clit stimulated.

Bry reversed again, pulling out slowly, and Fia couldn't help the whine she let out at the loss of the glorious fullness inside her. She needed him deep, and she knew he was good for it.

When he started pushing inside her again, she pressed back against him. "I need…all of you. Please."

"Fuck." His fingernails bit into her hip, but she relished the effect she had on him. The way he almost vibrated with tension behind her.

Sinking into her slowly, he kept going this time until his hips were flush against her ass, and his entire length was buried inside her.

Fia's eyes must have been a mile wide with how he felt deep inside her. The last couple of inches of him had made her realize what had been missing with her previous lovers. The depth felt so fulfilling, and just feeling him there was enough to make her teeter on the edge of what promised to be an epic orgasm. She was truly made for this man, or perhaps he was made for her.

Lowering down onto her elbows, she pushed her pussy even more firmly against him. It allowed him to sink into her another half an inch or so, and she gasped and shuddered when something unlocked inside her and the first lick of her orgasm made her channel seize Bry's cock in an iron grip.

"Fuck, Fia. You're perfect!" His shouted words ended in a roar as his thick shaft started jerking inside her, filling her with his hot cum.

His pulsing member sent her flying, her whole body shaking with the intense pleasure surging through her in waves. Nothing had ever felt this good. So deep, so satisfying, so earth-shattering.

It lasted for what felt like a long time, but she had no idea how much time had actually passed when she finally blinked her eyes open.

She was on her side with Bry lying behind her, holding her close with a hand pressed to her belly. At some point he had pulled out or perhaps slipped out when he softened. Her thighs and pussy were drenched with a mixture of his cum and her juices.

He kissed her just behind her ear, and the feel of his soft lips made her smile. "How are you feeling, redbird?"

"Fucked."

He laughed. Moving away from her, he rolled her onto her back before leaning in and kissing her slowly. But it didn't stay slow for long. His tongue swept into her mouth as his hand curled around her neck. Then, he was suddenly on top of her, his hard cock poking into her stomach while he plundered her mouth.

Heat surged through her, and she wrapped her legs around him, grinding her heels into his ass. How it was possible that she wanted him again so soon after exploding with pleasure she had no idea—but she did.

Bry broke the kiss and pushed up on his hands, grinning down at her. It put his magnificent shoulders, arms, and chest on display, and she absently licked her lips as she let her eyes feast on his amazing body.

"Eyes up here." His gravelly voice was filled with amusement.

Laughing, Fia met his smiling eyes. "What? I'm not allowed to stare at your chest?" She put her hands on his shoulders before sliding them down over his chest toward his abs. "I've admired your body from a distance for a long time, wanting so badly to touch you. And I'm going to touch you every chance I get from now on."

"I like the sound of that." His breathing hitched

when she wrapped a hand around his hard cock and started stroking him.

"When are you going to claim me?" Fia stared up into his hooded eyes. "I know that's one of the reasons they put us out here. It allows us privacy, and I guess it allows them peace and quiet. Although, your roar earlier must've been loud even inside the farmhouse."

"And your screaming wasn't?" He grinned before he suddenly scooted down, and she lost her grip on his straining shaft.

Her eyes widened when she realized what he intended, and she clamped her hands on either side of his head to stop him. "I need a shower before I'll feel comfortable having your mouth on me."

He raised his gaze to hers without moving his head. "As long as I get to wash your beautiful body."

She shivered at the mere thought of him touching her everywhere. "Okay, but the same goes for me."

He smirked. "Deal."

Before she even knew what was happening, he had thrown her over his shoulder and was carrying her to the bathroom. Once there, he turned on the water in the shower but made no move to put her down.

Fia wriggled against him. "You can put me down now."

His hand landed on her ass with a crack, and she sucked in a breath when her channel clenched in response. "I'll put you down when I'm good and ready, redbird. Until then…" His finger was suddenly between her legs, circling her clit.

"Bry." She tried to squeeze her thighs together to stop him touching her sensitive nub, but it didn't make any difference. His hand was already lodged between her legs, making her squirm with building pleasure. Her mate obviously liked taking charge, and it was driving her crazy in a good way.

But she wasn't against retaliating and driving him crazy as well. She used one hand to reach around him and grab his heavy cock and the other to cup his balls between his legs.

"Fuck, Fia." His glutes tightened, making his ass look even better than usual.

She suddenly had an urge to put her teeth marks on his butt cheek but with the way he was holding her and their height difference she couldn't reach it. Instead, she stroked her hand up and down his cock while massaging his balls gently, trying to ignore the way he was manipulating her pleasure nub so expertly, sending her barreling toward another orgasm.

She was just about to tip over the edge when his hand disappeared from between her legs. "Bry, that's cruel." Her voice was whiny with how desperate she was for him to keep playing with her.

***

Bryson's jaw was clamped shut as he tried to hold off his orgasm. He had wanted to tease her while waiting for the water to heat, but as usually happened with Fia it backfired. Instead of allowing him to take control, she had grabbed both his shaft and testicles and with her soft hands playing with him, he wouldn't be able to control his need to come for much longer.

She let go of his parts when he pulled her back over his shoulder. He wrapped his arms around her thighs when his face was level with her breasts and latched onto one of her nipples, sucking and biting the tight peak.

"Bry, that's…" Her hands gripped his head as she squirmed against him.

After giving her other nipple the same treatment, he pulled his head back and raised his gaze to hers. "Wrap your legs around my waist, redbird. I want to see your face when you explode around my cock."

Her eyes widened, and he almost expected her to protest, but then she grinned and did what she was told.

With one hand under her ass, he adjusted her position until his dick was lined up with her entrance. Loosening his hold on her, he let her sink down onto his cock.

Bryson growled, and his eyes just about bugged out of his skull when she took all of him without pause.

Her eyes lost focus as she moaned her pleasure, and it was a miracle he didn't come right there and then.

"Fuck, you're dynamite, woman." After walking into the shower, he pushed her back against the wall before capturing her lips in a deep, demanding kiss.

But less than ten seconds later, Fia tore her mouth from his. "Move, Bry. Please. I need you to move. I'm dying here."

Bryson chuckled, knowing exactly what she was going through. He had been trying to stall to regain some control. The last thing he wanted was to come before she did, but he couldn't refuse her plea.

Supporting her thighs with his hands, he started thrusting into her, adjusting his angle until her nails bit into his shoulders, and she mewled every time he hit that extra sensitive area inside her.

It didn't take long before she screamed his name,

and her pussy clamped down on his dick so hard he saw stars. He staggered when his orgasm slammed into him, and he roared as he pumped his seed inside his mate. His instincts kicked in and his jaw stretched over her shoulder close to her neck, before he pierced her soft skin with his teeth.

Another violent orgasm had his knees buckling, sending them both to the floor. Something nicked his clavicle and the intensity of his pleasure increased, making his whole body spasm with sheer ecstasy.

Bryson was still breathing hard when his scrambled mind finally reassembled into something approaching normal function. After cracking his eyes open, he blinked to regain focus.

Fia was straddling his thighs where he was sitting on his heels on the floor. His arms were wrapped around her, holding her tightly against him, and her head was resting on his shoulder. If it wasn't for her right hand caressing his bicep, he might have thought she was asleep or passed out.

"Are we mated then?" She lifted her head to stare into his eyes.

He gave a slow nod as he tried to swallow down all the emotions her question brought up in him. "We are. Are you happy about that?" She had already told him she wanted him, but his shoulders still tensed while waiting for her response.

A happy smile spread across her face, and he sighed in relief. "Yes. I've wanted to be yours since I met you, but I was scared you didn't feel the same about me." Her expression sobered. "And I was afraid I would end up being just another woman on your long list of conquests. I knew I wouldn't be able to survive that, or at least my heart wouldn't."

"Oh, Fia." He carefully brushed her wet hair out of her face before gripping her head with both hands. "Please forgive me for being such an idiot. I should've shown you from the start how much I truly wanted you and been open about the fact that I didn't want anyone else. Just the thought of another woman turned me off, whereas the thought of you had me so hard I thought I was going crazy at times. But most of all I just wanted to be near you, spend time with you, get to know you. I was too proud to admit it, though—to anyone. Because I thought it would make me look weak to be so utterly obsessed with one woman."

Fia's arms wrapped around his neck. "I'll forgive you, Bry, if you can forgive me for putting a spell on you to suppress the mating bond. I understand that's on par with a mortal sin among shifters, but I hope you can forgive me anyway."

Nodding, he let his love and happiness show in his smile. "I've already forgiven you for that. It hurt when I realized what you had done, but it didn't take me long to understand why and that I was making a mistake by running away. I had already turned around and was on my way back here to you when Amber found me."

He leaned in and pressed his lips to hers in a soft kiss before pulling back. "I love you, redbird. And I feel honored to have you accept me and become my mate." His brows furrowed when he suddenly remembered something and tried to look down at his clavicle, but he was unable to see the spot without a mirror. "Did you bite me?"

She winced and looked down. "I wouldn't call it a bite. It's more like I graced you with my tooth. I'm sorry."

"No, don't be sorry." A huge grin spread across his face as his heart fluttered in his chest. He put a finger under her chin and lifted until her eyes met his. "You marked me. I love it. I didn't expect you to do it, that's all. I mean, you're not a shifter. If you had been, it would've been instinctual, but it isn't for you."

"You love it?" Her eyes widened, and she started smiling before she suddenly frowned. "Does that mean it will leave a permanent scar?"

Bryson nodded. "Yes, for everyone to see. I can't wait to show it off."

"But it kind of distorts your tattoo. I mean it cuts into the picture, not by much but enough to be noticeable."

He laughed. "Even better. Then everyone will notice it and know I'm taken. Shifters don't scar, so everyone knows that if you have one, it's a mate mark."

Fia's smile returned. "I like that. A visible sign that you're mine if anyone's ever in doubt."

"Exactly." Bryson crushed his lips to hers. When her lips parted, he pushed his tongue between them and explored her warm, wet mouth. It reminded him of something else he would like to do to her. His cock was hardening, ready to play, but before that he wanted to eat his mate's pussy until she had no voice left to scream his name.

CHAPTER 24

Henry paced in the corridor upstairs in the farmhouse outside the room where Eleanor was resting. She hadn't woken up even once since they'd found her early that morning. Sabrina had checked her again but couldn't find any trace of the spell Amber had put on the beautiful vampire. Whatever was keeping her unconscious or sleeping didn't seem to have anything to do with what Amber had done to her, unless there was something they were missing.

They had managed to transport her to the farmhouse in Trevor's car, after covering her in several layers of clothing and a blanket. Henry had been reluctant to even try it, but after observing her for a while and noticing she didn't seem to suffer from the daylight streaming in through the door and the broken window, he had concluded that she should be fine as long as no part of her was exposed directly to the sun.

Stopping outside her bedroom door, he raked his fingers through his hair in frustration. He wanted her to wake up so he could make sure she was all right. It was early afternoon, and she might just need sleep, but none of the people in the house were familiar with vampires' needs or could tell if she was just sleeping or if something was seriously wrong with her.

There was another reason he wanted to talk to her as well, but it would have to wait until he knew she was fine. He wanted to ask her why she had bitten him. And more specifically why he had reacted the way he had to her bite. He had come harder and faster than he had ever done in his life. And although he was reluctant to admit it, he wanted to experience it again, preferably at a time when he was able to give her something in return.

Henry started pacing again. There was a conflict going on inside him about the whole episode. His mind was telling him he should forget about Eleanor to avoid getting swept up into something that might prevent him from finding his true mate, but his body was telling him to stop listening to his mind for a change and live a little. And in this his body might be right.

His mind had dictated his actions for several years, making sure he kept his eyes on the prize at all times, his prize being his true mate, even though he didn't know whom she was or if he would be lucky enough to meet her at all. Everything he had done in the last few years was grounded in his wish to be worthy of his mate. Taking on the pack who sorely needed an honorable alpha, supporting the weak and scared in the pack to enable their confidence to grow, and disciplining the assholes who had used weaker members of the pack for their own convenience and pleasure. He considered it his duty as an alpha to support and build people, but at the back of his mind had been the thought that it would also earn him his mate's love and loyalty.

Logically, Henry knew that a true mate would love him for whom he was, and even if he failed in one of his goals, she would still be his, but he couldn't shake the fear that she wouldn't approve of him for some reason. Growing up with parents who tolerated but didn't really love each other might be one of the reasons for his fear, even knowing that his parents weren't true mates and their mating had been arranged by their packs.

It wasn't common knowledge, but his mom had been in love with someone else when she had been sent to mate his dad, and those feelings hadn't died with their mating. It had led to a horrible start for them, and although they had learned to tolerate each other, they had never grown close. But despite their turbulent relationship, his parents had agreed on one thing, to make sure everyone else thought they were happy together. Their fake smiles and show of affection had become practically unbearable as he grew up and realized what the falseness meant, and it was one of the reasons he wanted so badly to find his true mate, the one person in the world he would be perfect for and who would be perfect for him.

Stopping again, he stared at the door to Eleanor's room. She wasn't the mate he was looking for, but he couldn't forget what had happened between them and how it had made him feel. One thing was the surprising orgasm, but there had been something more. A sense of connection beyond anything he had ever felt before, a feeling that she would keep his secrets safe if he ever chose to share them. Closing his eyes, he shook his head to try to dispel the need to go to her, lie down beside her, and pull her close.

The problem was that he didn't know whether his reaction to her and need to be close to her was due to some kind of bond she had forced on him. It felt real, but that didn't mean it was. No matter how much he wanted it to be.

"Fuck!" Henry spun and headed down the stairs before he could change his mind. His behavior was crazy and desperate. He had to get a grip, and the only way to do that was to find something to distract him.

When he reached the bottom of the stairs, he heard voices in the living room. Upon entering the room, he saw Leith and Sabrina on a couch with Hugh and Kynlee seated across the table from them. Trevor and Jennie were nowhere to be seen, but the new man, Gawen, was standing in front of the large windows staring out over the green fields.

Henry frowned as he stared at the man's back. Gawen hadn't said much since he emerged from the forest following Fia, Bryson, and Trevor back from their encounter with Amber. The man had asked if he could join them, and even though Bryson had opposed the idea, they had offered Gawen to come back to the farm with them. He had been a victim of the evil bitch, as well, and he might have been dead if Fia hadn't protected him. And Gawen obviously knew it.

Walking closer, Henry took in Gawen's tall and broad form. He wasn't as tall as Trevor, or as broad as Bryson, but he was a big man.

"How long were you Amber's prisoner?" Stopping

beside Gawen, Henry turned his head to look at him. The others might have already asked him that question while Henry was upstairs, but hopefully the man wouldn't take offense at being asked again.

Gawen's brows pushed together as he continued to stare out the window. "I'm not quite sure. I can't remember much from the last couple of years. Someone captured me and did something to me that scrambled my mind. But I don't know if it was Amber or someone else. I can't remember ever having met the woman before, but today is the first day my mind has been clear since I was captured."

Henry's eyes widened as he stared at the other man. That was worse than he had expected. "I'm sorry for what you've gone through. Where are you from? Have you called your family and friends to tell them you are okay?"

Gawen looked down at his feet. "I...haven't."

"You can borrow my phone." Henry pulled his phone out of his pocket and held it out for Gawen to take.

But instead of accepting the phone, the man finally turned his head to meet Henry's gaze. "No, I mean I don't have any family or friends to call. I'd already been alone for many years when I was captured."

Henry wasn't sure what to say to that. Had Gawen chosen to be alone or was it forced on him? And would it be okay to ask him about it? The man had volunteered the information, though, which might mean he would be willing to share more about himself if asked.

"That sounds lonely. Was it by choice?" Moving his gaze to the fields outside, Henry waited for Gawen's response. He couldn't imagine how it would be to be all by himself. But then he never had been.

"Yes and no. I'm...different, and the people in my pack didn't like that. When my mother died... Well, there just wasn't anything left for me there. I didn't fit in, so I left, searching for another group of shifters that was more accepting. But I never found one. And then I was captured."

Henry nodded slowly. Unfortunately, he wasn't surprised. He didn't know how Gawen was different from other shifters, but he knew most shifters didn't accept people who didn't fit the norm. It was a custom that had survived from the old days when a pack member's weakness would put the whole pack at risk. But it was an old-fashioned view Henry didn't share, and that he worked hard to eradicate in his own pack.

"You're welcome to join my pack." Henry turned to look at the man next to him. "All I ask is loyalty to the pack and respectful behavior toward every other pack member. I don't care about disabilities, ethnicity, what you believe or who you love, but I do believe in respect and honesty."

Gawen's eyes had widened as Henry spoke. "That sounds like...a haven, and too good to be true. I would be stupid not to accept your offer."

Henry chuckled. "Does that mean you accept?"

The man nodded softly at first before the motion turned more decisive. "Yes, I accept." Gawen suddenly dropped to his knees, facing Henry. "I pledge myself to you and your pack. I will do whatever is necessary to ensure your safety and every other pack member's safety. I'm yours to command."

Henry was a bit taken aback at the formal pledge. A

simple *yes, I accept* would have been enough, but he wasn't going to tell Gawen that. Not yet anyway. He didn't want to belittle the man's show of respect. Smiling, Henry put his hand on the man's shoulder. "Rise, Gawen. And thank you. I'm sure you'll be a valuable member of my pack."

Gawen rose. "I'll do my best."

"It might be a few days until you meet the rest of your pack, though." Henry frowned. "We're trying to take down Amber, but she's proven herself to be more powerful, ruthless, and difficult to track than we had expected. But nevertheless we need to destroy her before she destroys us."

Nodding, Gawen glanced at the others sitting on the couches. "Yes, Leith told me about that. And I'll help in any way I can."

∞∞∞∞

Fia sighed in contentment. It was getting dark outside, and they had spent hours in bed having sex after they mated. And each time had been better than the last with the mating bond doing its magic.

It was incredible how she was able to feel Bry's pleasure blending with her own, and it drove her crazy each and every time, sending her tumbling into a world of pleasure with him right there with her.

They had been spooning for the last fifteen minutes or so, and Fia had been enjoying the feel of his large body behind her. It suffused her with a different type of pleasure, from the love and utter devotion she could feel from him through their bond.

Bry's large hand on her belly suddenly moved down

between her legs, his middle finger sliding over her clit before it dipped inside her.

There was an immediate spark of pleasure, but she couldn't help the hiss that escaped her at how sore she was. She hadn't really noticed it before, but after the number of times they had fucked, it wasn't a surprise.

His hand disappeared, before he rose on his elbow to stare down at her. "You're sore."

She nodded. "I'm sorry. I think I might need a little break."

Bry chuckled, before giving her a quick kiss on her lips. "Don't be sorry. I think my balls could use a break as well. They've been running on empty for a while now. And no wonder. We've been fucking more times than rabbits during mating season."

Snorting, Fia shook her head at him. "Rabbits don't have a mating season."

"I know. But if they did, we would still have them beat." His eyes were sparkling with amusement as he smiled down at her. "How about we clean up, get dressed, and join the others for some food?"

"Yes." Fia nodded. "That sounds good, and hopefully, it will keep me distracted from how amazing it is to have sex with you. Lying here with you naked behind me is tempting me to ignore how sore I am."

Bry threw his head back and laughed. "Thank you, redbird. I'm going to work hard to make sure you feel the same in fifty years. And a hundred." His eyes were filled with love when he met her gaze. "And right back at you. Don't be surprised if I walk around with a permanent erection from now on. That's what you do to me."

After showering separately to avoid ending up back

in bed, they got dressed and left the barn. There was light pouring out of all the windows on the ground floor of the farmhouse, making it look like none of the others had opted to get some sleep yet.

Fia and Bry had just stepped into the hallway when they heard a gasp. It sounded like it came from the kitchen, and they had just reached the entrance to the room when Jennie stormed out and almost crashed into them. Her eyes were a mile wide and her complexion paler than usual.

"What's wrong?" Fia frowned as she took in Jennie's expression before her gaze dropped to the phone in the blond woman's hand.

"Come. Something's happened." The woman hurried toward the living room.

Fia's whole body tensed in apprehension as they followed Jennie.

"Turn on the news." Jennie barked out the command as soon as she entered the living room.

Hugh frowned before he grabbed the remote and turned on the large television.

"...as you can see behind me." The male reporter was staring into the camera with a serious expression on his face. And in the distance behind him was a massive blaze, the flames reaching far above the forest surrounding whatever it was that was burning. "Witnesses almost two miles away heard an explosion before they saw the fire in the distance and called the emergency services."

The scene changed to show footage taken from a drone or a helicopter. It showed a large house completely engulfed in flames with walls that were all buckled outward like they had been hit by an immense force from the inside of the structure. There was no doubt there would be little left to salvage after the fire was extinguished, and whatever evidence remained of the source of the blast would be difficult to find.

"That's Jack's mansion." Trevor was standing beside Jennie with his arm protectively around her waist. "I hope no one was home when it started. Jack might be an asshole, but I don't believe all his panthers are the same."

"Fuck." Bry's lips were pulled back in a look of horror. "I wonder what happened, but I guess it might be days before we'll know the answer to that. Callum should keep an eye on the investigation." He turned to look at Leith.

"I agree." Leith nodded. "It might be a tragic accident, or something related to Jack's drug trade, but I would still like to know just in case."

Fia studied Bry's worried expression. "I take it you're talking about Jack, the panther alpha who kidnapped Steph?"

Nodding, Bry met her gaze. "We are. And I seriously hope this has nothing to do with Amber, but we won't know that until we know what set off the explosion. If the cause is ever established at all."

Fia nodded slowly as thoughts raced through her head. Her grandmother had written several journals detailing magical practices she had encountered throughout her life, as well as stories she had heard from family and friends about the use of magic. Fia had read through them a few times, and they had helped her practice her own magic and explore her abilities.

Her grandmother's journals didn't include all there

was to know about magic. There was no doubt more spells and abilities existed in the world than those her grandmother had encountered. But Fia had never heard of anyone being able to set off an explosion of any magnitude purely with the use of magic. Unless magic was only used as the source of ignition, sort of like a magical match.

"I'd like to know what Callum can find out as well." Fia glanced at Sabrina, who nodded back at her. "I've never heard of magic strong enough to cause something like this, but I don't know everything, and different witches have different abilities. Although I think if Amber had the ability to blow shit up, she wouldn't have waited until now to use it."

"At this point I'm not ready to put anything past that bitch, though." Sabrina's eyes narrowed. "She'll do anything she thinks supports her mission. And if someone gets in her way, she won't hesitate to dispose of them. Unfortunately, this will only escalate until we manage to take her down, and she has the advantage that she doesn't really care if human's find out about shifters."

"Why do you say that?" Bry's brows creased with concern as he stared at Sabrina.

The blond witch swung her gaze around the room before she spoke. "An autopsy has already been carried out on several shifters she has killed, and there will be more after this fire if there are any bodies to be retrieved. Every autopsy increases the risk of discovery. The more anomalies are found, the harder it will be to dismiss them as mistakes or contamination."

"Fuck." Trevor shook his head, his jaw tense. "You're right, but we do have people specializing in manipulating forensic evidence, DNA tests and the like. They need to up their game, though, to make sure we stay safely undetected."

Sabrina nodded. "They do. And until we know what happened at Jack's mansion, we have to assume Amber was behind it. Which means every pack and clan should increase their security to make sure she doesn't do the same to them."

Fia lifted her gaze to Bry to see him turn pale before his expression changed into one of determination. "We're leaving. I have to talk to my clan. In person."

EPILOGUE

Bryson felt calmer after talking to G, instructing him to increase security and keep an eye out for Amber in and around the village. He would feel even better after having talked to his clan members himself, and he would do that as soon as they arrived.

But he was also feeling excited at the announcement he was going to make. Glancing at his true mate sitting in the passenger seat beside him, he reached out to put a hand on her thigh. The most amazing woman in the world was his, and he couldn't wait to formally introduce her to his clan. They already knew her, of course, but not as his mate.

"What are you planning? I'm not sure I like that wicked grin on your face." Fia lifted an eyebrow at him with a small smile on her lips.

He laughed. "I'm not planning anything, just looking forward to introducing you to everyone as their queen."

She snorted. "You're their alpha not their king. So

how can I be their queen? That doesn't make sense."

He shrugged. "It does to me. You're my queen so it makes sense you're theirs as well."

"Not sure I follow your logic." She put her hand on the one he had placed on her thigh. "Why don't you just introduce me as your mate? That's enough. Isn't it?"

Bryson just smiled. He was going to introduce her as his true mate. That was a given. But she was going to be more than that to his clan.

The electronic gates swung open, and he drove down into the underground car park beneath the house. The entrance wasn't visible behind the tall gates, so most people didn't even know the lower level existed.

After pulling into his parking spot and turning off the car, he turned to face Fia. "I want everyone to know you are more than just my mate, redbird. You're my alpha queen, and your word is law just as mine is. If you give them a direct order, they have to comply as if the order came from me."

Her eyes widened as she stared at him. "But I don't know the first thing about being a clan leader."

Smiling, Bryson let his love for her show in his eyes. "You will in time. You will be part of every important discussion and decision from now on. I don't expect you to know everything from the start, but you will learn, and I think it will be good for the clan that your perspective is included when decisions are made. Many view my leadership as formal and rigid, even though I feel it has its advantages. But it doesn't mean it can't benefit from a softer touch, and I think you can provide that. Together, I think we can lead the clan better than I've been able to do by myself."

Fia's mouth was hanging open by the time he stopped speaking. She clearly hadn't expected this from him.

Almost a minute went by before she snapped her mouth shut and swallowed hard. "I didn't see that one coming. I guess I expected everything to just stay the same, with the only difference being that I would be living with you from now on. But you have clearly thought about this. When did you find the time for that?"

Bryson grinned and winked at her. "It's been swirling in the back of my mind since I realized you're my true mate. I want you to be a part of every aspect of my life from now on, and I want to be a part of every aspect of yours. Exactly what that means is something we'll need to discuss, but we have plenty of time for that. You're not made to play second fiddle, redbird. And that makes me happy. I might like bossing you around in the bedroom, but in everything else I want you to be my equal."

Her smile grew until her face shone with love and happiness. "You're an amazing man. Do you know that, Bry?"

He laughed. "Please remember that when I piss you off for some reason. Because it's bound to happen sooner or later. I'm still a stubborn and proud man and polishing those edges might take a while."

Fia laughed. "I'm sure the same can be said about me in many ways. But I kind of like your edges. The way you take charge and go for what you want is part of what drew me to you in the first place. And if all else fails, I can always follow Sabrina's advice and take my clothes off." She winked at him.

Bryson threw his head back and laughed. "Good advice." Winking back at her, he let her see the desire in his eyes. "And keep that in mind, because I'm planning to take charge of your pleasure and make you explode on my cock as soon as you're up for it."

"Of course you are." Fia curled her fingers around his hand. "But first you're going to introduce me to your clan, and I'd like to get that over and done with. It's making me nervous." Her expression sobered, and he could see the concern in her eyes.

Bryson gave her what he hoped was a reassuring smile. "It's nothing to worry about. Trust me. A lot of them already love you, and they'll be happy you are my true mate. Come. Let's do this."

***

Fia's heart was racing in her chest when she walked into the elevator with Bry. He might believe everyone in his clan loved her and would accept her, but she wasn't so sure. Her conversation with G after she sent Bry running from her was still vivid in her mind, but Bry didn't need to know that.

No sooner had the elevator doors closed behind them than Bry pressed her up against the wall and covered her lips with his. Soon her heart was racing for an entirely different reason, and she started hoping he would change his mind about introducing her to his clan and instead take her directly up to his bedroom.

But when the elevator doors opened and he broke their hot kiss, she could see they were on the ground floor. And some of his clan members were standing right outside the elevator, waiting for them.

After taking her hand in his, Bry turned away from her and headed out of the elevator, and she had no choice but to follow him. She pasted a smile on her face, but her apprehension turned it into a stiff grimace.

People pulled back to give them space, but everyone's eyes were on their clasped hands. Some smiled and some looked confused, but there were also those who frowned and one of them was G.

The second in command gave a firm nod in Bry's direction, but he didn't even acknowledge Fia with a glance. "I've gathered everyone as you instructed, Bryson, except the ones out patrolling."

"Good." Bry returned G's nod. "But before I address the new safety procedures, I have an important announcement to make."

Fia's mate turned his head to stare into her eyes with so much pride and love in his gaze that she couldn't help the happy smile that split her face. "I've found my mate, my true mate. I've claimed her as mine, and she's claimed me as hers. You will honor and obey her like you do me."

Bry swung his gaze around the room until it came to a stop with a frown. Fia followed his gaze to see G staring back at Bry with defiance stiffening his features and his arms crossed over his chest.

Bry's eyes hardened, but before he could say anything, Fia put her hand on his chest to stop him. "Bry, don't—"

"Fia, I will handle this." Bry's voice was firm, and he didn't look at her while he spoke. "G. You look like you have something to say. Speak."

"This woman"—G waved his hand in her direction

with a look of disgust on his face—"committed a heinous crime by using magic to hide the fact that you are true mates. She should be punished for her crime instead of being accepted into the clan. Keep her in your room for your pleasure, but she's not our leader and never will be. She doesn't even call you by your real name for fuck's sake. She clearly has no respect for you or anyone else in this clan."

Several people gasped, but Fia lowered her gaze to avoid seeing their looks of horror and accusation. This was even worse than she had expected, and the only sensible thing for Bry to do was to keep her as a slave in his room like G had suggested.

Bry's hand tightened around hers. "What Fia did, she did because of my disrespectful behavior toward her. I pretended to take women to my bed after I met her two years ago, even though the only one I felt any desire for was her. If I had openly denounced other women, I might've won my true mate sooner. The only one to blame for this is me."

Fia's jaw dropped in disbelief, and her eyes snapped up to Bry's face.

His eyes were truly menacing as he stared at G. "I fucking love her nickname for me. It's uniquely hers and something I cherish. Fia will have your respect, or you are no longer a member of this clan."

Bry suddenly turned to her. Meeting her gaze, he dropped to his knees in front of her. "You're my alpha queen. I have claimed you, as you have claimed me. I have never kneeled in front of anyone in my life, but I kneel to you as the ruler of my heart. I'm yours forever, mind, body, and soul."

Fia was too shocked to do anything but stare at

him. And judging from the complete silence in the room, she wasn't the only one.

G's voice broke the silence. "Well, I'm not going to be part of a clan that has a leader with a broken spine. You're no longer the alpha you used to be, Bryson."

Bry rose and turned to G. "No, I'm not. Fia has made me a better alpha, and I'm confident it will help make this a better clan for everyone."

G's lips twisted in disgust, but before he could respond, the man standing to his right spoke. "I think I speak for most people here when I say that we have been waiting for this day. The day when our alpha would find his mate and settle down. You have always been a good leader, Bryson, and I am convinced that finding your true mate will make you an even better one. You have my loyalty and respect like you've always had, and from this day my loyalty and respect extend to Fia. Her love for you and her power as a witch will make our clan stronger."

People nodded and mumbled their agreement. Everyone except G.

"Thank you, Ian." Bry nodded at the man who had spoken before turning his focus back on G as his alpha power suffused the room. "Leave. You're no longer welcome here. You have thirty minutes to pack and get out."

G looked like he wanted to object, but then he obviously decided against it. Tightening his lips into a hard line, he spun and forced his way through the people crowding the room.

"Ian." Bry nodded in G's direction. "Please make sure G leaves peacefully."

"Of course." The man gave a sharp nod before

turning to follow G.

Fia breathed a sigh of relief, even though she felt bad for her mate. G had been Bry's friend for a long time. It must feel awful to lose him like this.

Looking around, she gave the clan members surrounding them a tentative smile. Bry had chosen her over G, which didn't surprise her, but the fact that everyone else had done the same was more than she had expected.

Bry suddenly turned to her with a wicked grin on his face. "It's time, Fia."

She frowned as she met his gaze. "Time for what?"

"To give them what they're waiting for." His hand cupped the side of her head, and his thumb reached beneath her chin and tipped her head back.

Fia lifted an eyebrow at him. "And that is?"

"This." He grinned before his lips descended on hers. His greedy mouth pushed every thought from her mind, except the love and desire pouring into her through their mating bond.

∞∞∞∞

Henry couldn't take it anymore. Dawn was fast approaching, and Eleanor still hadn't woken up. Bryson had opened his eyes almost immediately after Sabrina had removed the spell affecting him, and that was almost twenty-four hours ago. There was something wrong with her. There had to be. Why else would she still be unconscious or sleeping?

He pushed the door open to her bedroom. He had told himself not to bother her until she woke up, but that was while assuming she would open her eyes within the hour or at least as soon as it got dark. But his assumption had been wrong.

Entering the room, he stared at the beautiful woman on the bed. Her features were relaxed in sleep, and her full lips were slightly parted. The sight of his T-shirt still covering her naked form was more thrilling than he wanted to admit.

Was it his imagination or had her position changed a little? He could have sworn her right hand had been next to her thigh earlier, but now it was close to her head.

After walking over to the side of the bed, Henry sat down next to her. She looked to be in her twenties by human standards, but since she was a vampire, it was impossible to tell. For all he knew she was ten times that age or even older. So there was a fair chance she was older than him.

He reached out and tucked a stray lock of chestnut hair behind her ear. It didn't want to stay there, though; her springy curls apparently had their own opinion of where they wanted to be.

Henry started and his eyes snapped to Eleanor's when her hand suddenly clamped around his wrist like a manacle. They stared at each other for a couple of seconds before he smiled. Her expression was unreadable, but at least she was finally awake.

Before he knew what was going on, he was flat on his back on the bed with his wrists locked in an iron grip just above his head. Eleanor was straddling his hips and staring down at him with a wicked grin spreading across her face.

His lower body's reaction to the close proximity of her pussy was immediate, and the color of her eyes changed with the hardening of his cock. Soon they were red and glowing.

"Eleanor." His voice was husky. "I'm happy to see you're awake. It took quite a long time, and I was getting worried about you."

Her delicate brows pushed together while she seemed to consider what he was saying. "How long?"

"Almost twenty-four hours."

Her eyes widened, and sitting back, she let go of his wrists. Several seconds went by before she spoke. "Were you the one who brought me back here? And"—her hands fisted in the T-shirt she was wearing before she lifted it to her nose and inhaled—"gave me your shirt?"

He lifted his head and stared at the black curls between her legs that had been exposed when she lifted the T-shirt. *Oh fuck.* His shaft turned to steel immediately and started throbbing with how much he wanted to tear his pants open and sink into her. What was it about this woman that turned him into a horny beast?

Her sudden laughter had him raising his gaze to hers. "You look like a starving man." She moved forward until she was on her hands and knees above him, smiling down at him. "And a very enticing one at that. I don't think I've been this tempted by anyone since…forever."

Henry swallowed hard, his response right there on his tongue. *I want you too.* But he wasn't going to tell her that. He wasn't going to say anything that would give away how much he wanted to forget about everything else and dive into a relationship with Eleanor. Even if all she wanted was to feed from him, he knew he would enjoy it.

Frowning, she moved to the side and sat down next to him on the bed. "I ran into the fucking witch." She shook her head slowly with an irritated expression on her face. "What are the odds? I just ran in a random direction, and somehow I ended up right in front of her. And she took control of my mind before I even realized who she was. And that's all I remember. Were you the one who found me?"

Henry nodded. "Yes, me and Fia. You were naked and lying next to Bryson. The two of you were positioned to look like you had been intimate, but your scent told me otherwise."

Eleanor cocked her head. "Bryson. He was one of the people who rescued me at the cabin. How did Amber get ahold of him?"

Henry lifted up on his elbows. "Same as you I imagine. He ran and was somehow picked up by Amber. Can you remember if she had her daughter with her when you met her?"

Raising her gaze to stare at a point on the wall, she shook her head. "All I can remember is Amber suddenly being there and taking control of my mind. I can't remember seeing anyone else around but that doesn't mean there wasn't any."

Her gaze lowered back to his. "Thank you for finding me and bringing me back here. And for helping me even after what I did to you before I left. I'm sorry. I should've made sure you agreed. The only excuse I have is your looks and scent, and the way you seem to radiate decency and kindness. Those are personality traits that are a much bigger turn-on than you might think. At least to someone like me who's inherently wicked."

Frowning, Henry shook his head. "Why do you think that? No one is inherently wicked. It's all about choice—what you choose to do. And I forgive you."

She gave a soft chuckle. "Spoken out of true kindness. Thank you." Her right hand reached out toward his face, but it stopped about an inch before connecting with his cheek. She pulled her hand back as her eyes filled with sadness. "You won't have to put up with me for much longer. I'll leave as soon as night falls. It's too close to dawn right now for me to go anywhere."

Before he even knew what he was doing, Henry grabbed her hand. "Please stay. I..." He stopped when he realized what he was about to say. Pronouncing that he was drawn to her as well was exactly the opposite of what he should do. Eleanor was beautiful, and she had his body all revved up, but she wasn't his. She wasn't even a shifter. Not that it really mattered what she was, but he had never heard of a shifter and a vampire getting together before. Perhaps because vampires were typically solitary creatures.

***

Eleanor felt a thrill run down her spine at his spontaneous reaction. The fact that Henry wanted her to stay filled her with warmth and an urge to do as he wanted. But this amazing man needed someone better than her in his life. Someone who would truly cherish him for whom he was. And all she would do was corrupt him.

This time she didn't stop herself when reaching for him. Cupping his cheek, she gave him a warm smile. "I wish I could, but it's better for everyone if I leave.

You'll find a mate soon and be happy like the other couples here."

His eyes widened with astonishment. "How do you know I'm looking for my mate?"

She laughed. "Every shifter is. But with you I can sense your longing for her even though you haven't met her yet."

He nodded as his gaze dropped to her bare knee. "I have wanted to meet my true mate for some time, but it's a rare thing among shifters. I can hope, but chances are I'll never meet her. Most shifters end up mating someone they are attracted to instead of their true mate."

Eleanor frowned at the sadness in his voice. She hadn't spent a lot of time with shifters, but based on her observations, there were a lot of happily mated couples who weren't true mates. Finding your true mate obviously wasn't essential for happiness. So, why did it seem that way for Henry?

Perhaps she could do something for him. Something that would cheer him up, if only for a little while.

"Henry." She brushed her fingers along his jaw until her fingertips were beneath his chin. Tipping his head back, she gave him a warm smile. "I—"

Eleanor was suddenly weightless, the bed disappeared from beneath her, and she seemed to be stuck in the air for a moment. Then, a massive roar hit her, and she fell and smashed into things on her way down.

It felt like minutes of being hit by one thing after another, but it was probably over in seconds. And another few seconds went by before the realization of what had happened sank in and made her jump to her feet in the rubble surrounding her. She was covered in cuts and bruises, but they were already healing and would be gone in less than a minute.

An explosion. The house had just blown up, or at least the section she had been in. The rest of it seemed to be mostly intact. And thankfully there was no fire.

Henry.

The bed they had been on was half buried beneath rocks from the stone walls and debris of all kinds, but there was no sign of the handsome shifter.

Fear threatened to choke her as she started rummaging through the rubble. She picked up the damaged bed and threw it onto the lawn, but Henry wasn't beneath it. He had been right beside her when the explosion hit, though, so in theory he should still be close by. Which meant he was buried deeper down in the wreckage of the house.

Eleanor started clearing away the debris quickly and methodically. A shiver raced through her body, and she knew all too well what it meant. The sun was only a minute away from clearing the horizon and bathing her in its deadly rays. Which meant she had less than a minute to find Henry.

---THE END---

BOOKS BY CAROLINE S. HILLIARD

Highland Shifters

A Wolf's Unlikely Mate, Book 1
Taken by the Cat, Book 2
Wolf Mate Surprise, Book 3
Seduced by the Monster, Book 4
Tempted by the Wolf, Book 5
Pursued by the Panther, Book 6
True to the Wolf, Book 7 – May 2023
Book 8 – TBA

Troll Guardians

Captured by the Troll, Book 1
Saving the Troll, Book 2
Book 3 – TBA

ABOUT THE AUTHOR

Thank you for reading my book. I hope the story gave you a nice little break from normality.

I have always loved reading and immersing myself in different worlds. Recently I have discovered that I also love writing. Stories have been playing in my head for as long as I can remember, and now I'm taking the time to develop some of these stories and write them down. Spending time in a world of my own creation has been a surprising enjoyment, and I hope to spend as much time as possible writing in the years to come.

I'm an independent author, meaning that I can write what I want and when I want. I primarily write for myself, but hopefully my stories can brighten someone else's day as well. The characters I develop tend to take on a life of their own and push the story in the direction they want, which means that the stories do not follow a set structure or specific literary style. However, I'm a huge fan of happily ever after, so that is a guarantee.

I'm married and the mother of two teenagers. Life is busy with a fulltime job in addition to family life. Writing is something I enjoy in my spare time.

You can find me here:
caroline.s.hilliard@gmail.com
www.carolineshilliard.com
www.facebook.com/Author.CarolineS.Hilliard/
www.amazon.com/author/carolineshilliard/
www.goodreads.com/author/show/22044909.Caroline_S_Hilliard

Printed in Great Britain
by Amazon